FAST FALLS THE NIGHT

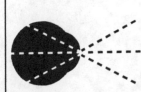

A BELL ELKINS NOVEL

FAST FALLS THE NIGHT

JULIA KELLER

THORNDIKE PRESS
A part of Gale, a Cengage Company

Farmington Hills, Mich • San Francisco • New York • Waterville, Maine
Meriden, Conn • Mason, Ohio • Chicago

Copyright © 2017 by Julia Keller.
A Bell Elkins Novel.
Thorndike Press, a part of Gale, a Cengage Company.

Thorndike Press® Large Print Reviewers' Choice.
The text of this Large Print edition is unabridged.
Other aspects of the book may vary from the original edition.
Set in 16 pt. Plantin.

LIBRARY OF CONGRESS CIP DATA ON FILE.
CATALOGUING IN PUBLICATION FOR THIS BOOK
IS AVAILABLE FROM THE LIBRARY OF CONGRESS

ISBN-13: 978-1-4328-5081-4 (hardcover)

Published in 2018 by arrangement with Macmillan Publishing Group, LLC/St. Martin's Press

Printed in Mexico
1 2 3 4 5 6 7 22 21 20 19 18

For Susan

ACKNOWLEDGMENTS

On August 15, 2016, I happened to be visiting my hometown of Huntington, West Virginia. The following morning, I discovered through news accounts that the day had a cruel distinction: Twenty-eight heroin overdoses, two of them fatalities, had been recorded in Huntington in a single four-hour period.

I was stunned. This was not the town I knew. This was not the town in which I had been born and raised, spending many long, wistful hours watching the coal barges slide along the Ohio River.

Alas, it was.

Huntington's real-life catastrophe was the catalyst for this fictional account. What would happen, I wondered, if the people of Acker's Gap suffered a similar series of tragedies, compacted into a small space of time?

For their wisdom and friendship, I am

pleased to thank Lisa Keller, Holly Ann Bryant, Ron Rhoden, Carolyn Alessio, Marja Mills, Ann C. Hall, and Joseph Hallinan.

At Minotaur, I continue to be guided and inspired by Kelley Ragland. And there is no better advocate for an author and her work than Lisa Gallagher. I am deeply and everlastingly grateful to both of these extraordinary women.

Abide with me; fast falls the eventide;
The darkness deepens; Lord with me
  abide.
When other helpers fail and comforts flee,
Help of the helpless, O abide with me.
> — REV. HENRY FRANCIS LYTE, 1847

She loved her own little town, but it was a
heart-breaking love, like loving the dead
who cannot answer back.
> —WILLA CATHER, *LUCY GAYHEART*

This story takes place in the course
of a single day.

DANNY

The woman asked to use the bathroom. Danny Lukens was 99 percent sure of what she wanted it for — and it had nothing to do with the usual uses to which bathrooms are put. He said yes, though, because it wasn't worth arguing about. He had a long night still ahead of him. He had just started his shift. He didn't want any trouble.

"Okay, thanks," she said.

Her speech wasn't slurred, which surprised him. Then he realized that he shouldn't have been surprised. The slurring would come later. Right now, she was honed to a clean, brittle edge, polished to a gloss of pure longing. No wonder the "Okay, thanks" had come out intelligibly. She was too sharp, too attuned to her life and its attendant miseries. Slurring — not only her words, but also her world — was the goal, not the current reality. In a few minutes,

13

she would be able to relax into the newly made mess of herself. The beautiful ooze.

"Back there," he said, pointing. "It ain't locked."

Whatever she did in the bathroom was her business. Not his.

She nodded and moved away from the counter. He took a quick mental snapshot with his sideways glance, just in case she trashed it and his manager asked him for a description of her to give to the sheriff. *As if,* Danny thought, *they'd be able to find her again if she didn't want to be found.* Addicts were ghosts. They drifted in and out of people's lives, just as they drifted in and out of their own lives.

He sort of knew her and he sort of didn't. He had seen her before, most likely, but he didn't have a precise recollection of it, and they all ran together in his mind, anyway, the faces and the skinny bodies. She had been in here before; again, he didn't remember it, but the odds favored it. This was a small town. Not that many places to go. She wore cutoff denim shorts and a too-tight black T-shirt with the word PINK splayed across her chest in — *Duh,* Danny thought — pink letters. She was very, very thin; her arms and legs were like tiny white PVC pipes. She had a long narrow face, scraggly blondish hair with black roots, and dead eyes. Her eyebrows were charcoal smudges. She was barefoot. She was — how old? Danny couldn't guess. Maybe eighteen. Maybe forty.

Did it matter? It did not.

Until she came in, he had been alone since his shift started at 11 P.M. Chuckie Purvis, the guy with the shift before his, had reported that it had been slow all night. Which was strange, really, for August. Usually August nights brought an unbroken line of customers: smartass kids, say, out for midnight rides in dusty pickups, buying gas and beer, shedding waves of look-at-me bravado, slapping a fake ID down on the counter like the winning card in a blackjack game. Or truckers craving a can of Red Bull and a flap of conversation. Or sometimes it was deputies from the Raythune County Sheriff's Department. They had a habit of stopping in, too, at intervals throughout the night, propping a black-holstered hip against the front counter and slowly unwinding the brown wrapper from a Snickers, alternating bites with observations about how anybody in their right mind would've gotten the hell out of this state a long time ago. No question about it. Once the last chunk of candy was chewed and swallowed, they would use

15

the tip of their tongue to pry out the nut pieces from their back teeth.

The Marathon was a natural gathering place. It was the only station in these parts open after 11 P.M., except for the Highway Haven up on the interstate. The Marathon was closer to Acker's Gap, the county seat. At one time there had been a Lester Oil station even closer, but it shut down last year, the front glass window replaced by sheets of yellow plywood. The pumps and the underground tank had been hauled out, leaving open holes and a trough gorged with trash and rainwater. Husky weeds had colonized the long cracks in the asphalt.

The Marathon, though, was still going strong.

Danny's favorite deputy was Jake Oakes. He liked Charlie Mathers, who had retired a while back, well enough, and he didn't mind Steve Brinksneader, Charlie's replacement. Jake, though, was the best; he was the one Danny most admired, most looked forward to seeing during his shift — or any other time, for that matter, which was weird, because Danny wasn't the kind of guy who liked authority figures. That had been his whole problem back in high school, and the reason he had to drop out: He couldn't stand it when somebody tried to tell him what he could and couldn't do. In study hall one afternoon in his junior year, he spat at Mrs. Pyles, the civics teacher. She had told him to quit talking and do his work. Witnessing him being called out that way, some of the other guys laughed at him. That was *not* okay. And so when Mrs. Pyles marched down the aisle in his direction, surely intending to repeat her reprimand, he stood up and sent a ginormous wad of spit right in her eye. It was worth everything that came after — being expelled for the rest of the year — just to see the look on the old bitch's face, the shock and the fear. By the time the school year rolled around again, he was out on his own. To hell with her. To hell with all of them.

Jake, though, he respected. He never made Jake pay for his Snickers. Yet so far tonight there had been no sign of Jake. No sign of anybody. Just this woman. Danny didn't see a car outside, which meant that wherever she had come from, she had walked.

It had been a strange summer. The heat never really settled in. Throughout June and July and the first two weeks of August the weather seemed to be in a sort of trance, a holding pattern, as if it was waiting for a secret signal to let loose and intensify, prompting a moist and insistent misery.

That is what usually happened. Not even the cooler air in the mountain valleys was any match for the sudden descent of the wipe-out heat of August. This year, though, things were different; temperatures remained moderate. And yet people could not quite trust the moderation. They waited nervously for that final blast, for a day when a red, pitiless sun stuck to the sky like a wet lollipop on a sidewalk. It was like expecting a call with bad news and listening always for the phone to ring.

Danny looked toward the short hallway leading to the bathroom. He wondered how long he should give her — the station only had the one bathroom, and both women and men had to use it — before he fist-knocked on the door and muttered, "Hey," followed by, "you okay in there?"

Chuckie Purvis had gotten in trouble last month for not checking on a trucker whose name turned out to be Gil Trautwein. Trautwein had stumbled in through the double doors at about 2 A.M. on a very busy night, lurching past the counter and into the bathroom. According to Chuckie, he was sweaty, disheveled, grimacing, and he clutched at his shirtfront, mumbling about how "goddamned awful" he felt, and how it must be the flu. Forty-five minutes later, after several other customers had come up to the counter and complained that the bathroom door was still locked, Chuckie unhooked the key from the bent nail under the counter and went to investigate. The bathroom door could be secured from the inside with a little push-button lock, but the key overrode the button.

Chuckie had knocked, called out, knocked again. Silence. Then he shouted. More silence. Finally he used the key. He found the trucker curled up on his side next to the toilet, pants puddled around his ankles, his skin the color of sliced beets. Apparently he'd had a heart attack or a stroke or a seizure — Danny never heard any confirmation about which it was — and he damn near died. Chuckie called the squad. The paramedics hauled the trucker out of there on a rattling gurney. Later Chuckie got an earful from the regional manager, Brady Sutcliffe, and now the instructions were clear for all employees: Give them twenty minutes in the can and then go check. No matter what you find, do not touch them.

Like you have to tell us that, Danny thought. *Like some guy passed out by the shitter is so freakin' irresistible.*

He liked this job. He liked the fact that he had regular company — customers coming

19

and going, unless it was a night like tonight, with that odd stretch of nothingness until the girl came in — but he never really had to get to know anybody, and they didn't know him. Mostly you were your own boss. Danny had never had a serious problem on his shift. Chuckie had once been held up at gunpoint — what was it about Chuckie and bad luck? — but it turned out that the guy's gun was a fake and the deputies caught him down the road. He was a meth head and stupid to boot. If he'd had a real gun, Jake Oakes told Danny, he'd have blown off his own pecker. He was that dumb.

So maybe it's my turn for some trouble, Danny thought. *My number's up.*

He stood in front of the bathroom door.

"Hey," he said. He started out with a mild tap, using a flat hand and not a fist. What if she was — well, sick with some kind of female thing? Something embarrassing?

If that was the case, then she could tell him so. Through the door. He would be able to hear her plea for privacy.

"Hey," Danny repeated.

He waited.

"Just need to know," he said, raising his voice, "that you're okay in there."

Nothing.

Now he pounded. He made a fist and he

rammed it against the gray metal door. Four times — *boom boom boom boom* — in quick succession.

"Come on," he said. "Don't make me get the key, okay? Just tell me you're okay and I'll leave you be."

Nothing.

Danny was pissed. He liked things to go as planned. His pleasures were simple: He enjoyed standing behind the front counter, arms crossed, looking out through the glass toward the gas pumps. He liked to watch the bugs nosing in and out of the wedge of light dropped by the bulb up on the high pole at the edge of the lot. He liked it when somebody pulled in and bought their gas with a credit card and then pulled out again without even looking his way; he and the customer were like two people stuck on separate islands, never acknowledging each other. Night after night Danny was on his own here, and he was totally in charge, yet there was very little to do, which was the perfect combo: authority without duties. He also liked having his days free to do as he pleased. That suited him just fine.

And now: this. The woman in the bathroom. Doing God knows what.

Okay, so maybe God wasn't the only one who knew. Danny had a pretty good hunch himself. She was skinny and from the look of her, she was well on her way to being dope-sick. He knew the signs. Heroin was as common as stray cats around here. It was swiftly replacing the pain pills, because heroin was so much cheaper. Sure, it was also a lot more dangerous — but you couldn't argue with the math.

He had to get her out of his bathroom. Had to get her moving on down the road, even if that road led nowhere. At least it wouldn't be here.

"Last chance," he yelled at the door.

Nothing.

Danny returned to the front counter. He was bending over to find the key on the bent nail when it occurred to him that it was high time for Deputy Oakes to pay him back for all those free Snickers. He would call Jake, make it his problem. He knew Jake's schedule. He was working tonight.

Fourteen minutes later, a black Chevy Blazer with the county seal branded on its flanks pulled up in front of the glass. The vehicle juddered and then was still, as if a cord had suddenly been snipped. Danny watched as Jake Oakes unfolded himself from the driver's side. He was a big, black-haired, sturdy man, and his brown deputy's uniform made him look even bigger; the fabric fit tightly across his chest and his taut stomach, and snugly encased his thick thighs. It was a hot night but Jake Oakes always looked cool and sleek, no matter what the temperature was.

"Evenin', Danny," Jake said. He had gotten the greeting out of the way before he even reached the counter. He showed Danny his palm, wiggling his fingers. "Gimme the key."

Danny retrieved it. He had filled in the details for Jake during the phone call: A woman wouldn't come out of the bathroom. Possible overdose. "On my way," Jake had barked back, sounding abrupt, almost mean. Danny had known him long enough not to take offense. Jake was a nice guy, but when he was focused on his job, nothing else mattered.

Danny followed him down the corridor.

"Ma'am, this is Deputy Oakes." Jake stood in front of the door. He kept his voice at an ordinary, business-as-usual pitch. Danny figured that Jake didn't want to scare her if this wasn't a "situation," if she was just hanging out. "You've got thirty seconds," Jake said. "Tell me you're okay or I'm coming in."

The only noise was the hum of the refrigerated case on the other side of the wall, the

23

one with the assorted six-packs and racked cans of energy drinks.

Jake did not wait the full thirty seconds. He thrust the key in the lock.

"Coming in," he said. He twisted the key as he grasped the doorknob, pushing at the metal door with a meaty shoulder. Danny leaned to the left so that he could see around the deputy's broad brown back.

She was lying faceup in the middle of the floor, her head partially blocking the round gray drain in the center. Her limbs extended straight out from her body, stiff as sticks. Her face was a bluish color. Her mouth was slack; foam leaked from one side of it, glistening on her chin. Her black T-shirt had rolled up, exposing both her concave belly and a wet red sore next to her navel. The syringe had slipped out of the swollen wound and rolled into a lane of cracked grout separating the yellow tiles.

"Damn," Danny said in a whisper. There was more awe than shock in his tone.

Jake dropped to his knees and checked for a pulse, thrusting two fingers up under her flaccid chin. He used a thumb to prop up her eyelid. The pupil was dilated. He didn't bother yelling at her or shaking her shoulder or slapping her face to revive her. She looked to be long past the point at which

24

that sort of intervention would be effective. He did the only thing he could, Danny figured, under the circumstances: He used his radio to call the paramedics, keeping his voice low and calm, his description specific and succinct.

He had seen this before, Danny knew. Many, many times. They had talked about it, on one of the few occasions when their conversation turned serious. Talked about how Jake and the other deputies handled more overdoses these days than car accidents.

Now they waited for the squad.

"Look at her left wrist," Jake said. He stayed where he was, kneeling on the sticky floor beside her. "Must be left-handed. Left wrist's clean. Right arm's a mess. She uses the left to inject herself." He waved his hand toward the prime access spots: ankle, belly, groin, thigh, between the toes, under the fingernails.

Danny squinted. Her left wrist was indeed white and delicate, like a fluted piece of fine china. The rest of her was filthy and nicked with scars and ablaze with oily dark sores, but not that left wrist. It looked like the wrist of a little girl.

Jake was muttering again. "Such a waste. Such a fucking goddamned waste."

Danny shrugged. Jake didn't usually talk like that. In fact, Jake had told Danny that you couldn't get emotional about these things. Anger and sorrow were useless. Worse than useless: They made a person sloppy. You took your eye off the ball and you couldn't handle your job. If by some miracle this woman lived, she would, Danny knew, be doing this again another night, in another dirty bathroom. Again and again. And so would all the others. Rinse and repeat. It wasn't worthy of anybody's grief. Nothing was ever going to change. There was nothing special about any of this, Danny told himself; there was nothing special about this woman, or about this night.

He was wrong.

BELL

She couldn't remember the last time she had slept through the night. Surely at some point she had experienced a golden, unbroken road of sleep — everyone had, right? At least once? As a child, perhaps? As a teenager, when she had exhausted herself by a constant headlong flight from anything that threatened to touch her, tame her, hold her back? There must have been a night when she slept long and seamlessly and well. But she had no memory of such a thing.

Bell Elkins placed the bookmark in her book and closed it. Had anyone asked her just then, she could not have come up with a single detail about the plot of the paperback with the shiny, curled-back cover currently perched on her right knee, the story she had allegedly been absorbing for the past hour. Nor named a single character. Her eyes had moved methodically over the

27

pages, but nothing stuck. Late-night reading, reading undertaken in lieu of sleep, could be like that. It was empty, pointless motion, a surface activity that never engaged the depths of her mind. Busywork, aimed at passing the time.

And speaking of time: What time *was* it?

She looked up at the wooden case clock on the mantel. She had sensed that it was after midnight because — well, because even without a clock she could always feel when midnight slipped by, like a dark wind brushing her cheek. But after that milestone, the rest of the night fell back into a blur.

The clock settled the matter. Not quite two.

She was disappointed. She had hoped that more of the night would have vanished by now, without her having to know about it. That was the trouble with insomnia — along with all of the other things, of course, such as the fact that it left her weary and grumpy during the subsequent workday. It made her hyperaware of the passing of the minutes, the hours. Time was a great problem for Bell Elkins. She had trouble chopping it up into its constituent elements — past, present, future — because time to her was a continuous black ribbon and she couldn't figure out where to make the cut.

One night, she had watched the second hand on that mantel clock perform its dutiful loops until she realized — startling herself — that twenty-four minutes had gone by. She had been thinking about the past. She did that a lot. The process always reminded her of washing out a filthy bucket, one crusted with mud and sticks and sadness. She scrubbed it and soaked it, and then she filled it with water and swirled the water around in it, and then scrubbed it and soaked it again, over and over, knowing — well, hoping — that sooner or later it would rinse clear.

She could not identify the precise origin of tonight's insomnia. Sometimes it was easy. She was a county prosecutor, and there was always something to worry about. Always a case pending, always a judge to be placated or a jury to be persuaded. She was always facing a can't-put-it-off-any-longer decision about whether to charge a certain defendant and, if she charged her or him, what that charge ought to be. She always had to balance the probability of success against the expenditure of resources — because Raythune was a small, poor county. Her staff consisted of two assistant prosecutors and one secretary. They had to count every paper clip.

But the sleeplessness that bedeviled her at present might not be about work at all. There were other possibilities. She lived with a constant sense of apprehension, a kind of itchy, nervous, fluttery buzz that, at some point, had been inserted under her skin without her knowledge or consent. Her older sister, Shirley, lived with it as well. They had discussed it many times. Neither had been able to shed the vestiges of a violent past, vestiges that included a fear-induced vigilance. And vigilance was a hard habit to break. Relaxation felt dangerous. If they let down their guard, they were asking for trouble — and they would have no right to complain about that trouble, after the fact, because they had made themselves vulnerable. And they had done it voluntarily.

Then again, her restlessness might emanate from the ongoing quarrel she was having with her boyfriend, Clay Meckling. "Boyfriend" was a ridiculous word. But the other words didn't work, either. "Partner" was jumping the gun. "My guy" sounded like a 1950s song lyric. "Gentleman caller" was ludicrous and Victorian. "Lover"? Not lately. Neither one of them had been in the mood. Not while Clay's challenge still echoed: *So what's the deal, Bell? I want to marry you. I've said it until I'm tired of saying it. If you don't see that happening, you need to tell me so.* He didn't want to wait anymore. She couldn't blame him.

But she also couldn't get herself there. By all rights, she should cut him loose, let him find someone else. Someone who would make him happy.

So why didn't she do that?

It was 2:03 now.

She unhitched her gaze from the clock so that she could look around the living room. She liked everything she saw. Other people might not understand that, given its degree of dishevelment, from the battered brown couch to the coffee table with the nicked edges, to the lamp with the frayed and cockeyed plum-colored shade, to the cracked and slanting hardwood floor, and then on to the low arch, its beige plaster chipped and flaking, that linked the living room and the foyer, and over to the weather-warped front door. The sole item of furniture in the foyer was an antique desk — "antique" being a nicer way of putting it than "older than dirt" — and sitting in the middle of that desk was a stout manual typewriter with CORONA stamped above the top row of keys in dull gold. The typewriter was a gift from Ruthie Cox, who had been her best friend in Acker's Gap. Ruthie died

31

last year, leaving Bell the beautiful machine. They had shared a wariness of technology, an unease about the liberties it took in so many lives.

This house always seemed smaller at night, and pugnacious in the way of all runts, as if the corners drew themselves in ever so slightly to make a tighter seal against the pressure of the dark. The house had her back. It protected her. If the house could somehow figure out how to keep her anxieties on the other side of its walls, it would do so. She was sure of it.

This was the first house she had ever owned by herself. The others had been jointly owned with her husband — now ex-husband — Sam Elkins, and they were in various upscale sections of the Washington, D.C. area, where she had lived during her marriage, and where Sam still lived. This house was considerably smaller and shabbier than any of those. And it happened to be located in Acker's Gap, West Virginia, not some fancy suburb in Virginia or Maryland. But she didn't care. She reveled again and again in the simple forthright joy of the realization that this was *hers* — all of it, every nail, every plank and stone, every tile and joist and dusty corner, every scratch and stain, everything from the faulty furnace to the disintegrating roof to the lopsided front porch to the rickety back stoop. She didn't care about any of those flaws. She cared about the fact that this house belonged to her. And to no one else.

So things weren't altogether terrible. She had much to be grateful for. Her daughter, Carla, had ended a period of restlessness and enrolled at George Washington University. She was undecided about her major — which was another way of saying that she was majoring in everything. Her e-mails to her mother were filled with the verbal sunbursts that came from a newly awakened and continually challenged mind. Bell knew better than to tell her how much she loved those e-mails and looked forward to receiving them. That would make Carla far too self-conscious.

Her gaze switched back to the mantel clock: 2:05 A.M.

She heard a train whistle in the distance. It was a stretched-out, lonely-sounding moan that tailed off into a sigh of solemn wistfulness. Something clunked against the roof; chances were, it was a black walnut released from the tree that hung over the back half of the old house. On late-summer mornings she would find the fist-sized yellow balls dotting the yard. Sometimes the hard shells split open from the impact of the long fall, and chips and shreds of black nut meat littered the grass like the visible remnants of her dark dreams.

The minute hand shifted: 2:06 A.M.

She had returned to Acker's Gap eight years ago, law degree in hand. It was a rescue mission. Her hometown was in trouble, slammed by unemployment as the coal mines shut down, one by one, and ripped up by drug addiction and stunned into lethargy by — the worst foe of all — hopelessness. By the cast-iron conviction that nothing would ever go right around here. It wouldn't because it couldn't. It couldn't because it wasn't meant to. It wasn't meant to because — well, look around. Just look around. Could you doubt it? The circular logic of despair kept the people dizzy, turning around and around on the same small patch of muddy ground instead of moving forward.

She lived her life amid lives that didn't seem to matter to the outside world. Lives that didn't seem to matter, either, to the people who were living them. And that was one of the chief reasons why Bell had come back, and why she had chosen to run for prosecutor. The highest compliment you could pay to a place and its people, she believed, was to insist on justice. On the rule of law. To say to the dark anarchical currents that were always threatening to overwhelm this area: *No. I won't let that happen.*

She had done her best. Yet West Virginia still had the highest rate of drug overdose deaths in the nation. Raythune County Sheriff Pam Harrison would stop by the prosecutor's office every few days and share a grim statistic or two, just in case Bell had dared to let some optimism trickle into her mood. Newly emboldened gangs of drug suppliers continued their regular sweeps through the mountains, sowing their poison in the creases in the land, tempting discouraged people with a quick and easy bliss. A few days ago, a bedraggled old man — he had a scraggly beard and a too-big Army jacket and droopy pants and a lost look in his bleary eyes — had been hanging out in front of the courthouse, and when Bell went by he grabbed her by the sleeve and shouted in her face, "It's coming! It's coming!" She shook him off, but it was unsettling. She had never seen him before, but the old man seemed to be channeling her own grave apprehensions and clinging doubts. He reminded her of a soothsayer from a fairy tale, the kind she used to read to Carla when her daughter was a little girl, only far more sinister. His warning was strange and vague, but it matched up with Bell's growing sense of dread about Acker's Gap, her feeling that some final, terrible reckoning was at hand.

The clock hand jumped forward again: 2:08 A.M.

For a time, when she worked with the former sheriff, Nick Fogelsong, she had believed they were making progress. Then the heroin took hold. But she didn't give up; she fought back. Hard. She was still fighting, every damned day. She did what she could to help the new sheriff, Pam Harrison, hunt down the suppliers and get help for the addicts — but she had no answer for the despondency that made people reach for drugs in the first place. Sometimes she felt as if she was knee-deep in rapidly rising water on the lower deck of the *Titanic,* bailing it out with a rusty teaspoon.

If people did not care about their lives, about their health and their future, you could not make them care. Could you?

A glance at the mantel: 2:10 A.M.

Two days ago, she had received a phone call from an old friend in D.C. Elaine Mitford was a classmate from Georgetown University Law Center. Intimidatingly smart. Formidably successful. Dazzlingly

36

well-connected. With two other classmates, Grady Fiske and Abigail McElroy, Elaine was starting her own firm. She had leased office space on K Street. Prospects were bright. She wanted a fourth partner. "Mitford, Fiske, McElroy, and Elkins — how does that sound?" Elaine had said, putting a lively curl in her voice, a brisk shiver of enticement.

A year ago, maybe even a few months ago, Bell would have turned her down flat.

But now . . .

"Let me think about it," Bell had replied.

"Really?"

"Really."

"Not to pressure you, but we need to move quickly." There was even more excitement in Elaine's voice. "God, Bell — this would be *terrific.* Frankly, I didn't think we had a shot. If you're serious, though, I'll send you a detailed proposal."

"I'm serious."

Am I really ready to jump ship? That was the question she couldn't shake tonight. It blocked every path to sleep. She thought about Clay. She thought about a lot of things. Finally she made a bargain with herself: She would put off considering Elaine's offer for another day or so. And then she would make up her mind for good, having let all the probabilities and contingencies and pro-and-con arguments move around in her head unchaperoned for a short while.

She didn't want to give up on West Virginia. Yet sometimes it seemed to her that the mountains were slowly closing over her head, the peaks meeting and sealing. If she waited too long to leave, she would be trapped. When she had that vision, she had trouble catching her breath; she felt a little faint, a touch claustrophobic. Maybe the solution was simple: She needed to get out while she still could.

JAKE

Molly Drucker was pretty, but not in a conventional way. Not in the way that usually mattered around here. She was a little heavier than she ought to be, and she never wore makeup. Jake could not imagine her with lipstick or mascara, the massive application of which was the usual standard of feminine beauty in Acker's Gap.

He hated the fact that he was even thinking about her looks right now. It was crassly inappropriate. It made him feel oafish and small-souled and irredeemably male. He didn't mind that last one — totally out of his hands — but he didn't much like the first two. He wasn't a saint. But that didn't mean he had to be a jerk.

Still, he found Molly attractive. He always had. He had never counted, but he had probably worked at least two hundred accident scenes with her over the past four years, the length of time he had been employed by the Raythune County Sheriff's Department, and he never failed to think: *Damn, she's a good-looking woman.* He kept the thought to himself. She might be spoken for. He had no clue about her personal life. She didn't wear a ring, but that meant nothing. Paramedics — the savvy ones, at least — did not. Rings made it hard to put on latex gloves. And rings got in the way of the work. They could even be dangerous. If you found yourself inching down a rope into a well in which some toddler had tumbled — that had happened, just last summer — a ring could catch on something. It was a fast way to lose a finger.

So even without a ring, she might have a partner. He was too shy to ask. But he thought about her more often than he ought to, and in ways he probably shouldn't. She had a broad, serious face and lively black eyes and spirited-looking black hair that she kept clear of her field of vision with a blue bandana. Several hours into her shift, her hair would start to spring loose from that mooring of fabric, licks of it standing up around her face like a fierce dark corona. Jake put her age at about thirty-five. She had been a paramedic for ten years — he had asked her once, among the very few times he had risked a personal question — and she was good at her job. She was smart and she was poised and she was resourceful.

She was also African-American, which made her a distinct minority in this part of West Virginia. Yet the nature of her job meant that few people reacted to her race when she showed up at an emergency. Any reservations based on the color of her skin — and that was an unfortunate possibility in regions such as these, where it was, Jake knew, something they didn't see every day — were automatically pushed aside in deference to the fact that she was there to save a life.

Or at least to try.

Sometimes — tonight, for instance — she was too late.

Molly crouched next to the young woman in the Marathon bathroom. Jake stood behind her. There wasn't anything for him to do right now. For the time being, this was the sovereign territory of the paramedics. Molly's actions were quietly aggressive, even though the outcome was obvious. It had been obvious from the moment she had barreled in here, dropping the red plastic case filled with supplies onto the filthy yellow tile, checking for a pulse, at-

41

taching the bag-valve mask to the woman's face. Molly wore dark blue Dickies trousers, a light blue polo shirt, and black Converse sneakers. Her squad partner, Ernie Edmonds, was still out at the big, square, white-sided ambulance parked in front of the station, yanking the gurney out of the back. Jake was sure of Ernie's activity without actually witnessing it because he had worked scenes like this so many times with the two of them. The division of labor was practiced, absolute. Their routine almost never varied.

Gray skin. Needle marks. Feeble pulse.

Molly, Jake knew, was reading what she saw on the bathroom floor the way somebody else might speed-read a paperback thriller, alert for clues and patterns and spoilers. She whipped out a syringe and injected the contents of a yellow-capped vial of naloxone into the victim's thigh.

Victim, Jake thought. *Really? Victim? She did this to herself.*

He told himself to knock it off. *Not my call to make.* And not an observation appropriate to entertain if your job was public safety.

Rule number one: You don't judge.

At least not out loud.

He had sent Danny back up to the front counter. Danny hadn't liked that — he had scowled, twisting his lip — but Jake didn't care. This wasn't a circus. Plus, Danny needed to do his job, even if the kid would clearly rather be part of the excitement that went along with a dead body on the bathroom floor. There might be customers to attend to — although the presence of an ambulance in front of the station, its engine huffing like an overtaxed buffalo, the perky light on its top slathering everything in the vicinity with a relentless red pulse, would probably cut down on business.

"Pull the surveillance tape from when she first came in," Jake had called out to Danny's back as the young man clomped away. "Might need it for evidence."

Only half-turning his head to reply, Danny had mumbled over his shoulder, "Camera's just for show. Never did work. Ain't no tape."

Figures, Jake thought wearily.

He resumed his focus on Molly. He loved watching her work. She evaluated. She measured. She administered another shot of naloxone. She didn't make any noise, aside from a single grunt when she lifted and tilted the girl's head to check for injuries on the back of the skull, which could have occurred when she collapsed. Molly had already questioned Jake as he followed her in here, gathering the relevant facts without breaking stride: How long had she been in the bathroom? *Forty or forty-five minutes, tops.* ID? *Unknown.* Other information that might help? *Nope. Sorry.*

Watching Molly run through the rest of her protocols, he thought once again about how much he was attracted to her. And again he was ashamed, given the dire situation, and so he forced his mind to alight on something else: on, for instance, the abject filthiness of this floor. Jake had used the toilet in here many, many times — that was the reason he stopped in at the Marathon, although he knew Danny Lukens chalked it up to the promise of conversation and free candy — but he had never really looked at the floor before. Not like this. Why would he? Why would anybody? The grime was systemic. There wasn't a single square inch that looked clean. The room smelled just as you would expect it to: It smelled of piss, and of the bleach with which Danny or one of his colleagues attempted, regularly and ineffectively, to mask it. It smelled of rot. It smelled of mildew. But it was the specific and disgusting appearance of the floor that preoccupied Jake just now.

What would it be like, to die on such a floor?

Because the girl was clearly dead.

That was what he called her in his mind — "the girl" — even though he knew it was politically incorrect, as well as technically inaccurate. She was not a girl. She was a woman. Young, yes, but a woman. An adult. Yet somehow, he thought, it was always easier to refer to a woman of any age as a girl. And maybe it wasn't an insult, after all. Maybe it wasn't rank sexism. Maybe it was because people wanted to see all females, at their cores, as unformed and malleable and promising. Men were disposable. But women were special, potentially salvageable, regardless of how many years or in how many ways they had abused their bodies.

"What do you think?" Jake said. What he meant was: *Is she going to make it?*

Molly answered without looking up. She didn't stop working. She was checking the girl's arms and legs for any other recent injection sites, running two gloved fingers up and down the ashen skin.

"Don't know."

He wondered if Molly noticed the floor, too. How gross it was. How a smeary, yellow, snot-like film made it slippery. How the brown crud in between the tiles could have been regular dirt or possibly human feces. Impossible to say, really, without a lab test or a good long sniff — and who the hell would ever want to bend down close enough to do it?

Molly's cool relentlessness always impressed him. No matter where they were — and he had worked with her in some wretched, rackety, godforsaken places — her focus on her job was steady, implacable. It annoyed him that he had allowed himself, just a moment ago, to think about her in a way that veered well outside the lines of the professional.

And yet he was drawn to her. One of these days he might just summon the nerve to ask her out. For a meal, maybe. Wouldn't matter where. As long as it was far away from dirty floors and used syringes. And dead addicts.

Ernie was back. He didn't dawdle, but he wasn't hurrying, either. He had one hand clamped on the end rail of the gurney, waiting for Jake to step clear of the doorway.

"Helluva night," Ernie said, in a flat voice. He was in his mid-forties — or so Jake guessed — and he sported a luxuriant handlebar mustache the color of brown mustard. Both curling ends of it stuck out from his face in a manner that Jake found somewhat comical, but he had a hunch that this was not a man who allowed himself to be laughed at, or even teased in a mild, friendly way. There was an air of prickliness about Ernie Edmonds, a simpering pride belied by his sloppy appearance. His trousers were a size too small. They probably hadn't been when Ernie first purchased them, Jake told himself, but they surely were now. The waistband was folded double in front to accommodate his soap-bubble belly. Unlike Molly, he wore his light blue polo shirt untucked. His sneakers had no laces, effectively turning them into slippers.

Ernie's radio spat out a gob of static and a rushed muddle of words, to which he responded, "Copy that." Molly turned and peered up at him, too focused on the task at hand to have listened to the call, asking him with her eyes to fill her in. "Another overdose," Ernie said. "Burger Boss parking lot." He jerked his head at Jake, a rough signal that meant the deputy needed to get out of his way, to move even farther back out of the doorway and into the room, toward the grimy toilet. Ernie bumped the gurney over the threshold. Only about 10 percent of it fit in the small space. They would have to make do.

"Jesus," Molly said. "Not our run, right? Somebody else handling?"

"Yeah." Ernie fiddled with the hardware

47

on the gurney. His movements were not infused with any sort of intensity. Neither he nor Molly would say so out loud, but this was now officially the Land of the Lost Cause. Urgency was pointless. The girl on the floor was gone. She had died before they arrived, and she would be just as dead when they dumped her on the gurney and her arms flopped over the sides and they picked up those arms and piled them back on her motionless chest. She would still be dead when they shoved the gurney into the rear of the ambulance and slammed the doors. And yet the siren would still scream and the red light would still turn around and around on top of the vehicle, awakening people needlessly from their sleep.

It was all part of the charade, Jake thought. All part of the little show they had to put on — but a show for whom? For God? So that He'd know they were still trying? So that He wouldn't get fed up and just abandon the area, leaving them to deal with all this crap by themselves? Maybe. But Jake had another theory, which he had never shared with anyone: The dramatic urgency of first responders — red lights, yowling sirens, the stepped-up pace and the terse talk — was a piece of misdirection. It was a tactical dodge, a way of delaying an acknowledgment of their collective failure to drag the victim back to this side of the line. They had lost, but if they kept fighting, or looked as if they were, the loss might not sting quite so much. They had done this so many times, the three of them; they had seen the same sort of waste. Felt the same sort of drag-you-down futility.

"Gotta run," Jake said. Molly and Ernie had a backup team, but he didn't. Steve Brinksneader was working a multicar accident on Savage Ridge Road. Jake needed to be heading out to the Burger Boss to deal with two more unconscious bodies. Another squad of paramedics would meet him there.

Jake would have to scoot around Ernie to get out of the bathroom, but Ernie didn't budge. He was too busy looking at the girl on the floor. He ran a tongue around the inside of his mouth, making his mustache quiver. He frowned.

"I know her," Ernie said. "That's Sally Ann Burdette."

Molly did not comment, which tipped off Jake that maybe she, too, had recognized this girl, but wasn't letting herself think about it. Not while she was working.

Unlike Ernie and Molly, whose families went back several generations in Raythune County, Jake had lived here only a few years. Faces didn't spark a long train of associations in his mind. The only Burdette with which Jake was acquainted was a county commissioner. "Any relation to Sammy Burdette?" he said.

Ernie nodded. "You bet. This gal's his niece."

"Was," Jake said.

"Was," Ernie agreed.

SALLY ANN

They thought she was gone but she wasn't. They thought she was dead but she was still alive. She could hear them. She couldn't see them and she couldn't feel anything, but — for a few seconds more — she could hear them. The sound was loud and then it wasn't loud, like the sound of a train going by; first it's soft and then it's really LOUD and then it fades away again. There was a name for that. She knew the name for that. She did. She loved learning new things. She was good at school. Well, she was for a while. Then she wasn't anymore.

What did they call that thing where the sound changes? She knew. She really did know the name and if she had more time, she'd remember it. If she had more time, she'd do a lot of things.

They didn't know what she knew.

No one did. No one would ever know

51

what it felt like to be her, to watch your life like you're watching the fish waggle around in the big glass tank at the Petland out at the mall. Back and forth. Back and forth. She'd watch those stupid fish and she'd think: *That's me, that's it. That's my life. Back and forth. Same old shit, over and over again.* If she tried to get anywhere, change anything, do something, she failed. It never worked out. She had a boyfriend once, back in high school, named Johnny Ehrlich — everybody called him Lick, because of the way you said his last name but also because of the dirty joke — and when she told him (BIG MISTAKE) about her plans to get out of Acker's Gap, he grinned at her, which was sort of gross to look at because most of his teeth on top were gone and his face was caving in on account of it. He would surely look like a wrinkled old man before he was twenty-five. He'd said, "Yeah, *right.*" And that just went right through her, like somebody had shot her in the heart with an arrow: Yeah, right. Like it was a joke. Like she was a joke. Like everything was.

Lick gave her the heroin. First time. Somebody said heroin would feel like being kissed by Jesus. Wow. Those words made her shiver and dance inside, even before the heroin itself did. Just the sound of the words. Some words, certain phrases, did that: She felt them all the way down to her toes. They made her toes curl, in fact. Her English teacher, Mrs. Mason, once told her that she was good with words, that she had a "gift" for them (that was the actual word she used) and she really ought to think about trying for college and being an English major and becoming an English teacher or a writer. Or both.

She wished Mrs. Mason had never said that because there was nothing worse than somebody telling you that you had a gift for something. That they believed in you. That you could do it if you tried. When they said that, it just made it easier for you to disappoint them. Aunt Dot was always doing that: giving her compliments. Then she had to live up to them. Which was impossible. Aunt Dot could rot in hell for all she cared.

Lick said he also heard that heroin was like a ten-minute orgasm. Right again.

Tonight was a mistake. She knew instantly that something was wrong. She'd realized that and then there was a long Nothing and then she heard them working on her and at some point, before the next long Nothing, she thought:

Doppler.

That was it. That was the thing with the

train and the sound, the coming-toward and the going-away. She had been good in school, not just in English but in science, too, and sometimes she thought she might —

CHARLIE

3:14 A.M.

Charlie Mathers poked at his shirtfront with a pudgy index finger. Yep: bingo. A dime-sized drop of melted ice cream had landed right next to the third button up from the bottom of his shirt, at the point where the swell of his belly reached its mushy apex. He had experienced considerable initial difficulty in finding the spot, despite having actually witnessed the ice cream sliding off the edge of the spoon, because the only source of illumination in the living room right now was the stubborn blue stupor of the TV set.

He frowned. He made a soft clucking noise with his tongue. He would have to notify Doreen about the spot, so that she could pre-soak his shirt in Shout to ensure its removal during the regular wash cycle. His wife had tried to wise him up, again and again, about chocolate: It was a killer, laundry-wise, and if he didn't want his clothes to look as if they'd come down with a bad rash, he would have to either alert her to the presence and location of every stain, every time — or give up his late-night gorges.

Charlie chose the former. Eating ice cream directly out of the carton while Doreen slept upstairs, a *Law & Order: Special Victims Unit* marathon unspooling before him courtesy of one of those upper-tier cable channels whose name he could never recall, was now his nightly routine. He enjoyed the linked chain of incidents of make-believe mayhem, a reliable supply of fictional havoc running back to back to back to back to back. Charlie couldn't get enough of the show. He loved the thing they did between scenes, that ominous two-beat chime (*bomp bomp*) that not only tied off the just-concluded tragedy but also warned of worse to come. He never tired of the murders and assaults and suspects and clues and false trails and last-minute twists and cynical dialogue, interrupted only by commercials for lawyers specializing in bankruptcy protection, or for hair-removal products (aimed at women), or hair-restoration products (aimed at men), or for bathroom cleaning supplies (aimed at everybody).

The current episode was a beaut, which explained his most recent spillage. He'd been massively preoccupied. The gap between the lip of the carton and Charlie's open mouth had not been vast — it was mere inches — but his eyes were welded to the screen and its depiction of Stabler and Benson caught up in a fiery argument over the best way to interrogate a twitchy punk who may or may not have raped and murdered a twelve-year-old girl. And Charlie had paid the price. A majority of the final delectable spoonful from a half-gallon carton of X-Treme Chocolate X-Plosion, his favorite flavor by far, had landed *on* his stomach instead of in it.

"Dang," Charlie said. In truth, his regret was inspired more by having missed that last lovely taste on his tongue than by the making of a new stain.

Dang was his most extensive foray into the forest of epithets. He never ventured any deeper. Thirty years as a deputy sheriff in a rough, dark county filled with rough, dark people — real-life bad guys, not the fake ones on TV — and still he had never developed the habit of casual cursing. Doreen always said that that was what she'd first noticed about Charles Comstock Mathers, and what had drawn her to him:

He was a gentleman. He did not take the Lord's name in vain. He touched the front brim of his hat when a lady passed him on the sidewalk. Yes, he had his flaws: He was overweight and unrepentant about it, and he was far too gullible, especially when it came to the purchase of self-help books and CD series, and he could be rather silly at times, and he would never rise higher than deputy in the sheriff's department of Ray-thune County, West Virginia. But he was a good man. And so, twenty-seven years ago, Doreen Sharpley had accepted his offer of marriage, a decision that had benefited both of them, bringing a mutual happiness and contentedness that — or so it seemed to Charlie — would forever elude Benson and Stabler, who were not married to each other, of course, but who *should* have been, at least in Charlie's opinion. Benson and Stabler had been sweet on each other for years. You could just tell. That's why they fought so much. Stabler eventually left the series — that is, the actor playing him did — hence Charlie liked these early episodes best, when the two of them went at it like cats in a bag. Fortunately, the older shows were the ones most likely to end up in marathons.

"Dang," Charlie repeated.

He moistened his fingertip and dabbed at the spot. When he told Doreen about it in the morning, she would surely sigh and shake her head and mutter something about how *civilized* people ate ice cream out of a *bowl* and not out of a *carton* in *the middle of the night* — but she wouldn't really be mad at him. It was a performance. A little show. He knew that. She didn't mind his slovenly habits. Those habits guaranteed that he needed her. And Doreen needed to be needed. Charlie had figured that out by their second date.

Hey, Charlie thought. Maybe that was the issue with Stabler and Benson. They were too independent. Neither one needed the other.

His attention shifted from the brown dribblet on his shirt to the TV screen. Stabler had just stormed out of the precinct, swinging his suit jacket over his shoulder and bolting away while Benson was in the middle of a sentence, and she was none too happy about it. Charlie could read her hurt feelings right on her face: the slowly widening dark eyes, the slightly parted lips, the grim set to her long jaw. Nobody could push her buttons the way Stabler could.

Geez, Charlie thought. *Get a room, you*

two. He grinned at himself. He was a rascal.

When the landline rang, he was still so deeply involved in his ruminations about Stabler and Benson and their long-smoldering, non-romance romance that his entire body bounced and shuddered. If he had been holding the ice-cream spoon, he would have dropped it in his lap, making yet another stain for Doreen to contend with.

The phone lived on the small end table next to his recliner, alongside the remote. Charlie grabbed at the slender plastic stalk — it was a cordless, with identical brethren distributed around the house at convenient locations — and mashed the answer button with his thumb, cutting off the next ring so that it wouldn't wake up his wife.

"Yeah?" Charlie said. His voice was gruff. He didn't care about sounding cordial. If this turned out to be some drunk who had misdialed, he'd let the bum have it.

"Charlie. Hey. It's Jake. Figured you might still be up."

Charlie relaxed. "You figured right." He reached for the remote and muted the TV. He didn't turn it off; he needed the light.

Jake was his former colleague and still his good friend. They had worked side by side as deputies for the last few years of Charlie's career. They still kept in touch, even though Charlie wasn't on the job anymore, and Jake knew he would be awake. Charlie talked a lot about his fondness for *Law & Order: Special Victims Unit* marathons that ran so reliably through the night. When Jake was working the night shift, he checked in from time to time, asking advice, testing out theories. Jake wasn't too proud to admit that Charlie knew a hell of a lot more about law enforcement — and especially law enforcement in Raythune County — than he did.

"What's going on?" Charlie said. He kept his tone light and breezy, the default setting for his conversations with Jake, who was a bit of a rascal himself.

"Just a minute." Odd. There was nothing breezy about Jake's tone.

Charlie, by now more than a little puzzled, heard a noise through the receiver that he recognized: the sticky bramble of static from a police radio. Jake was talking to a dispatcher, asking a question. The words were too muffled for Charlie to make them out. He strained to isolate and identify the rest of the background noise: Tangled-up voices, high and low. Rattles. A heavy hum. The hum sounded like a truck engine stuck in an overworked gear. Charlie could envision the low successive puffs of exhaust, each one exiting the tailpipe like a proud fart.

Charlie waited. He had no choice.

The good news was that there had been no commotion from the second floor. Jake's call had not awakened Doreen. If it had, a predictable series of sounds — the soprano squawk of the warped floorboards on her side of the bed, a slight creak throughout the old house as she padded barefoot across the hardwood, the slozzy gurgle of a flushed toilet, because Doreen's first stop when she got up, no matter the time, was the toilet, same as his was — would have sparked and wheeled directly over Charlie's head.

"Okay." Jake was back on the line. "Got some trouble."

"Yeah?" Charlie said. They hadn't talked for a few weeks. Charlie, like most newly retired people, had resented that at first, missing the contact, but then he realized how busy Jake was — as busy, frankly, as Charlie had been when he was on the job — and let it go. They would talk when they talked. If Jake needed him, he'd be here.

Apparently he needed him now.

"Yeah," Jake said.

"Do tell."

"Three overdoses. One fatality."

Charlie sighed. "That's rough. But come

on. We've seen that before, right? Two or three ODs per week. It's bad, but it's not shocking. Not anymore."

"You don't understand. I'm not talking about *days*. I'm talking about a couple of *hours*. They've all come since midnight."

"Jesus."

"One at the Marathon. That was the fatality. The other two're here at the Burger Boss. Place is closed up tight but they were passed out in the parking lot. Not in a car — right out in the middle of the damned lot. And get this — the body at the Marathon was Sally Ann Burdette. Sammy Burdette's niece. That's what I was told."

"Jesus." Charlie was aware of the fact that he had already said it once. But surely there would be no harm in the repetition. Of all the words you could be excused for repeating, that had to top the list.

He had known Sally Ann Burdette from the time she was a tiny little girl, "no bigger'n' a minute," which is how her Uncle Sammy put it back then. Charlie's head instantly filled up with memories. He couldn't stop them from coming.

As a rambunctious five-year-old, Sally Ann would ride her red tricycle on the sidewalk ringing the courthouse while her aunt Dot — Sammy's sister — finished up work at

63

the bank down the street. Sally Ann was the daughter of Clyde Burdette, the older brother of Sammy and Dot. When Clyde's much younger girlfriend announced she was pregnant, Clyde fled the state, unable to handle "the kid thing," as he said to Dot during a quick, apologetic call made from a pay phone somewhere in New Mexico. He wouldn't say specifically where he was, afraid that Dot might sic the law on him. But of course Clyde had miscalculated in this matter — as he had in so many other matters, too. Dot didn't want Clyde back. She adored her niece and was more than happy to raise her, which is precisely what she did, with love and care, after the girl's mother had made it clear that she, too, was completely uninterested in parenthood.

Charlie always wondered what had made Sally Ann turn out the way she did. It could not have been for lack of affection, because Dot Burdette cherished that child. But the day came when Sally Ann was no longer a bright-eyed kid on a tricycle, riding around and around the courthouse, singing a little song to herself, but a shaking, shuffling, emaciated teenager with blank eyes and rusty sores on her arms. Her appearance told Charlie — told everybody — that she had fallen victim to the Appalachian virus:

drug addiction.

Jake was still talking. Charlie didn't know what he had missed, but he felt pretty sure he could figure it out from context.

". . . and so the paramedics just left," Jake said. "These two might make it. They got 'em Narcanned in time, I guess. Sheriff told me to sit tight until she gets here. Thought I'd call you while I was waiting."

"Okay." Charlie was a little surprised at himself. Why wasn't he more upset? He knew how distraught Dot Burdette was going to be about her niece's death. Sammy Burdette would be upset, too, but it was Dot who commandeered his thoughts. He could imagine her face, owned by sorrow. It was going to be hell for her. So why didn't he feel that swishy motion in his gut, that anticipatory dread of watching bad news wreak havoc on decent people?

Well, maybe it was happening. Maybe retirement was finally settling into his soul. Changing him. Doreen had said it would. She had predicted that the day would come when Charlie heard about a tragic blow — the kind that involved law enforcement, the kind for which, a few months earlier, he would have felt responsible for softening for anyone hit by it — and he would feel distant from the event. Aloof. He would care, but not in the same way. Because it wasn't his lookout anymore. Sure, he would be concerned about his friends and their troubles, but as a regular person now — not as a deputy sheriff. Was that the situation here? He hoped not. He had seen it happen to Nick Fogelsong, the former sheriff. He didn't like it in Nick. He didn't like the hint of it any better in himself. It might make life easier in the long run, but in the short, it felt like laziness. And cowardice, too.

Jake's voice broke into Charlie's thoughts. "Do you think I should I start warning folks?"

"Not following you."

"I mean — this looks like a bad batch, right? That just got delivered? Shouldn't we be sounding the alarm?"

"Hmm," Charlie said, to indicate a fair degree of skepticism. Skepticism morphed into sarcasm. "So you aim to warn drug addicts that shooting heroin in their veins is not such a good idea, after all? Downright bad for their health? Maybe they'll want to rethink their life choices, in light of this new information, and maybe watch the carbs while they're at it? Eat more veggies? Jake, my man — *listen* to yourself. How useful you think that'd be?"

"Okay, forget the addicts. How about the

dealer? Whatever's been added to his supply is killing people. We've got to stop it."

"Sounds mighty ambitious."

"Damned straight. If we can't get folks to listen, we can at least track the source. Arrest the dealer. Maybe even stop the supply coming in. Get it off the streets."

"Tall order."

"Didn't say it wasn't. Just said we ought to get started." Jake's voice was impatient.

"I think you need to chill out."

"Really."

"Yeah. Know why? Number one — there's really not a damned thing you can do about it. Number two — as terrible as this all looks right now, the truth is, it's probably a fluke. A temporary spike in the numbers. You might not have another overdose for a week or so. You know what I mean. They come in waves, right? Always have. The thing is, you can't overreact. Got to keep a sense of proportion. So here's what you do. Take care of business there. When your shift's over, go home. Get some rest. Have a nice meal. Good for what ails you. Chances are, it'll all die down. Settle out."

"Spoken like a guy who's retired." Jake had calmed himself. Charlie could hear it in his voice. "Any other advice, old man?"

"Sure. Watch a little TV." Charlie chuckled. "I recommend *Law & Order: SVU.*"

Several hours from now, when Charlie remembered the fact that he had laughed right then, he would wince. His stomach would turn sour. And it wouldn't just be his acid reflux kicking up.

He had missed the signs, missed everything. If somebody had been trying to send him a private signal about what was to come, a whisper, a murmur, he had ignored it, drowning it out with his damned stupid donkey-snort of a chuckle. He had been a deputy sheriff for enough years to know that there were always early clues to a coming catastrophe. Hints and glimmers. But you had to be attuned to them. You had to be on the lookout. You had to listen. You had to be sharp. You could not be relaxing in a recliner with a belly full of chocolate ice cream, poking at the stain on your shirt, wondering when Benson and Stabler would finally figure out they belonged together.

SHIRLEY

7:14 A.M.

"You can't smoke in here."

Shirley Dolan flinched, acknowledging the reprimand with a quick grimace. *Duh.* Of course. Smoking was forbidden everywhere these days. You'd create less commotion if you pulled out a hand grenade and flicked at the pin with a thumbnail.

"Right," she said. "Yeah."

"Sorry."

"It's okay." She shrugged. What had she been thinking? Well, she *wasn't* thinking. That was the problem. Digging into the pack with a curled-up index finger had been a reflex, a response to stimuli. The stimuli? Her nerves. They felt as if somebody was plucking them like ukulele strings. Somebody who didn't know how to play but was just messing around.

The pack went back into her purse. She dropped the purse on the floor, using her left heel to wedge it under her chair. To keep it out of the way. Out of her reach. So that she didn't forget and go for a cigarette all over again. It had been that kind of day. That kind of week. The kind when you forget things. Screw up. Repeat mistakes.

Hell. It had been that kind of life.

"So," he said. He leaned back. Just a little bit. Not a full recline. Still, the chair moaned in protest; the springs and the ball bearings weren't new. Nothing in this office was new. The furniture was clean, neat, but old. Broken-in. Well-used. She appreciated that. There would be something off about a preacher's study that featured shiny new stuff, right? Something borderline hypocritical. With all the dire needs in these parts, all the suffering — kids going to school hungry, old folks sitting in the dark to shave a few cents off the electric bill — you don't want to see a man of God with a fancy new sofa and a leather recliner. No, sir.

Placed on the front of his desk, facing out, was a short orange bar of polished wood with a carved line of swirling letters: *Rev. Paul Wolford.* Must have been a gift, she thought. The kind of thing he couldn't refuse to display, because he was polite, and he wouldn't want the gift-giver to think he was ungrateful. Even though it probably embarrassed him — having his name out there like that. As if he was bragging. She was just guessing, but still.

The desktop also was home to a small brass lamp with a beige shade. Pens and pencils, lined up next to a desk calendar. No computer. She liked that. It made him seem more human, somehow. More ordinary. Accessible. Not some saintly creature who would judge her from on high.

"Yeah," she said. "Well." Now that she was here, she couldn't figure out how to talk about it. How to get started.

"No rush," he said. "Whenever you're ready."

She nodded.

Time passed. The silence should have been awkward, uncomfortable, but somehow it wasn't. The early morning sun slid into the room through the middle third of the tall window off to the right, the part not blocked by the faded curtains hanging from either side. A pillar of listless gray light lay across the carpet.

"Can I make an observation?" he said, after a minute had sloughed away.

"Sure." He could do whatever he liked. This was his office.

"First thing you told me, when you sat down, was that your sister's the county prosecutor. Belfa Elkins."

Shirley shrugged. Yeah, she had said that. Right off the bat, so he would know. It was a crucial part of what she was here to talk about.

"And so," he went on, "you don't want to embarrass her. You both live right here. That means that when you have a problem — you don't have a lot of places to go. Must make you feel pretty lonely sometimes."

Shirley's hands were stacked in her lap. She looked down at them, noting the paleness of her sun-wrecked skin, and noting, as well, the way her wrists jutted out of the cuffs of her chambray shirt, the material thinned from a million washings, give or take. Same basic shade as her jeans. She was fifty-five years old. She had a bony butt and a pleated face and stringy yellow-gray hair that fled down her back. She was, in other words, as old and used-up as the décor in this office.

"Yeah," she said. She nodded again.

"But you're worried. You're not a member of this church, and so you're thinking — 'He doesn't really have time for me.' "

Shirley didn't reply and so he added, "Do I have that about right?"

"Yeah."

It was his turn to nod. His tone was

cordial but businesslike, which she found reassuring. She was suspicious of instant friendliness from strangers. People who were nice to you always had an agenda. An angle. "Okay," he said. "First off — relax. You're fine. I'm glad you came in today. There's no requirement that you be a member of Rising Souls Church before I'll try to help you."

"That's what Connie said you'd say. She goes here. Connie Boyd."

"Is that who gave you my name?"

"Yeah. We work together, me and Connie. Over at the auto parts store." Shirley took a thumb and turned it sideways, rubbing it against her bottom lip, first in one direction, then back the other way. It had become a nervous habit. Especially during the times when she had tried to stop smoking. She wasn't trying anymore. But the lip-rubbing habit stuck. "I'm having a hard time these days," she went on. "Got something on my mind. Connie — me and her talk a lot — Connie said you'd be the person to go to."

"Well, I hope I can justify her faith in me. And yours, too."

"She said you're a good man. She told me about you and your wife. About how you help out anybody who needs it. No questions asked. You let a man live in the church basement, isn't that right? A veteran who's had some trouble?"

"That's Eddie Sutton. But he earns his keep. Works on the furnace when it needs it — which is just about one hundred percent of the time." Paul smiled a whatcha-gonna-do? smile. "Sweeps the walks before Sunday service. Keeps the pews dusted. So it's not charity. More like barter. He gets room and board and whatever money we can spare."

"Still. Pretty decent of you all to do that."

"Everybody needs a helping hand from time to time. Everybody's got challenges — Eddie more than most. He saw a lot of terrible things over in Afghanistan. It's been hard for him to keep a job." Paul nodded to himself, as if he had just done a quick internal recount of the man's problems and was surprised all over again at the total. "He's trying to support a child, too. A little girl. Eddie and the girl's mother aren't involved anymore. Never were, really. But he wanted to do the right thing. He's that kind of man." He scooted his chair closer to the desk. "And if you're wondering why I'm telling you all this — it's just to drive home the point that everybody has times when they need help. So don't feel funny about being here."

Shirley liked Paul Wolford, a fact she

found surprising. When her friend Connie had suggested the minister as a confidant, Shirley had groaned and put up her hands as if she was warding off gunfire; her experience with religious people had not been positive. But Connie pushed. *You'll like him,* she said. *He's not like a regular preacher. He doesn't do much preaching, for one thing. Outside of Sunday service, I mean. Does more listening than talking.* That sounded good to Shirley. But she would withhold final approval, she told Connie, until she had laid eyes on the man.

Now she had done just that. Paul Wolford was handsome — you'd call him that, no question. Clean-shaven. Chiseled jaw. His eyes were the shade you find in amateur paintings of the ocean — an intense, unalleviated blue. His hair was thick and straight and acorn-brown; no matter how often he shoved it up and off his forehead, a soft chunk of it flopped right back down there again, like the hair of that movie star. The one with the English accent. His name was — yeah, Hugh Grant. That was it.

There was an earnestness about Paul Wolford, she thought. Like he wanted to make the world right for everybody and even if he couldn't, he wanted to be on the record as having tried.

Sitting there in the battered chair facing his desk, all at once Shirley decided to trust him. She had to trust somebody.

"Things started to go bad for me at the start of the summer," she said. "Broke up with my boyfriend. We'd been sharing a place, so I had to move out."

"Ending a relationship is hard."

"Yeah. Yeah, it was. He's a singer — he's real good — but he wouldn't work at any other kind of job, even when the singing wasn't bringing in much cash. I guess I got tired of supporting the both of us."

"Understandable."

"Yeah. Connie helped me think it through. Helped me find another place, too. But this other thing . . ." Shirley let the sentence die a natural death. She started a new one. "Connie stopped me before I got very far. Said it was too much for her. She was over her head." Another pause, longer this time. "Kind of tough. Talking about it, I mean."

He lifted his hand and gestured with it. "Would you like some coffee? A glass of water?"

Shirley shook her head. She was enough of a disruption in his day without making him wait on her.

"Just give me a sec here," she said. She broke off eye contact, pretending a sudden interest in whatever might be happening outside the window. She couldn't really see anything. Just feeble sunlight struggling to push through the dusty panes.

She had showed up at the door of the church a few minutes before seven. She didn't know what time somebody might come along and open the place. The sign said the church office was open from nine to noon on Mondays and Wednesdays, and this was Monday, but she wasn't here for church business. Or was she? She didn't know how much ground the phrase "church business" actually covered. And maybe they opened up the place earlier for non-church business. Whatever. She didn't care to wait anywhere else. They could throw her out if they didn't want her here.

A moment later she had heard a scuffling sound on the other side of the big wooden door with the tarnished brass studs. The door swung open. She recognized the man right away, from his photo on the church Web site. It was Reverend Wolford. In his right hand he held a short red leash. At the end of it quivered a small dog, a chubby brown-and-white terrier whose paws had clearly done the scuffling.

Startled, the man had blinked a few times, and then he smiled.

"Good morning," he said. "May I help you?"

"Hope so."

"Well, I hope so, too. Hang on. Let me ask my wife if she can walk Gil. Get me off the hook." At the sound of his own name, the terrier had reared up on his hind legs, begging for his walk. He was so close. He could see the grass. Shirley figured he could probably smell it, too.

"I didn't mean to come to your home," she said. "I thought this was the church."

"It's both. The rectory's attached." Paul inclined his head. "I come through the sanctuary sometimes. When I'm taking Gil out. I just like the feel of a church without any people in it. Especially in the morning. We've only got the one stained-glass window, but it faces east and — wow. It's just beautiful. It's like the whole world is getting a second chance, you know?"

Shirley had nodded, because a nod seemed to be called for. In truth, she did not remember what a church felt like in the early morning. Or any other time of day. She had not been inside a church since she was a little girl, when certain relatives — an aunt and uncle she now referred to exclusively in her mind as "damned hypocrites" — would come by on Sunday mornings and

78

pick up her and Belfa and take them to church. Uncle Chester and Aunt Bess knew very well what was going on in that trailer, the one the sisters lived in with their pig of a father, but they didn't do anything about it. They were scared of him, too. And so they told the girls to bow their heads and pray and ask God to make them more obedient, better behaved, so that they wouldn't make their daddy mad. That, Uncle Chester insisted, was the crux of the problem: They pushed his buttons. Set him off. *Better ask the Good Lord to help you learn to keep your mouth shut,* Aunt Bess would say, holding Shirley's upper arm in a grip as tight as a tourniquet, *and not be such a smart-aleck. You girls need to learn to be humble. And grateful that your daddy takes care of you. Since your mama done run off like she did.*

There was more to the story about what had happened to their mother. Shirley knew that now. There was always more to every story than what you were told as a child.

Shirley had occasionally gone to the nondenominational service run by the prison chaplain, but that was in a square beige room with folding chairs and no windows. Hence no light. Of any kind.

"Be right back," the minister had said. The dog reluctantly let himself be dragged away.

When Paul returned a few minutes later, his wife was with him. She was short and portly, a vivid contrast to his height and leanness. She had a shelf of dark hair and round, gold-rimmed glasses.

"Jenny Wolford," the woman said. She shook Shirley's hand with a brisk friendliness that was also somehow impersonal, which Shirley appreciated. "It's my turn to walk Gil, anyway." She smiled. "His name's short for Gilead. I'll let you and Paul have some privacy." And then she was gone, taking the leash from her husband in such a smooth and seamless way that Shirley was barely aware of the handoff.

He led her back through the sanctuary. Shirley had an impression of old wood and long splintery benches and a gray flagstone floor — the floor looked chilly, even in August — and yes, a stained-glass window, rising behind the altar in a radiant blaze of reds and yellows and blues. She consoled herself with the thought that she probably wasn't the first person to show up on the church doorstep; others before her had surely appeared at an odd hour and asked to talk to the minister. Both Paul and Jenny had seemed thoroughly at home with the interruption, with having their day scrambled by a surprise visitor.

She followed him through a paneled corridor and into his office. He motioned her into a chair. He took the one behind the desk and waited for her to fill him in. After their brief initial conversation, during which she told him who her sister was, Shirley had stopped. She was unsure about how to go on. She asked him for a moment to collect herself. She did not feel pushed or rushed, and that enabled her to find a way forward.

She shifted her gaze back to his face. "Okay," she said. "I'm ready."

He waited.

"I have a lot going on," Shirley said. "First off, like I said — my little sister's the prosecutor. Belfa Elkins. She goes by Bell."

"I've heard of her. Impressive woman."

"Yeah. She is." Shirley let the pride rise in her voice. "If you knew how we grew up — if you'd seen what we had to put up with, the both of us, if you'd seen the miserable SOB who called himself our father, you'd . . ." She expelled a brief jet of air. "Never mind. Let's just say that my sister's a good example of what you can do if you work real hard. Make the right choices."

"I'm sure that's true."

"And I don't mind saying — before we go any further — that I didn't always do that. Make the right choices, I mean. Made a lot of mistakes in my life."

"Just like everybody else."

"Well, mine were pretty big. I spent some time in Lakin." Lakin Correctional Center was the women's prison in West Virginia. Shirley spoke the next part quickly, to get it over with. "For killing our father. Donnie Dolan. So that he wouldn't hurt us anymore." She looked down at her shoes. When she raised her head again, she added, "And for burning down the trailer. Where we lived."

She waited for his reaction.

"Okay," he said.

"Been out of Lakin a few years. Me and Belfa — we get along fine. Wish I saw more of her. But she's real busy. All the time." Restless, eager to get to the point but also apprehensive about it, Shirley shifted her feet forward and backward on the floor. "Anyway, I got something I need to tell her. That's the real problem here. But I don't know how."

"What do you think will happen if you tell her?"

His question surprised her. "Don't you want to know what it is first?" she said.

"If you want to share it — sure. But before we get into that, I'd like to know why you're reluctant to talk it over with her."

Shirley pondered. "She'll be upset."

"Are you sure that's all it is?"

Again, he waited. She liked the careful, respectful way he handled silence. He seemed to know when to hold off and keep his mouth shut and when to speak, when to move the conversation forward.

"I just don't have the right words," Shirley said. "But I gotta tell her. And I gotta tell her real soon."

He was distracted. Someone had come into the office. Shirley turned her head. His wife stood in the threshold.

"So sorry to interrupt," Jenny said. "Paul, when you're finished here, you need to call Dot Burdette. She said it's urgent. Sounded really upset."

"Okay." He nodded. "Thanks, Jen." As soon as his wife had cleared the doorway, he returned his attention to Shirley. "We can take as long as you need. Don't feel rushed. I get calls like that all day long. You're my priority right now."

She felt a small blush of pleasure. It was nice to be someone's priority.

"Maybe you could meet your sister for lunch sometime," Paul went on. "Or better yet — write her a letter. Not an e-mail. An actual letter. Write it out by hand or type it on a typewriter and take it to her house.

83

You could watch her while she reads it. That way, you won't have to say anything out loud if it doesn't feel right. But you're there. If she wants to discuss it."

Shirley licked her lips. They felt dry and rough. "You still don't know what it is."

"It sounds private. You don't have to tell me unless you —"

"I'm dying."

He seemed to absorb the information through his skin. He shuddered. "Oh, my. Oh, my." He closed his eyes. When he opened them again, he locked onto her eyes. She appreciated the fact that he didn't look away. Looking away surely would have been easier.

"It's the cancer." She blurted the words. "Your sister needs to know. And like you said — the sooner, the better."

Shirley realized he had misunderstood. "That's not the thing that's hard to tell her."

He was confused now. She could tell from his face. So she quickly spoke again, her words coming in a rush: "It's something else. Something different. I lied, okay? I lied to everybody. I can't lie anymore. It's over. That's what I've gotta tell her — that I'm all through with the lying. I have to speak the truth. It's going to tear her apart, but I have to do it. I can't . . ." Her throat was suddenly much too dry. She coughed, swallowed.

And then she told him the rest of the story.

Bell

8:57 A.M.

This would be a day like no other.

In the beginning, though, nobody knew what was coming. It was impossible to know.

Or was it? Surely she should have predicted it, the blunt consequence of a perfect storm of causes and effects: a chilling rise in the number of addicts, a surge in potency of the heroin coming up from Mexico, the ease of finding willing customers. Any sentient person — especially a county prosecutor, for God's sake, someone who knew just how rapidly the situation was deteriorating — should have seen it. Should have known.

But even if there *had* been an unmistakable omen, an in-your-face portent, Bell might have missed it. Because at the crucial moment that morning — the moment when she should have received her first inkling that something horrific was stirring in its cradle — she wasn't thinking about drugs or death or the myriad issues involved in public safety and the administration of justice.

What was she thinking about?

She was thinking about doughnuts.

Her secretary, Lee Ann Frickie, had brought doughnuts to the office this morning, an occurrence that was, if not unprecedented, certainly highly unusual. Lee Ann was decidedly anti-treat, and militantly anti-sugar; she had once grabbed a Little Debbie Oatmeal Creme Pie out of the hands of Deputy Charlie Mathers mere seconds before its insertion into his widened mouth, declaring as she did so that he could thank her later for saving his life. Charlie did not see it quite that way. He was surprised, and he was angry, and he never quite forgave Lee Ann. She later apologized for startling him and perhaps acting impetuously — but she would *not* apologize for attempting to safeguard his health.

Yet the moment Bell walked through the door, Lee Ann rose from her desk and handed her a buff-colored circular confection upon which the honey-glaze had already cracked, like a mirror whose structural integrity had recently been breached by a slight tap, creating an interlocking network of polyhedrons that straddled the whole. As a consequence, the doughnut was shedding small cloudy flakes of sugar. Lee Ann had wrapped it in a napkin, but the fractured bits of deliciousness slipped over the napkin's edge in a constant messy sprinkle.

"Here you go," Lee Ann said. She had passed the mandatory retirement age for county employees some years ago, but no one seemed to care about that, least of all Lee Ann. She wore her hair in a gray bob. She was straight, tall and very thin; she claimed to prefer kale to cake, and her slenderness meant that it might actually be true. She had served six county prosecutors — all male, until Bell improbably was elected to the post — but would never, even when pressed, offer up an opinion as to which boss was her favorite. It seemed clear to most observers that her rejection of an easeful retirement meant that Bell Elkins topped her list, but there was no independent confirmation of that hunch from the only person who knew for sure: Lee Ann.

Bell stared at the doughnut. For a moment she was too flummoxed to move. She stood there, doughnut in one hand, briefcase in the other, and tried to solve this first mystery of the day. Her initial hunch — and she could be forgiven, surely, given Lee

Ann's age — was that her secretary must have suffered a mild stroke. Only a stricken and ailing brain could account for the fact that Lee Ann had cast her lot with something that actually tasted good. Or that possessed any taste, period.

And then, just like that, the mystery was solved.

"It was my turn to get the doughnuts for church yesterday," Lee Ann said. "Clean forgot that attendance goes way down in the summer. I bought too many. Hate to waste 'em."

So that was the explanation. The only thing Lee Ann disliked more than indulging in sugary snacks was squandering resources.

Bell continued on into her office. The prosecutor's suite was on the first floor of the Raythune County Courthouse, an immense stone behemoth that presided over Acker's Gap like a stern grandparent, reeking of iron judgment and encroaching decrepitude, gradually unraveling at the edges. Behind it a sawtooth-topped black mountain blocked a large part of the sky and hence the sun, so that, no matter the season, the courthouse felt chilly in the natural shadow. There was a time when Bell had referred to the courthouse as her second home. But as her workload had increased, and as her ability to delegate had decreased, she had tallied up the hours one day and realized it was actually her first. That place with the living room and bedrooms and kitchen was now the runner-up.

She set the doughnut on the edge of her desk. She didn't have the heart to tell Lee Ann what every doughnut aficionado knew: They didn't keep. Unless you ate a doughnut within a few hours of its creation, it quickly grew brittle and stale. A day was an eternity in the life of a doughnut. The dandruff-like spillage from the cracked glaze told Bell all she needed to know about Lee Ann's little gift: By now it would be a hard flavorless glob.

And so it was that when her cell rang, Bell was not thinking about the deep, abstract themes that usually engulfed her each morning in the first few minutes when she sat down behind the oak desk. She was not thinking about crime and punishment, or the universal propensity for selfishness and greed, or the violence bred by the dismal economic plight of the people who had elected her. She was not thinking about justice or injustice, or life and death, or suffering and redemption.

She was thinking about doughnuts.

The foolishness of that, accidental though

it was, would haunt her for a long, long time.

"Elkins." She hadn't bothered to look at the caller ID. It didn't matter who was on the other end; she would answer. That was what being a public servant was all about. You didn't get to pick and choose whose problems you responded to.

"Morning." The word was a friendly one, but the tone was blank and plain, with no embellishment to suggest actual affection. It was not that Sheriff Pam Harrison was unaware that her manner of speaking struck some people as offputtingly rude; she simply didn't care. She had a job to do. Social niceties did not register on her personal list of Things That Matter.

"What's going on, Pam?" Bell's voice was slightly more cordial than the caller's, but not by much. In the beginning she had attempted to forge a closer bond with Pam Harrison; she had been rebuffed so many times — not harshly, but with no question about Pam's desire to keep her colleague at arm's length — that she no longer bothered. If the sheriff was on the line, it was about business. Might as well get right to it.

"Rough night." Pam's voice was a straight line. It never changed to accommodate the nature of the information being conveyed, be it tragic or routine. "Five overdoses. One fatality."

"Damn. *Five?*"

As bad as it was, it wasn't a record, and thus Bell felt no premonition. A year and a half ago, the total number of overdoses on a single night was seven. Six of the seven had hailed from a single notorious, troublemaking family: the McAboys from Hawksbridge Hollow. No one died. *More's the pity,* Bell had thought at the time, and she knew she was not alone in that sentiment. She also knew it was the kind of thing you couldn't say out loud.

"Yeah," Pam said. "The fatality, by the way, was Sally Ann Burdette."

Bell winced. She had gone to high school with Dot Burdette. The first time she met Dot's niece, Sally Ann, Bell instantly knew the kind of trouble the girl was in; the runny red eyes and the unhealed sores on her arm and her fidgety demeanor could all be filed under the category "dead giveaway." But there was nothing Bell could do about it. Nothing Dot could do about it. Nothing anyone could do about it — until Sally Ann herself made the decision to change her life.

The window on that possibility, Bell thought grimly, was now officially and permanently closed.

"Okay," she said. "Thanks for the heads-up." She pulled the cell from her ear to check the time, wondering how many minutes would elapse before Dot called her, bereft and wailing. She and Dot were not close friends, but she knew that she would be among Dot's first calls. Dot would want to make sure the prosecutor's office was ready to pounce on whoever had sold her girl the drugs. Family members had to blame somebody. You couldn't blame a dead person, even if the dead person had injected herself with a lethal dose of heroin.

The sheriff was talking again. "Looks like a bad batch. Laced with something a lot more powerful than these folks are used to."

"Should we start tracking down the source?"

"We know the source."

Pam had a point. It was an infuriatingly well-established fact that drug gangs — mostly from Mexico, according to FBI reports — made regular trips to the area. They were, Bell thought, like peddlers from a couple of centuries ago, those canny con men who sported big smiles and practiced lines of snappy patter. Instead of horse-drawn wagons that swayed and clinked with pots and pans hanging from hooks on the side, the dealers tooled around in Trans

Ams and Chargers with small plastic bags packed in the glove box. And they didn't bother with patter. They didn't need to.

"True," Bell said, "but somebody's getting the stuff into the hands of the addicts. Somebody here in town, I mean." The gangs were wholesalers, not retailers. They relied on local help for distribution.

"You think we should find out who sold it to Sally Ann and the others."

"Yeah. Maybe they don't know what they're selling — the fact that it's so deadly, I mean. And if they *do* know, they probably don't give a damn. But we can try. Addicts use what they buy within minutes after buying it. More than likely, there's a single dealer who just finished selling the batch to these victims. We identify that dealer and shut him down."

The sheriff began speaking again before Bell had concluded her final sentence. "We don't usually pursue this kind of thing, and you know why," she said. "One word. Resources."

"I get it. But come on, Pam — five overdoses."

"That's a lot, I'll grant you."

"So let's do something about it."

Bell was surprising herself. She had not felt this passionate about anything in quite a while, least of all anything to do with concern over addicts and their self-inflicted miseries. She had enough on her plate just trying to achieve justice for the wholly innocent, for the people who *hadn't* regularly summoned their own misfortune like someone whistling for a dog from the back porch.

There had been a time, of course, when such a situation would have automatically kicked her conscience into high gear. She would have demanded — not requested, *demanded* — that they do everything they possibly could to hunt down the local dealer. And she would have rallied others to the cause. But the warrior part of her had diminished over the years. It was still there, but it had been systematically ground down. Trimmed back. Worn away, like a shelf of rock exposed to wind and water and time. Bell had spent too many years trying to fight the problems in Acker's Gap: bad schools, bad roads, no jobs. Now that drugs were added to the mournful list, she felt even less motivated to jump in, waving her sword. She still did her job, but she did it mostly by the book now, methodically, calmness in her heart. No more wild crusades with fire in her eye.

And yet here she was, asking Sheriff Harrison to find a needle in a haystack. *Make that a syringe in a haystack,* she corrected herself.

Maybe this was a last-gasp thing. A dramatic sign-off. A final gesture before she pulled up stakes for D.C. and the law partnership with Elaine Mitford. A way of going out with a bang instead of a whimper.

Or maybe it wasn't so narrowly personal, after all. Maybe she was just tired of the idea that some lives were disposable, that some lives didn't count as much as other lives did. That addicts, because they were addicts, didn't matter.

"You find that dealer," Bell declared, "and I'll prosecute him."

Pam's short silence meant she was contemplating ways and means. "Let me poke around a little bit," she said. "Collier County's been going through the same thing in their jurisdiction. I'll see if I can find some links."

Bell had another call coming in. She clicked off with the sheriff, who didn't mind abrupt endings. She actually preferred them, Bell knew, to articulated good-byes.

"Elkins."

There was no reply. But it was a darkly occupied silence — that is, Bell could sense the living presence behind it. A check of the caller ID confirmed her hunch.

"Dot, I'm so sorry," Bell said. "I just heard about Sally Ann. I'm so very, very sorry for your loss."

Suddenly the silence ended. The ensuing noise was like nothing Bell had ever heard before, an eerie shriek that scraped against the outer edge of the recognizably human.

"Oh, my God." This was followed by an urgent, guttural gasp and a repetitive flurry of words. *"Bell. Bell. Bell. Bell."*

"Where are you? Can I —"

Dot interrupted her. "They said — they said she . . ." There was a hard rasp as she took in a breath and then forced it out again. "My baby. My Sally Ann. She's gone."

"Is there anything I can —"

"Yeah. Yeah, there's something you can do. You can find out who gave those drugs to my little girl. She didn't know. She didn't know what she was taking. Do you hear me? She didn't."

"Are you at your house? Is someone there with you? I can come over if you need me."

"I already called my pastor. Reverend Wolford." Dot's voice bristled with bitterness. "And he'll tell me, right? Tell me why God did this to me. That's his *job,* right? To explain to me what kind of God would do this — would let Sally Ann suffer. She was

97

a good girl. She just trusted the wrong people, okay? And then it got to be too late. But it *wasn't her fault.* She was just a kid." A sob. "My sweet little girl. What kind of God would be this mean? This cruel? He must hate me. That's got to be it. He hates me. Well, then I hate *him,* too. The *bastard.*"

There was fury in Dot's tone, a stoked-up anger rich and raw. Gone was the elegant, clipped, even slightly arrogant mien of the bank vice president, the woman whose nails were always perfectly manicured, whose hair was always sculpted and tinted a metallic shade of white-blond, the woman who had always, in Bell's estimation, held herself apart from her tattered hometown, as if she only stayed here out of pity, and out of a desire to give lesser mortals a glimpse of what they might aspire to. That woman had disappeared. This one had a voice reaching deep into the flinty past of her ancestors from the hills of West Virginia, smearing itself with the mud of coarseness and casual brutality.

"You *get them,* Bell — you hear me? I *mean* it. You *get* those SOBs who sold it to her and then you leave me in a room with 'em, you got that? Just give me a minute. That's all I need." Her voice seemed to drop an octave, becoming even darker and harsher. "I'll rip out their eyeballs, is what I'll do, and then I'll saw off their balls and I'll jam 'em down their throats so hard their balls'll be popping out their assholes. Swear I will."

Bell let her talk. She let her rant. She had heard worse, much worse, before. The prosecutor's office, Bell knew after so many years on the job, was always the low spot in the drain. It was the place where the shock and the hate and the sorrow and the ravenous desire for revenge all collected in a tangled snarl. Bell accepted that. She was only half-listening, anyway, which did not mean she was indifferent, but only that Dot's anguish had filled her with new sense of purpose.

They had to find out who was selling the tainted heroin and stop it — fast. Sally Ann might have been the first fatality, but she wouldn't be the last.

JAKE

9:12 *A.M.*

He lifted his face from the basin and stared at his reflection in the bathroom mirror. Water dripped from his chin. He had filled the sink and then used both hands to scoop up the water and fling it repeatedly into his face. Quite a lot had spilled on the floor, and splashed the pale green tiles on the wall between the mirror and the vanity, but he didn't care about that. His face was burning up. He thought he might have a fever. He quickly overruled that, however. He didn't have a fever. What he had was a job. A job that was mostly okay, and occasionally deeply satisfying — but that sometimes left him hollowed out with fatigue.

This was one of those times.

After clearing the scene in the Burger Boss parking lot, Jake had taken a short break. He had parked his Blazer at the edge of a steep ridge. He liked to look at the mountains late at night, their darkness set against an older and even more immense darkness — the darkness of the sky. He had given up smoking five years ago but damned if he didn't miss it at times like these: sitting alone in his vehicle on a summer night, window down, mountains rising up in front of him. The presence of a cigarette, the glittering tip, the slow burn, the hot bitter taste of tobacco on his tongue, would only have enhanced the moment.

He had not had to make the notification, the one that went to the next of kin. Sheriff Harrison had taken care of it. Jake had made plenty of those visits himself, endured the shock, the disbelief, the anger. Once, an old lady had taken a swing at him. It wasn't personal, he knew; she had formed a fist out of pain the moment she'd heard that her husband was dead. So he knew how to do it, how to deflect not only the blows but also the screams, or the fainting, or the cursing, or the whatever. He knew the ropes. Still, he wasn't sorry when Harrison took over this time. Told him she'd handle it. Turns out she knew Dot Burdette personally. Thought it might be better, coming from her. That's what she told Jake, anyway. He knew the truth: It wasn't going to matter who it came from.

He'd sat in his Blazer for a good long time, watching the mountains, thinking about the girl on the bathroom floor. And then his radio had crackled. His stomach heaved, right on cue. It was never good news.

Two more overdoses. This time, the victims had been discovered in a culvert next to Sayman Street, near its intersection with Elderberry Road. Jake arrived there in less than fifteen minutes, whereupon he interviewed the driver who had come upon the grisly surprise. The driver had told his story in a shaky voice: As he rounded the big curve, the headlights of his Toyota Tundra had nosed along the side of the road and picked out a couple of ragged lumps that didn't look like they belonged there. He pulled over. His first clue that these were people and not piles of trash had come when one of them tried to sit up. *Nearly scared the bejesus out of me,* the driver admitted. *Got to go home and change my underwear.* Jake wrote it down just like the man said it. Word for word.

Shortly thereafter the paramedics arrived. It was Molly and Ernie again, a circumstance that caused Ernie to look at Jake and mutter the totally expected wisecrack, "Long time no see," because it had been less than an hour since they had had their little rendezvous in the Marathon bathroom. The victims, a man and a woman, were lucky: They had been found quickly. Molly squirted naloxone up their noses, reviving them in minutes. Soon they were up and talking. Instead of answering Jake's questions about the source of their supply, they cursed and complained about the naloxone. Along with saving their lives, it had blocked their bodies' absorption of the opiates, hence they had been robbed of an anticipated pleasure and were thrust immediately into the hell of withdrawal: stomach cramps, fever, the shakes.

Jake gave them the boilerplate warnings. They told him to go to hell. Molly chimed in, explaining that they really ought to let the paramedics take them to the hospital, just to be sure they were okay. They told her to go to hell, too. Jake watched them stumble on down the road. Somewhere along the way he had lost the capacity for surprise about any aspect of human behavior.

Then Jake had put the final flourishes on his report, released the driver, said good night to Molly and Ernie, wishing them a quiet end to their shift. "You, too," Molly had replied. Jake tried and failed to find something personal in her tone, something special, something more than just one professional being cordial to another. On his way home he had called Evelyn Munden, an ER nurse at the Raythune County Medical Center. The two girls who had overdosed in the Burger Boss parking lot were still hanging on. Their names, he found out, were Patty Mercer and Jewel Kannel. The names meant nothing to him.

Eyes still closed from the dousing he had given his face, he groped for the towel hanging from the towel rack. He rubbed at his forehead, his neck, and his cheeks, feeling the rapid encroachment of his beard, the new black bristles scraping against the towel. He really ought to shave. Save himself the trouble later. But he was too tired right now.

God, am I ever.

Five overdoses. One fatality. A bad night, you bet. But far from the worse he'd ever lived through. So why did he feel the way he felt right now — jazzed-up, jumpy, uncertain, half-afraid to turn the corner of the next five minutes of his life, because something terrible might be lying in wait for him there?

Routine tragedies were part of the job. Jake had been on duty the night a year and a half ago when a Honda Odyssey had crossed the centerline and gotten itself poleaxed by an eighteen-wheeler. Four people in the car. Three dead, one critically injured. The truck driver, too, was severely hurt and later died. And then, a month ago, two teenaged boys had wrapped their Dodge Charger around a tree out on Nash Pike. One died at the scene. The other one's brain injury would keep him in a coma for the rest of his life. No matter how wildly the comatose kid's mother wept and caterwauled and demanded that *somebody better do something about this and I mean RIGHT NOW,* the boy wasn't going to wake up. Ever.

So, yeah. He knew a little something about dealing with death and misery. He saw them all the time. Somehow, though, the drug overdoses felt different. They took more out of you. Maybe it was because you didn't really know where to put your sympathy. Addicts craved that sympathy; they used it to get what they wanted from their families. Jake had seen that in action, when he'd taken addicts home. The younger ones, that is. The teenagers. They seemed to love the horrified look in a mom's or a dad's eye, the disbelief, the appalled pity. Pity was catnip to an addict. They knew just how to use it for maximum manipulation.

Jesus, I'm as cynical as old Charlie. He'd be proud.

Jake dropped his tired butt down on the seat of the plaid recliner in his living room. He was in his boxers and undershirt. He had stripped off his deputy's uniform, wadding it up and flinging it down the basement stairs. That was his idea of housekeeping: wad and fling. At the end of the week, he would go down and pick up the items and stuff them into the washer. Throw in a Tide pod. The basement had a cracked concrete floor and cinder block walls and massive platoons of spiders. At one point, when he had first purchased this house, he had made plans to finish the basement; he intended to turn it into a sort of man cave with carpeting and a wet bar and a big sloppy leather couch and a ginormous TV set. But he didn't. It was one of a thousand things he meant to do but never got around to.

He was thirty-four years old — still a young man — but he had an old man's sense of regret, of having left too many threads in his life dangling. When he contemplated any sort of change these days, from fixing up his house to asking Molly Drucker if she would like to get a plate of eggs after their shift one of these mornings, he was stymied by a sense of futility. Things seemed rigid in his life, as fixed and permanent as those mountains that he spent too much time staring at in the velvety darkness.

He knew he ought to grab some sleep, because he was on the night turn again tonight. But he was too keyed up for that. His face was still wet from the good soaking he had given it at the bathroom mirror, in a ritual that was, he surmised, probably an attempt to wash off the stain of the night. He understood that because he tended to do it every morning when he returned from his shift. Stripped down to T-shirt and boxers, he felt less naked, somehow, than he had been just a few minutes ago in his uniform. The uniform and the responsibilities it deposited on him — the duties, the knowledge — made him feel vulnerable and exposed.

He had never intended to go into law enforcement. It was his father's idea. His mother, Pauline, died when Jake was twelve years old. When he told people that fact about himself, the reaction was always the same: A soft light came into their eyes, particularly the eyes of women, as they envisioned a poor motherless boy, far too young to endure such sorrow, forced to face the world without the comfort and guidance of maternal affection. But it wasn't like that at all. Jake did not correct them, but he felt guilty about reaping their concern under false pretenses. Pauline was a disaster as a mother. She was selfish and conniving. She resented the hell out of him — the unwanted child whose birth had ended her youth and pinched off all her hopes of leaving Beckley, West Virginia. She had gotten pregnant with Burt Oakes's child when she was seventeen, and everybody told her she had to marry him, and so she did — but she didn't have to like it. She never mustered the initiative to walk out on him, which is what she very much desired but also very much feared to do, because she had no money and no job skills, and she took out her frustration on Burt and the boy. It was a kind of slow-acting poison, that frustration. Jake's memories of his mother always involved a billowing tuft of reddish hair, a pair of narrowed eyes, and a cigarette plugged in the side of a scowling mouth, a tentacle of smoke crawling up her lean cheek as if the smoke itself was trying to flee the scene in the quickest way available. When he started fourth grade, his mother got so that she couldn't keep any food down. The flesh seemed to fall off her like sheets of mountain ice in the spring melt. By the time she went to a doctor, she weighed less than a hundred pounds.

The diagnosis: inoperable stomach cancer.

Jake remembered the day his father told him the news. He searched his father's face for a clue about how he ought to react. There was no clue. He was on his own. His mother was dead in two months. His father bought him a black wool suit for the funeral. Jake remembered more about the suit than he did the funeral: The trousers were cuffed, which made him feel like he was wearing ankle weights, and the coat was as heavy across his shoulders as he imagined chain mail would have been on a jousting knight. They were studying medieval times in school.

When Jake was nearing the end of his senior year of high school, his father sat down with him at the kitchen table. He wanted to talk about Jake's future. It was only the second time Burt Oakes had sat down like that with his son — the first was when he told Jake about his mother's illness. Both times Burt acted strangely; he moved more slowly than usual, an air of portentousness pushing down on his limbs as if the very air had suddenly become burdensome. Burt was an accountant with the gas company. He and Jake had rubbed along for the half-dozen years that had passed since Pauline's death. Their interactions were basic, serviceable. Burt Oakes was a quiet man who seemed to draw out the quietness in others, like rice does water; Jake had seen him quell furious emotions in other people simply by remaining calm, by looking at them with a placid, level gaze, a gaze that revealed a mild puzzlement as to what all the fuss was about.

On the day Jake's future was decided, his father sat with his elbows on the table, fiddling with an empty coffee cup, tracing the shape of the tan ceramic handle with his index finger. "So," his father said. "End of the month, you graduate, right?" He didn't say it in a pointed or challenging way. Jake, who sat across from him, shrugged an affirmative. "And then what?" his father said. Jake's reply: "Don't know." His father's finger had reached the bottom of the handle's wide curve and now started back up at the top again. "I hear," Burt said, "that the police are hiring. All you need's a high school diploma. You're in good shape. Shouldn't be a problem." It was true: Jake played football and baseball. He excelled at both. He was tall and rangy; his long body seemed to hang from his shoulders like something on a hanger, diving in sharply at the waist. His arms and legs worked together in a smooth, natural rhythm.

"Okay," Jake had said. "I'll look into it." He was hired right away. He stayed with the Beckley Police Department for twelve years. Gradually he cultivated a new personality: cheerful, outgoing, gung-ho. Quick with the quip. He discovered that people asked you fewer questions about yourself if you seemed happy and chatted with them in an abstract way. They left you alone — whereas if you were quiet and brooding, they were relentless. They poked and prodded and tried to entice you into personal conversation. He married a woman named Nancy Barron, an English teacher at the Catholic high school, St. Joseph's, but after less than a year they both realized that the marriage was a mistake. She didn't love him and he didn't love her. The divorce was simple because there was no emotion and no money; in other words, there was nothing to argue over, nothing to be bitter about. When Jake heard about the opening in the Raythune County Sheriff's Department, he filled out the paperwork right away. He was ready for a change.

And now here he was.

Jake looked down at his right hand. It was splayed on the plaid armrest. An old scar kinked across the back of his palm. When he was fourteen years old he had caught his hand on a barbed wire fence. The cuts had seemed routine, superficial, but they became infected and left him with a quirky line of scars.

Lesson learned: Like it or not, you wear your life.

New job, new people. At first he was sure he had made a mistake. He thought Charlie Mathers was a clown and a goofball and a fat, useless fool, and he thought the prosecutor, Belfa Elkins, was a bitchy know-it-all. Her assistants, Rhonda Lovejoy and Hickey Leonard, struck him as incompetent losers. But a funny thing happened as the months passed and as Jake watched them do their jobs. He got it. He began to understand why each of them followed the path they did: Why Charlie presented himself as an easygoing, amiable fellow who sort of rolled and squeaked along harmlessly as if he sported the tiny wheels of a kid's toy instead of feet, and why Rhonda and Hick were apt to answer a question about courtroom strategy with a long story about somebody's second cousin and the night his bluetick hound dog had puppies in the back seat of a Pontiac.

Law enforcement in a place like Acker's Gap was fluid and untidy. There were no square corners, only curves. Jake's hometown wasn't a large city, either, but it was a city, and the difference between police work done against the backdrop of sidewalks and neighborhoods and a deputy sheriff's duties in a largely rural county was profound. There were the distances, for one thing. Those nights he parked on the ridge with the engine off, watching the mountains, he was inclined to contemplate the enormous spaces between things out here, the vast gaps and the spreading vacancies. You had to fill those spaces with something. It was your choice, it was each man's and each woman's right to pick, but it had to be *something:* God or sex or money or family or work or food or hopelessness. Or alcohol and drugs.

He reached for a notebook. He kept one on the table next to his recliner, along with a pencil. He made a list of the small-time dealers he could recall off the top of his head. Jake and his colleagues knew who the dealers were. The trick wasn't in the knowing. The trick was in catching them in the act, and then deciding if it was worth all the aggravation of hauling somebody in for selling ten dollars' worth of tramadol. These

were not major distributors; these were local people who had been caught selling a
few pills here and there, or heroin when they
had it, and then went right back to it once
they were released from jail:

RAYLENE HUGHES
TAMMY KINCAID
JEB SAWYER
LEO SMITH

He drew a line through Sawyer's name.
Sawyer, he remembered, had died four
months ago. Jet Ski accident out on Charm
Lake.

He looked at the remaining three names.
One of them, most likely, was the distribu-
tor of the tainted heroin. He would check
them out today, one by one. He sent Sheriff
Harrison a short text to that effect.

The doorbell startled him.

What the hell?

He wasn't expecting company. Anybody
who knew him well enough to come by
without calling first would also know he had
worked the night shift; he would be sleeping
now. Ideally.

Jake started toward the front door. Then
he remembered that he was in his underwear. He made a quick detour toward the

staircase, grabbing a pair of gray sweatpants that hung over the banister. He yanked them on. Tied the drawstring. Whoever it was would have to deal with his T-shirt; he didn't have a shirt handy.

He opened the door.

Molly Drucker stood on the front porch, her face shiny with tiredness because, like him, she had worked all night. The skin around her eyes was pouched and the eyes themselves were a little cloudy. She had taken off her bandana, and her hair had asserted its fundamental independence. She was still in her work clothes; the polo shirt was rumpled and the knees of her trousers were stamped with dirt. Jake knew the origin of that dirt. She had had to kneel in the ditch to save the last two overdose victims.

For a quick, strange second he doubted what he was seeing. It felt way too much like an odd and beautiful dream, arising directly out of sleep deprivation and his own deep hopefulness. She seemed to have materialized from the sheer force of his desire.

Because he realized, as he stood there with his hand cupped sideways on the edge of the open door, that no matter what else he had been thinking about since he got home this morning, he had also, behind the screen of those surface thoughts, been thinking about her.

But it was real, all right. It was Molly Drucker. Jake's heart gave a little leap in his chest as reality insisted it be recognized.

"Hey," he said.

"Hey." She was embarrassed. He could tell. She raised her eyebrows up and down, in what seemed to be a silent, rueful acknowledgment that her being here was a tad peculiar, and she spun her gaze around the small porch. A corn broom slanted in the corner. The only furniture was a single lawn chair. The floorboards needed repainting. That job was on Jake's list, along with making the man cave in the basement. And about ten thousand other projects, too.

"I had your address," she said, "from that time you invited me. To your party."

Right. His party. Back when Charlie had announced his retirement, Rhonda Lovejoy had persuaded Jake to throw a party for him, even though party-throwing was not the sort of thing Jake Oakes did. His decision to host was predicated on the fact that he saw it as the perfect opportunity to ask Molly to his house — *Just a small group of us getting together for Charlie, it'll be people you know* — and Molly had said, "Maybe."

116

He gave her his home address. But she didn't show. The next time they worked together, she told him that something had come up. A family thing. "Sure, no problem," he had said, covering his disappointment with breezy nonchalance.

And now here she was. On his front porch.

Jake let a crazy idea spiral up from the center of his mind. Maybe she was here to tell him that she had been thinking about him, too, and that she wanted to get to know him better. Sure, it would be tough — interracial couples were not exactly common around here — but dammit, life is short, and if they enjoyed each other's company then it shouldn't matter what other people . . .

"So I'm sorry to just show up like this," Molly said, "but I've got my brother Malik with me. He wanted to talk to you."

Jake leaned to one side, to see around her. A white Chevy Silverado was parked at the curb. A young black man sat in the passenger seat, his right arm hanging out the open window. He wasn't looking at the house; instead he looked straight ahead. His hair was cut very close to his scalp and his profile seemed soft, tentative, not settled or permanent. Jake was brought up short again by just how little he knew about Molly's life. He didn't know she had a brother. Did she have any other siblings? He didn't know if her parents were still living. Or who her friends were. He didn't know where she'd gone to school or why she had stayed in West Virginia.

"Okay," Jake said. He had no idea what was going on here, but he didn't need to know. This was Molly. At his house. "You guys want to come in?"

"Yeah. Thanks. I'll get Malik."

He watched her descend the porch steps with that grace and rhythm and nimbleness he had admired from the first moment he saw her. Yet he was also annoyed at himself for taking specific note — *Here we go again,* he thought — of her body and the way she moved through the world. His mind should have been on higher things, right? On hunting drug dealers and saving lives and keeping the peace and all of that. He was a deputy sheriff. But he was also a man, a human being, and a thickness came into his throat while he observed her.

He realized all over again just how much he was attracted to her — her body, yes, but also the abstract essence of her, and the competent, strong woman she was at her core, a fact of which he was certain because he had worked with her, and nothing tells

118

you more about somebody, he believed, than working with her — and he also realized how much it hurt, this longing inside him, this constant, constant yearning.

BELL

10:10 A.M.

"Carfentanil."

Collier County Deputy Kyle Hunsacker said the word slowly and carefully, as if the syllables themselves were dangerous and by all rights should be handled with heavy gloves and tongs.

She remembered the first time she had seen the word written down. It was two years ago, in a report from the governor's task force on drug abuse prevention. "Carfentanil" looked instantly sinister, owing to its length and unfamiliarity. Back then, she wasn't sure how to pronounce it. Part of her wished she was still unsure; she wished she had no need to know anything at all about it.

"So that's what we're dealing with," Bell said. "Your best guess, anyway."

Hunsacker gave her a single solemn nod, like a pulse beat.

Somebody let out a short sigh. Bell was looking down at her notes when the sigh came, and so she couldn't be sure of the source; it was a natural response to this new and appalling information delivered at the outset of the meeting she had convened.

It might have come from Sheriff Harrison, who stood next to the closed door of Bell's office, arms crossed, the flat brim of her brown hat pulled so low that her chin was the most visible part of her face, or it could have emanated from Deputy Brinksneader, also standing, who occupied the spot on the other side of the door. He, too, still wore his brown hat, and he, too, had crossed his arms, and so the two of them looked like brown-uniformed, black-booted bookends, propping up the wooden rectangle between them. But the mystery sigher also could have been Hickey Leonard, the assistant prosecutor, or Rhonda Lovejoy, the other assistant prosecutor. They sat next to each other on the small couch across from Bell's desk.

Or the culprit might have been Bell herself. She had done that once during a county commissioners meeting — let out a sigh of despair without realizing that she had done so, causing Commissioner Sammy Burdette to glare at her and snap, "You got

121

something to say, Mrs. Elkins? I'd thank you to say it, then, and quit with the sound effects. This ain't Hollywood." Sammy liked her and respected her. His remark had been sparked by frustration over a shrinking county tax base, not animosity toward the prosecutor.

Hunsacker cleared his throat, ready for the next question. He had driven over here this morning at Bell's request, after Sheriff Harrison suggested he be included. Collier had had a rash of overdoses the previous week.

He stood in front of Bell's desk like a middle-schooler giving a book report: shoulders back, spine straight, iron set to his jaw when he was listening instead of talking. There was a chair for visitors, angled toward the desk, but no one sat in it; as long as Bell had been a prosecutor, she had never persuaded a deputy on duty to sit down. They always wanted to stand. Hick and Rhonda had chosen the couch, and so the empty chair took on an unnatural importance in the room — far more than it would have, Bell speculated, if somebody had just sat down in the damned thing. What was it about deputies and the necessity of standing at attention all the time?

If Jake Oakes were here, he would be

standing, too. He had offered to come in for the briefing, the sheriff had told Bell, but she said no; they could fill him in later. The office was crowded as it was. And Jake needed to start tracking down dealers, anyway.

"No doubt in your mind," Bell said.

Hunsacker nodded again. He was very young and very blond. His face was so pale it was almost translucent, and it glowed with a permanent pink blush. His uniform shirt had been ironed to within an inch of its life. Seconds after he entered Bell's office he had pulled a small blue spiral-bound notebook from his breast pocket. He referred to it as he spoke.

"That's what the tests showed in our case and this sounds mighty similar," he said. "We had twelve overdoses in a four-day period. Turns out the heroin had been cut with carfentanil. As you folks know, it's a hundred times more potent than fentanyl — the usual stuff they use to stretch out the heroin. It's used to tranquilize elephants, if you can believe that. We were just lucky not to have any deaths." He swallowed, setting his large Adam's apple into conspicuous motion. "I hear that wasn't the case here in Raythune last night."

"So where would somebody get it?"

Rhonda asked.

"You can order carfentanil off the Internet," Hunsacker replied.

Hick Leonard made a noise of black disdain in the back of his throat. "Always the damned Internet," he muttered. "You ask me, the devil's got a new right-hand man — and it's called the Internet." Hick was nearly seventy. He remained physically spry, but sometimes his age showed through in his attitude.

"So let's review," Bell said. She needed to keep them focused. "We've got heroin coming into Raythune County that more than likely has been laced with carfentanil. We'll be getting that confirmed by lab tests just as soon as they're available. From what I've read, a flake of it no bigger than your fingertip can kill you. Isn't that right, Deputy Hunsacker?"

"Right. In fact, we were told to warn first responders to avoid any skin contact with victims at the scene without gloves on. You can get it into your own system that way. So field tests of suspicious substances are strictly prohibited for the time being. Carfentanil is way, way too potent to take a chance with."

Bell started to ask another question, but was sidetracked by the sound of a text coming in on her cell. This was shaping up to be the kind of day in which she couldn't ignore a text. She picked up her phone and glared at the screen. The message was from Shirley. Her sister wanted to meet for lunch today at JPs. *Fine,* Bell thought. *Whatever.* She was annoyed at the interruption, but it wasn't Shirley's fault. Bell had encouraged her sister to come downtown more often, so that they could keep in better touch. Shirley didn't know that Bell was in the middle of a meeting.

Bell texted back *K* and returned her attention to the room.

"Mexico, right?" said Sheriff Harrison. "Same as always." She pushed herself off from the wall and moved a step or two closer to Bell's desk, tightening the circle. Her arms stayed crossed.

"Yeah," Hunsacker said. "That's the supply route — they come up from the Southwest. Usually there's a stop in Chicago and then they spread on down through Ohio and Kentucky and West Virginia."

"And heroin's a hell of a lot cheaper than pain pills," Hick said, "so that's what folks turn to now." He knew that every person present was aware of that fact. Sometimes, though, he needed to speak a truth just to have it on the record. Things that would have seemed astonishing a few years ago — regular, everyday people taking *heroin,* for God's sake — were commonplace realities now. Hick, Bell knew, was afraid that if he didn't declare them out loud every now and again, he and his colleagues would lose the keen edge of their outrage. They would start to accept the unacceptable.

Rhonda Lovejoy leaned forward from her seat next to him on the couch. She was wearing a hot pink pantsuit and white sandals. She was a heavy woman, and she planted her elbows on the tops of her thighs to accommodate the shift in her center of gravity. "So what did you all do?" she asked Hunsacker. "How'd you let the addicts know about the danger?"

"We didn't," he answered, "because we couldn't. Not enough personnel. We just waited it out. Let it blow over."

His meaning was clear: They had let addicts do what it was that addicts did, and then the paramedics had moved in, administered naloxone to save the lives that could be saved, and then everyone sat back and hoped that the next batch of heroin would be cut with something less deadly.

Silence held the room for a few seconds. Bell sensed that each person present was contemplating the implications of that strategy in light of her or his personal philosophy of law enforcement. Sheriff Harrison and the deputies — Steve Brinksneader and Kyle Hunsacker — probably approved; they were realists, having given up long ago on the idea that addicts might eventually see the light. They didn't waste their time or their energy on hope. They dealt with the problems set before them, one by one, working down each day's grim list. And frankly, the task of warning addicts that the current poison they intended to cram into their sweaty, twitching bodies was a great deal worse than the poison they typically crammed into their sweaty, twitching bodies *did* seem to reek of pointlessness. People never changed.

Rhonda and Hick, though, were prosecutors, and prosecutors had to believe, at least theoretically, in the possibility of redemption. They had to maintain a smidgen of hope — or else they would become so bitter, so jaded, and so sardonic, that they could not argue effectively with judges or make deals with defense attorneys or extract pledges of cooperation from defendants. If they operated like cops — believing the worst about people, always — they couldn't do their jobs.

Would Raythune County also wait it out,

allowing addicts to risk death? *Hell, addicts risk death already,* Bell reminded herself, *every day of their lives. They don't give a damn. Why should we?* She could argue the other side of the debate, too: *Because we're not like them. And one of the ways we know that is because we care about them — even when they don't care about themselves.*

She took a moment to look around at the people she had summoned to her office this morning. She had known Hick and Rhonda and Pam Harrison since she had taken this job. Deputy Brinksneader had joined the department some six months ago, and thus was relatively new to her, but her initial impressions were favorable. He worked hard. He seemed to have a good sense of the region and its ways. He had a big body and a face like a bulldog, complete with jowls and a bulbous ridge of flesh that sat across his eyebrows like a shelf. Only Deputy Hunsacker was a stranger, but he was so similar to the law enforcement professionals with whom she had worked for the past eight years — he was taciturn and earnest and resolute, with no wasted motion, and his refusal to sit in a chair made Bell wonder if his knees even bent — that she felt as if she did know him.

She was the center point in this room. She

was the unofficial but undeniable locus. Everyone was leaning in toward her, waiting, because it was principally her decision about what was coming next. Bell had expressed her opinion to the sheriff earlier, but this was a new venue, with a new audience for the debate: Would they begin a rigorous, all-out search for the local dealer who was handing out death as casually as Tootsie Rolls at Halloween? Would they abandon other cases in favor of an investigation whose only potential benefit was to addicts — and only peripherally to the hardworking, law-abiding people who constituted the majority of the citizens of Acker's Gap?

They might get lucky. Last night's emergencies might be the end of it. Perhaps other addicts, even now, were spreading the word on their own about the danger; there was a functioning network of users who did just that, protecting their fellow addicts, looking out for the mutually lost. A great deal of the naloxone administered to overdose victims these days, Bell knew, was done at the scene by friends and family members of the addicts — rather than by paramedics.

Yes, they might get lucky.

First time for everything, Bell thought grimly.

Sheriff Harrison's cell rang. She answered. She listened. Her face betrayed nothing about the content of the call. She ended it with a terse, "Yeah." Then she looked at Bell, but she was addressing everyone in the room. "Four more overdoses," she said. "One fatality at the scene. Squad's already there."

"So now we're up to two deaths and nine ODs," Bell said. "I don't know about the rest of you, but I'm ready to start thinking about this as a murder investigation. The dealer — that's our perpetrator."

There were nods around the room, some of them grudging.

"Word of caution here," Brinksneader said. "Don't forget that these folks take the drugs *willingly.*" It was the first time he had spoken at the meeting and there was a creak of petty complaint in his voice, like an old man who had just found the baseball that cracked his front window. "They're not what you'd call innocent bystanders."

"Never said they were," Bell replied. "But since when does the moral character of a victim affect how we handle the case?"

"I'm only saying," Brinksneader muttered.

Sheriff Harrison shot him a dark glare. Deputies didn't argue with the prosecutor. That was her job. Brinksneader took a sudden interest in the pattern on the area rug under his feet.

"Thanks for the report," Bell said to Hunsacker. She stood up and reached across her desk to shake his hand. "Appreciate you making the drive. I'm sure you have plenty to do back on your own patch, so we'll take it from here."

"Yes, ma'am. Anything else you need, give me a call." The blue notebook was dropped back into his pocket. The gesture seemed to free him up to make a personal remark. "You know what? My grandfather was a deputy in Collier County, too, back in the day. And the worst thing he ever faced was a bootlegging ring during Prohibition. Way up in the hills. He used to tell me how scary it was, going after those boys in the dark, knowing they had shotguns." He shook his head. "Can't imagine what he'd make of all this."

"Different world," Hickey said gruffly. "That's for damned sure."

As soon as Hunsacker cleared the door, the sheriff closed it firmly behind him. What she had to say was none of Collier County's business.

"Look," she said. "I know we talked about it before and it sounds like you've made up your mind, Bell. But Steve here isn't wrong.

We're way short of manpower. You know that as well as I do. Hard to justify chasing after some dealer whose only real victims are — well, low-life scum."

"So we just let them die. Is that right?" Rhonda said. She didn't say it nicely. Challenge simmered in her tone. Bell was surprised; Rhonda was usually a peacemaker, a smoother-over. Something was bothering her this morning. Surely the overdoses were enough to rile anybody — but Bell had the sense that it was more than that, too.

The sheriff started to defend herself. Then she shrugged. "Yeah, okay. Fine. Have it your way, then. That's what I'm saying. Let 'em die. And good riddance."

The words hung in the air, cold and stark.

Bell finally broke the silence. "I expect you to track down the dealer, Pam," she said quietly. "As long as I've known you, you've always done your job."

After a pause, the sheriff said, "Mind a question?"

"Shoot."

"Since when are drug addicts a priority around here?"

"Last time I checked," Bell said, "drug addicts were still human beings."

The sentence was out before she could stop it. She hated herself for saying it that way, for so blatantly playing the moral high card. Bell hated sanctimony in other people, and she hated it even more in herself. She had indulged in far too much of it during her first few months as prosecutor, all those years ago; she had been filled with righteous indignation and a priggish insistence on moral absolutism. She had been — she realized in embarrassed retrospect — insufferably pompous in her haughty rectitude. Nick Fogelsong was the sheriff back then and he had called her on it, setting her straight: *There's only room for one God,* he said, *and as far as I know, the job's already taken.* It took her a while, but she finally understood what he meant. It wasn't about compromise. It was about survival. And proportionality. And effectiveness. Another of Nick's favorite lines — *The perfect is the enemy of the good* — also haunted her, in a positive way. She had learned, over the years, that in a place such as Acker's Gap, you didn't always get your first choice in outcomes. Sometimes you had to settle for your second or third or fourth. Or fifth. And you couldn't get upset about it, or you would fume and stew your way toward an ulcer or a drinking problem or even an early grave.

She missed Nick. He still lived in Acker's

Gap and she saw him from time to time, but it wasn't the same. She had treasured him as a colleague and a confidant. He had taken a job as a security consultant for a chain of truck stops. The pay was better, the hours more reasonable, giving Nick more time at home with his wife, who struggled with serious mental illness. The change made sense in all kinds of ways. But part of Bell still resented his decision to leave before the job was done. Because the job would never be done.

Wait. Isn't that exactly what I'm *planning to do?*

Bell's attention returned to the here and now. The sheriff was looking at her, jaw taut, body tensed with a resentment that seemed to have taken up permanent residence in her spine. Bell could read her posture like a paperback: The sheriff felt free to ignore Rhonda. But she could not ignore the prosecutor. If Bell wanted her to pursue the case, she had to either comply or spend a lot more time arguing.

"Jake Oakes texted me a list of known dealers," Pam said. "He's on it." Her voice was as warm and inviting as a coil of barbed wire. "I'll keep you posted."

"Good. Thanks."

There was nothing more to say. The meeting was over. Pam opened the door — she moved stiffly, as if her joints had seized up in the last few seconds and she might snap a limb if she put any softness into her gestures — and left. Brinksneader followed.

Hickey rose. "No rest for the wicked," he said, hitching up his pants and buttoning his suit coat. "Got a preliminary hearing coming up."

Rhonda kept her seat on the couch. "A word, Bell?"

Bell nodded. She waited until Hickey had departed and then she sat back down behind her desk.

"Hell of a morning," Bell said.

"Hard to recall a worse one." Rhonda looked down at her lap. She'd linked her fingers there. She raised her face. "Need to ask you about something."

"Not surprised. Seems like you're not quite yourself today."

"I'm that obvious?"

"We've worked together a long time."

Rhonda nodded. "That we have."

She had been Bell's second hire. Hickey was her first. Bell had defeated him in the race for prosecutor, and then turned right around and persuaded him to come on board as assistant prosecutor. She needed him. He had practiced law in Raythune

County for half a century — longer than Bell had been alive. He knew the backstory of every man, woman, and child, not to mention every tree, road, and rock, in Raythune County. He himself had made the same case for Rhonda Lovejoy, minus the longevity: She was only thirty-four, but her knowledge of the region and its people was legendary, owing to the fact that her roots went deep and spread wide.

Among Rhonda's only flaws, as Bell had come to see, were a propensity to dress in apparel that was insufficiently conservative for the prosecutor's office, and a habit of collecting strays — people as well as pets — on account of an excessively tender heart. Last time Bell asked her about it, Rhonda had admitted to sharing her small apartment with two cousins visiting from out of town, three dogs, a one-eyed cat, and a guinea pig, along with a family of raccoons who showed up at her patio door every night and received a pie plate rattling with Purina Dog Chow.

There had been a time when Bell considered Rhonda more trouble than she was worth. She was still trouble. But she was definitely worth it.

"Not sure if you remember," Rhonda said, "but a while ago I told you about a child I was kind of concerned about."

"Need a little bit more to go on."

"I heard about her from Penny Latrobe — my great-great uncle's stepdaughter. Penny works as a cashier over at Lymon's. Called me last March. Said a woman had set up a little stand in the parking lot and was begging money to pay for her five-year-old's cancer treatment."

"So the child has cancer."

"Nope. At least Penny doesn't think so. She talked to the girl when Mama was busy taking somebody's money, and the girl said they were just playing. Then Mama got wind of the conversation and told Penny to go away and mind her own business. Got hopping mad. Penny got her name from somebody who recognized her. Raylene Hughes. She's a real piece of work."

"If the child isn't sick, that's fraud."

"Had the same thought myself. Turns out I know Raylene."

"You know everybody."

"Well, maybe. I went to high school with her. Lost track of her over the years. She moved in and out of the area, apparently. I'd hear things now and again — bad things, mostly. Seems like Raylene's generally always in some kind of trouble. And worms her way out of it on account of a pretty face."

"And now she's using her child to collect money under false pretenses."

Rhonda nodded. "Before I could get over there that day, Raylene and her little girl left. Must've gotten spooked. Penny didn't see them again for months."

"Let me guess. They're back."

"Yep. Penny called me this morning. They've been there since nine."

Bell picked up one of the dozen or so yellow pencils on her desk. She tapped the business end against the chipped and seamed woodgrain. "And?"

"And I thought I might head over there and point out to Raylene that she's breaking the law. Catch her in the act. If it's okay with you, I mean."

"You've got seventeen active cases, including an aggravated homicide. And we're chasing a drug dealer who's selling heroin filled with elephant tranquilizer." Bell paused to let the numbers sink in. "If this Raylene person is still on the premises, fine. But don't waste any time chasing her. We just don't have the personnel today."

"Okay." Rhonda stood up. "Appreciate it, Bell. You know how I feel about kids."

"Yes. I do." She decided that they knew

each other well enough for her to add another sentence. "Are you sure that's all this is?"

"What?"

"You don't sound like yourself when you talk about this woman. The bit about the pretty face. Do you have some kind of history with her? A fight over a boyfriend, maybe? Back in high school?"

Rhonda blushed. "No."

Bell waited.

"No," Rhonda repeated.

"Okay, then. You do what you're called to do."

There was relief in Rhonda's voice. "Thanks. And look on the bright side."

Once again, Bell waited. She wasn't aware of any bright sides.

"At least," Rhonda said, "it'll be a change, right? Totally unrelated to the drug crisis."

Bell gave her a level stare. Rhonda knew as well as she did that in Acker's Gap, things always seemed to be linked; all things were part of the same dark turning.

RAYLENE

A woman and a little girl occupied a small corner of the parking lot of Lymon's Market.

The woman, whose name was Raylene Hughes, stood with one hip cocked slightly forward of the other leg. Her long reddish-brown hair draped her narrow shoulders and framed her face in soft, delicate-looking scallops. She wore beige capri pants and a white cotton sweater. She was thirty-four.

Her five-year-old daughter, Marla Kay, sat cross-legged on the blacktop beside her. The blacktop glittered menacingly in the sunshine, like the flank of some exotic animal recently slaughtered on the African veld. Marla Kay, her mother could see, was having too much fun to mind the heat rising up from the lot's dark surface. The little girl was wearing a T-shirt, denim cutoffs, and sparkly plastic flip-flops. Her pink knees

140

grew pinker by the minute, and her scalp was baking like a casserole bound for a church potluck, but Marla Kay was oblivious to all of that. She was playing with an empty plastic two-liter container in which had formerly resided the sloshing brown contents of Dr Pepper. Sometimes she put the container on its side and spun it around; other times, she tried to balance it on its tiny snout. It always fell over and rolled some distance away, and Marla Kay, from her sitting position, had to stretch to retrieve it. When she stretched, she let out an exaggerated *uhhhh* sound that clearly amused her; she followed it up each time with a giggle.

"Stop that," Raylene snapped. She didn't look down at the girl. She was too busy scanning the lot. "Climbing my last nerve."

"Stop what, Mommy?"

"That noise."

"What noise?"

"That noise you been making."

"Okay."

"Good. And don't start back up again, neither."

The lot featured only two cars. This was a disappointment. They had been here for more than two hours and had had barely a nibble. Typically there were at least four or five cars at Lymon's at any given time, which meant at least four or five people — and usually more, because people often gave friends and relatives a lift to the grocery store — would notice Raylene and Marla Kay, and after that, the hand-lettered cardboard sign that Raylene had duct-taped to a yardstick. The yardstick was jammed into a black plastic trash can.

The sign read: PLEASE HELP MY LITTLE GIRL. SHE HAS CANCER. Raylene had helpfully provided a second black plastic trash can, into which the caring souls of the people of Acker's Gap were expected to fling nickels, pennies, and quarters.

"I won't," Marla Kay said. "I won't start up again."

"Good."

Marla Kay was a sweet-natured child. The lack of hair on her head made her look as fragile and friable as an insect pupa that had emerged too soon for its own good. Her skin was pale, a paleness emphasized by the sunburn that was inching across it like the gradual shadow of an eclipse. She was very thin; her legs and arms could have been mistaken for kindling. The thinness, Raylene hoped, would help sell the idea of her girl's tragic condition.

This had been a surefire moneymaker the

first time she tried it, and she hoped it would prove to be so once again. Yet with so few customers on the premises, the chance of collecting even a decent amount of cash today was small. Raylene was not happy. She was considering moving on — staking out another parking lot that adjoined another of the establishments in Acker's Gap or elsewhere in Raythune County. She'd had only a paltry few opportunities so far to let her hopeful smile leap into action, as she laid a concerned maternal hand atop Marla Kay's nubby scalp.

"Morning, ma'am," Raylene would say, when somebody did happen to wander by. Cheerfulness was key. People didn't like to be around the depressed or the downtrodden. Right on cue, Marla Kay would cough. Raylene had taught her that: *When I say hello to them, you cough. Or you let your head go slack to one side. Or you close your eyes like you got a bad headache. You gotta look real poorly, okay? Got it?*

Marla Kay was a good child, and by "good," Raylene meant "obedient." There was no other definition, to Raylene's way of thinking.

If the passerby showed the slightest inclination to hesitate, which could mean that she — women always outnumbered men in a grocery store parking lot — was contemplating a cash contribution to Marla Kay's medical expenses, Raylene would continue her well-practiced little drama: She would clasp her hands and look down, then look up at the sky, addressing an invisible authority with meek, humble reverence. "Dear Lord," she would say, in a quavering voice, "please open this stranger's heart and let her know how much Marla Kay is suffering. Please let her feel the pain that my baby is feeling — not for long, because I would not wish that agony on another poor soul, but just long enough so she will know. And help her to understand, Lord, that any contribution — no matter how small — can make a big difference. Thank you, Jesus." She liked to add a small sniffle. During her first few performances she had cried outright, but that was overkill. Raylene had learned through experience that people were unsettled by sobbing, and sought to distance themselves immediately from outsized displays of emotion. Far better to imply that you were holding back great torrents of feeling than to actively demonstrate them. She had taught Marla Kay the same thing: Swallow hard. Smile bravely.

After all that, only someone with a heart as black and hard as the surface of this parking lot could pass on by without first digging through a change purse for a few spare coins or — *Praise the Lord!* — an actual piece of folding money. The last time, Raylene had netted $647.18 over a three-day period. But that was March, when the cool morning air had caused Marla Kay to wrap her arms around her tiny little torso and shiver ever so slightly. *Jackpot,* Raylene had told herself back then, assessing the weather and the girl's beleaguered appearance that morning. *Ka-ching.*

Today, under a blue sky with cottony dots of clouds stuck here and there, the prospects for pity seemed severely reduced. When you added that to the general lack of customers in the lot to start with, there was ample justification for the thought rattling sadly around Raylene's head like the last pill in a prescription bottle:

We're screwed.

Honestly, she wondered why she had resumed the scheme at all. For the past few months she had been making decent money at the other thing. It was more dangerous, sure, but it was also more reliable. This was just plain pointless. And stupid, too. Apparently nobody gave a rat's ass anymore about a sick little girl. Heartless bastards. What kind of town was this, anyway?

A large woman in a bad wig was walking out of the store. Raylene started to cue Marla Kay to cough, but then she realized that the woman wasn't a customer. She was an employee. You could tell by the pink smock with the blue L on the pocket. Raylene recognized her; it was that nosy cashier. The one who had tried to talk to Marla Kay the last time. The one who had come out that morning and glared at them, before going back inside to resume her shift.

Bitch needs to mind her own damned business.

Raylene tapped the top of Marla Kay's head. The girl looked up.

"We're leaving," Raylene said. "Come on."

Marla Kay rose in one quick, fluid motion. That annoyed Raylene, and she gave her a mean glance of reprimand. She had told the girl over and over again: *When there's a chance that people are watching, you gotta move real slow. You're sick, remember? You hurt all over. You're suffering, okay? Suffering something awful. So act like it.*

Marla Kay was always forgetting. She loved to run and jump, and Raylene knew that the burden of trying to look sick and weak weighed heavily on her. The truth was that Marla Kay Hughes did not have cancer. She had never had cancer. She had not been

146

sick a day in her life.

"Where we going, Mommy?"

"Never you mind," Raylene snapped back. "And don't talk so loud. I told you and told you. Talk like it's hurting you to talk. In a whisper. And don't you forget to cough." There were a million things she had to make sure Marla Kay remembered.

The little girl nodded at her mother. She started to bend over and retrieve the Dr Pepper container, but Raylene clamped a hand on her arm and jerked her upright again.

"Leave it," Raylene said. "Got enough to carry as it is." She yanked the yardstick out of the trash can and handed it to Marla Kay. Then she stowed one trash can inside the other. She lifted the cans and started to move toward the road that ran in front of Lymon's. There was a secondhand clothing store across the street. Just in the past few minutes she had seen more cars going in and out of that lot than had visited Lymon's all morning long. The grocery store was visited mostly by women, but the clothing store clientele was fifty-fifty, and that was a good thing. Men sometimes were more generous than women. Not always — you would think so, with a cute little girl sitting there, the stamp of the cancer on her sad pinched face — but sometimes. Other times, men were even more suspicious than women. They'd look sideways at Marla Kay, holding their car keys in a hard cupped palm, and they'd pull their mouths to one side or the other, maybe comparing her in their minds to other people they had known with the cancer, a soon-to-vanish grandparent or an unlucky cousin.

Nobody trusts anybody anymore, was how Raylene put it to herself. *That's the problem with the world today. No trust.*

She looked back at the store. The cashier had gone back inside again. *Good.*

Raylene led Marla Kay to the edge of the road. In order to tote the yardstick the girl had first slung it over her shoulder, but her mother corrected her: She should drag it, like Jesus hauling the cross up Calvary. She was supposed to be exhausted. Weary from the chemo. Marla Kay did as she was told, wrapping her small hands around one end of the yardstick and letting the sign bump along behind her.

Before crossing the road they had to wait for an orange pickup to go by, its tires kicking up fist-sized squalls of dust. Orange was an unusual color for a pickup in these parts. Mostly trucks came in bold blunt colors like red or black. "Fuck-you colors," is how

Raylene's father, Tommy Hughes, had described them. Colors that told you what a man's made of. Colors that weren't sissified or wishy-washy. Even a blue truck was risky. Orange? Orange might as well be pink.

Raylene was reflecting upon that reality when another thought struck her: *Oh, no. No. This time of day? Couldn't be.*

But it was.

The truck made a quick, tight turn into the parking lot and then halted abruptly, and now Raylene noticed what was painted on the side in white letters: RISING SOULS CHURCH, along with a small white cross. The driver's door popped open. The man who pitched himself out was short and muscular, with a headful of stacked-up black hair and an angry face. Dark stubble outlined the sharp cut of his jaw. His jeans and his flannel shirt were stiff and clean, as if they belonged to somebody else; the boots, though, were scarred with filth and grit, and run over at the heels. They definitely belonged to him.

"Raylene," he said. There was an ominous undertone to his voice. He was walking toward her, fists balled at his sides. He hadn't bothered to close the truck door. Or even shut down the engine. His walk had a wobble to it, an appreciable lack of balance for which he compensated by keeping his legs spread wide, thereby increasing the width and stability of the base. It made him look somewhat bowlegged when he moved, as if he'd just slid off a horse. "Raylene," he repeated.

"Eddie, you leave us alone," she yelled back at him. "We can do what we like. We don't need no permission from you. So go away. If you had a real job and could give us some money — not scraps and leftovers from that church of yours — then I wouldn't have to be out here doing this. Beggin' like a damned dog. You ever think of that?"

"Raylene." He stopped about a foot away from her. "You said you'd quit this."

Her head whipped around. Had anybody heard him? He could ruin everything.

"You shut your damned mouth, Eddie Sutton," she said. "If you mess this up for me — if you tell a goddamned soul — I swear you'll never see your girl again. *Ever.* And I can do that. You know I can."

He shook his head. "This is shameful," he said. "Shameful and embarrassing. You know that."

"All I know," Raylene retorted, and her tone had a sauciness to it now, the same coy quality that, when she heard it in her daughter's voice, caused her to give the little

150

girl a quick smack on the bottom, "is that you better get the hell out of here."

Instead of answering her, the man looked down at the girl. She grinned back up at him. It made Raylene a little jealous, the way they related to each other. But only a little. She could see that the man and Marla Kay were living, just for now, in their own little world, the two of them. Raylene didn't like being left out of anything. Then the feeling passed.

"Hi, Daddy," Marla Kay said.

"Hey, sweet pea."

RHONDA

The world — even this one, small as it was — had its share of Raylenes: selfish, sexy, size-6 women who did as they pleased and took what they wanted and to hell with anybody and everybody else. They were attractive, and that settled the matter. They had their pick of men. They could get away with anything, no matter how outrageous. There was always somebody around to pick up the pieces.

Rhonda moved the stack of file folders from one side of her desk to the other. As Bell had just pointed out, she had a boatload of work to do. Each folder bulged with the massive paperwork attached to a particular case. She'd deal with it all later, after she got back from Lymon's. Right now, just for a minute or so, she wanted to wallow.

And that was okay, wasn't it? She didn't have to be cheerful *all* the time. Cheerfulness took effort. She never got any credit for just how much effort it took. Good old Rhonda: the hefty gal with the sense of humor. Everybody's pal. Need an errand run? A favor done? Call Rhonda. She won't have any plans.

Raylene wouldn't get those calls. Because a woman like Raylene *always* had plans.

Rhonda was feeling sorry for herself, and there were few venues more perfectly suited to self-pity than the assistant prosecutors' office in the basement of the Raythune County Courthouse. Was "office" even the proper word for it? Rhonda thought not. The word was too generous. Because this was a hole. A lowly, stinking, dirty hole. The county had run out of space on the upper floors, and so Rhonda and Hick were forced to do their work down here, at two shoved-together desks beneath a tube of fluorescent lighting that draped the place in a sickly blue pall. It was a narrow, low-ceilinged room with a cracked concrete floor and sticky walls and no windows. It was sweaty-hot in the summer, and so cold in the winter that water left in a glass would freeze overnight. No matter how often the custodial staff — on the day shift, that meant a stout, silent woman named Helene, and on the night shift, a moody, stooped-over man named James — cleaned it, dirt reappeared instantly, as if it was playing some kind of game with them. There was a constant sprinkle from the swaybacked ceiling; the misty ash and gritty flecks settled perpetually on the chairs and the lamps and the law books and the phones and the computers. Rhonda had once returned from a week's vacation and found that she could use the top of her desk like a sketch pad; with a few loops of her index finger, she could draw a picture or write her name in the thick gray dust, first, last and middle:

Rhonda Beauchamp Lovejoy.

Beauchamp was her mother's maiden name. There were Beauchamps tucked up and down the mountains around here. If you could somehow pick up the landscape and turn it over like a salt shaker, there would be a perpetual rain of Beauchamps, like dirt from that ceiling.

She sat back in her chair. Hick was in court just now. She was glad. She couldn't indulge her bad mood when Hick was around. He was a cynic — oh Lord, yes — but other people's cynicism brought out the optimist in him. It was perverse: All day long she was forced to listen to his dark mutterings, to his sour conviction that nothing good would ever come out of Acker's

Gap — but if *she* dared to express a negative thought, he was all over her, slinging affirmation after affirmation, pelting her with happy little nuggets of wisdom mined from the caves of *Oprah* and *Dr. Phil* and various sunny-side-up preachers.

It wasn't fair. If he could be bitter, why couldn't she? True, she was usually a happy person, and there were aspects of her life that she found deeply satisfying: her church work, her animals, those times in a courtroom when she felt as if justice had been done and she had helped to make that happen. But on the rare occasion — like right now — when her thoughts were dark and troubled and knotted-up with frustration, why wasn't that okay? Why couldn't she be granted the luxury of a bad mood now and again?

Her hometown was disintegrating, and damned if she didn't have a front-row seat for it. Drugs, poverty, violence, isolation. Lopped-off mountaintops. Crooked politicians. And con artists like Raylene Hughes. Granted, Raylene was pretty far down the list as far as grievous public nuisances went, but still. Using your child that way. And never getting punished for it, because you had a nice big bustline and a flirty way about you. And a line of bull that you could concoct while you batted your eyelashes at some besotted man.

Was she jealous of Raylene, as Bell had posited? No.

Okay: maybe. But it wasn't Raylene herself who sparked the envy. Rhonda didn't really know her. She'd seen her maybe three times since high school graduation, and never up close. Raylene's run-ins with the law had occurred in adjacent counties, not here in Raythune. It was more what Raylene represented: taking the easy way out. Preying on people's weaknesses. And using her looks to get out of her responsibilities. Rhonda could diet for the next decade and she would never — *never* — look like Raylene Hughes. Couldn't happen. Anything Rhonda wanted, she had to work for. Nobody gave her a damned thing. Especially not men. They didn't even notice her. They were too busy sniffing and pawing around the Raylenes of this world.

She was getting herself all worked up. And over something small and personal. She wasn't even thinking about the carfentanil and the overdoses, which she should have been, because that was her job. Her duty. And Rhonda Beauchamp Lovejoy always did her duty.

She had had a chance to leave, to live

somewhere else, which is more than most people from around here could say. She had a law degree from West Virginia University. Middle of the pack, grade-wise. That hadn't brought a ton of job offers, but it did bring some.

Okay: one. It brought one. In Roanoke. But she didn't take it. Instead she came back to Acker's Gap after law school. She didn't know what she was going to do, but whatever it was, she would do it here. Was it fear that had chased her back? Fear of leaving a place she knew so well? Maybe. She wasn't too proud to admit it. The offer from the new prosecutor, Belfa Elkins, had come out of the blue, and she took it. And here she was. The town was now eight years older than it was on the day she had walked into this office for the first time as assistant prosecutor, and so was she.

In another year, she and the town would be nine years older, and then ten, and then eleven, and then —

The phone's shrill ring interrupted her dismal arithmetic.

"Lovejoy. Prosecutor's office."

"Never mind. They're gone."

That was typical of Penny; Penny didn't go in for hellos or icebreakers such as "How are you?" She was blunt. Everyone on

157

Penny Latrobe's side of the family was that way. They weren't mean, only focused on what was right in front of them, like a cow and its next mouthful of grass.

Rhonda could picture Penny holding her cell in a big red fist, standing just inside the door at Lymon's in her stretchy polyester pants and her white socks and tennis shoes and her pink smock. She was a middle-aged woman, thick in the torso, who wore a blond wig to cover her baldness. Penny had buried two husbands and now was the sole caretaker of a third, a sweet man named Harve who was incapacitated by black lung disease. Every step he took cost him dearly. His sandpapery wheeze had been known to frighten small children.

"I went out to the parking lot and saw them packing up their stuff," Penny added, before Rhonda could jump in. "Wish you'd come when I first called you this morning."

"Had some things to take care of."

"Bet you did. I heard about the overdoses." Penny's job meant she often got the news early, from shoppers making small talk as they unloaded the canned peaches and loaves of bread and jars of mayonnaise from their carts onto the moving black belt. "Lord help us all."

Rhonda had no ready reply to that; the

Lord might or might not help, and she tended to think that He had decided to leave it to them to figure it out.

"If Raylene and her little girl come back, let me know," Rhonda said.

"Doubt they do. Pickings are pretty slim today. Customers few and far between. Nobody to beg from." Penny sighed. "Kind of worries me, the way business has been. You don't need a cashier if nobody's coming in to buy."

"I hear you. But things're bound to pick up." *There I go again,* Rhonda thought ruefully. *Upbeat again. Can't seem to help myself.*

"Could be." Penny did not sound convinced. "You know what?"

"What?"

"All those overdoses — well, it got me to thinking. There was a time when I didn't get it. I'd hear about people selling drugs and I'd say to myself, 'How can they do that?' But the worse things get around here, the more I think sometimes that I can almost understand it. Say you've got a bunch of kids to feed. Say you're four months behind on the rent and the landlord's knocking at your door. Maybe it's not so farfetched to consider . . ."

"You don't mean that, Penny."

"How do you know I don't mean it?"

"Because you're still worried about a little girl whose mother isn't doing right by her. That's how I know. You still care about this town."

A sigh of acknowledgment. "Guess so. And speaking of the child — I'll keep an eye out, just in case Raylene happens to drag her back here. Like you said."

"Can't hurt. Wish we had a deputy to spare, but we just don't. Not today."

"I get it. What with folks dropping in the streets and all."

A call was coming in on Rhonda's second line. "Gotta run, Penny. You take care."

"Will do. And I better go, too. I think I see an actual customer waiting for me to check her out. It's a miracle."

Rhonda laughed. "My best to Harve."

"You're a good girl."

She meant it as a compliment, but to Rhonda, it sounded like an epitaph chiseled on a gray headstone.

JAKE

11:37 A.M.
The call had come in on Molly's cell at 10:12 A.M., summoning her back to work for a double shift.

Christ, she had murmured into the phone. Her voice was low but Jake was able to hear her plainly. *Four more overdoses. Should've expected it, I guess.* Another squad — the one actually scheduled to be on duty right now — was handling the latest call, but that meant there would not be a spare unit to dispatch to any emergencies that might occur in the rest of the county. So Molly needed to clock in.

She would drop Malik back at home, she had said after her call ended, thinking out loud, and then she would go meet Ernie and gear up. Jake had offered to take Malik home, but Molly quickly said, *No thanks.* Jake did not quite know how to interpret her refusal; either she was reluctant to

161

intrude on his private time, or she didn't
trust him with her brother.

She and Malik had stayed at his house for
almost an hour. Malik did most of the talking — if that's what you could call it, Jake
thought, reviewing the visit in his mind after
the two of them had gone. Malik's speech
was an odd combination of normal sen-
tences interspersed with tongue-clicks,
abrupt sideways jerks of his head, hoots,
grunts, and other noises that sounded like
runaway hiccups. He was six years younger
than Molly. His hair had been razored so
close to his scalp that it was more of a
shadow than an actual color. His body was
oddly shaped; the top half was average-sized
but the bottom half was too big, and pudgy
and mushy to boot. His hips had a womanly
spread to them. His lower lip hung loose,
inviting a puddle of drool to linger in the
pink channel and occasionally spill over the
sides. That would prompt Molly to lift her
thumb and gently wipe the spit off her
brother's chin.

When Molly had first introduced him,
Jake put out a hand. Malik stared at it.

"No handshakes," Molly said. "He doesn't
like it. High-fives are fine — but no handshakes."

Then the three of them had moved into

Jake's living room. Molly and Malik automatically went to the sofa, and Jake slid back into his recliner, as if the seating arrangements had been agreed upon long beforehand. Malik was shy at first, but once he got rolling — look out. Over and over again Molly had to ask Malik to slow down lest his syllables become scrambled and fuzzed, the meaning lost in a confusing tumble of sounds. It reminded Jake of the time he visited his grandmother as a small boy and she sat at the kitchen table, typing on her Hermes manual typewriter. When she typed too fast, the keys would overlap in a dark metal snarl of crossed rods and stuck-together letters. She had to reach in and separate the keys, staining her fingertips with black ink.

"Just tell Jake what you told me," Molly said. "Take your time."

Malik's head wobbled. "Okay," he said.

The story he told was this: Two days ago he was walking around Acker's Gap, keeping his head down, looking for spare change or anything else somebody might have dropped and not noticed. Once, he told Jake excitedly, he had found a twenty-dollar bill. Jake nodded and gave him a thumbs-up. Malik had liked that; he offered a thumbs-up right back.

And then he continued his tale. He had checked out the Dumpster behind JPs, the diner a block and a half from the courthouse. Malik had often discovered great treasures back there, he explained, not so much *in* the Dumpster as close to it, stuff that gathered in a ragged little ring around the big green metal bin with the giant swinging lid on top. He had found, just this week alone, a wristwatch with a broken strap and a smashed face, a bicycle missing its tires, two golf clubs, one brown shoe, a blue plastic bucket, a seat wrenched from a van, and a cardboard box filled with six kittens. When he mentioned the kittens, Malik's eyes grew wide and his words began to speed up and lose control of themselves, like kids running too fast down a hill. Molly patted his knee and asked him to slow down, please, so that Jake could understand him.

"I took the kittens," he said. Frustrated, he looked at his sister; he did not seem to know quite how to describe what happened next. Molly nodded and reminded him: "You took the box of kittens over to the courthouse," she said, "and someone who worked there took them from you and promised they'd see that they got to the Raythune County Animal Shelter."

164

Jake had smiled at this, but his thoughts were darker. He was tired, he had had a busy night filled with death and the potential for more of it, and Molly had brought her brother to his house to talk about — *kittens?*

Really?

"Go on," Molly said, and Malik rocked back and forth, as if he were nodding with his entire body.

"Okay," Malik said. He had gone back to the alley behind JPs, he told Jake, to look for more stuff. By the time he returned, there were three dark men in the alley, standing by the Dumpster. They were smoking cigarettes. They did not see him, because they were very focused on each other; they were arguing. "And one of them grabbed the other man and he hit him and threw him down," Malik said. "They were all talking about money and about how the man on the ground needed to give it to them. The other man kicked the man on the ground." Finally, he said, the man on the ground gave them some money. It looked like a lot, Malik added. It looked like a lot of bills, folded over like a ham sandwich, with a rubber band around it. And then the other two men hauled him up. They handed him several small packages, each one wrapped in plastic. And then somebody else was coming down the alley. So the men went away. They did not run, but they were gone very soon, Malik said. "Molly told me about the bad men," he added. "And she told me about the drugs. Drugs are bad, too. The men are selling drugs."

"What do you think?" Molly said, addressing Jake. "When Malik says they were dark, he means Mexican. Hispanic. Not black." Jake nodded. Racial politics were simple around here: White was the default, always. West Virginia was about as diverse as a crayon factory that made only one color of crayon. If another shade showed up in the package, it was a mistake. Somebody had pushed the wrong lever on the production line.

"Because," Molly went on, not waiting for his reply, "it seems to me that Malik could be on to something. They might be part of that gang. The one from Mexico. The one that's been bringing in the lethal stuff. I would imagine they've gotten kind of care-less lately. It's just too easy. So I can believe they'd settle a dispute with one of their em-ployees in an alley, right? Maybe a dealer was holding on to part of the profits. Or something like that."

Malik grunted and pulled at Molly's shirt.

He was excited.

"I know, sweetie, I know," she said, settling her brother down. "I'll tell him." Back to Jake. "Malik's a pretty good detective," she said. "Show him, Malik. Show Jake what you picked up on the ground, after the men left."

Malik pulled a matchbook out of the back pocket of his jeans. "They used these," he said, handing it to Jake. "I watched them. Then they threw it down. Littering is bad."

Jake turned over the matchbook: STAR-LINER MOTEL, ACKER'S GAP, WV. The Starliner was a dilapidated, one-story strip of brick located far too close to the road, with only a narrow gravel parking lot separating it from traffic. The building's chipped cinnamon-colored façade was broken at regular intervals by an identical series of gray metal doors. Woods hemmed in the place on three sides. The STARLINER sign, raised up high on a rust-ravaged white pole, always featured at least two burnt-out letters at any given time, so the full name was never in residence; it was always ARLINE or STARL or, if the management was especially negligent, a simple LI E.

The joke about the Starliner — it was a joke made about all fleabag motels — was that its rooms were rented by the hour instead of by the night. Lately, though, the joke had lost its naughty relevance; such places were mostly used for drug transactions now, not romantic trysts. The rooms were rented by the week and the month to drug gangs. They were a one-stop-shopping location for local dealers to come by and top off their supplies.

Jake closed his hand around the matchbook in his palm, as if it were precious to him. In truth, of course, it was worthless. The information about what had happened in that alley might prove valuable, but the matchbook was a nonstarter, useless as any kind of clue about anything, but he didn't want to hurt Malik's feelings. Jake was puzzled; Molly must have known that it was useless, just as he did, and so why did she . . . .

She doesn't want to hurt his feelings, either. She was indulging her brother. Making him feel special.

"Okay, buddy," Jake said. "Thanks. I'll hold onto this."

"You'll get 'em, right?" Malik said eagerly. "You're gonna do that?"

"Gonna try." Jake put the matchbook down on the coffee table. He didn't just toss it. He was careful with his gesture, lining up the bottom edge with the edge of the coffee table. Making it symmetrical. It was another way of honoring Malik's contribution: treating his clue with respect. "Hey, would you two like some coffee?"

Before Molly could answer, her cell intervened with its sharp ring. That startled Malik. His body lurched to one side. Jake was half-afraid he was going to fall off the couch.

"Yeah," she said into the phone. "Yeah. Yeah. Okay. Got it."

She re-pocketed her cell and rose, reaching down for Malik's hand. She pulled him up beside her. "Four more overdoses. Jackson Avenue."

Jake knew the place well. The apartments on Jackson Avenue were notorious. Two T-shaped piles of pink cinder blocks spread out in a swampy area too close to the Bitter River. They were the last resort for people who had very little money and even less hope. Some of the apartments had been home to two and three generations of the same family, with each new passel of children facing a future bleaker than that of their parents, a steady winnowing-down of possibilities for a satisfying and meaningful life. Anyone who worked in law enforcement was familiar with Jackson Avenue. There were more calls from Jackson Avenue in a typical week — ODs, drunk and disorderly, domestic violence — than from the rest of the county in a month.

"You've got to be beat," Jake said.

"Sure. But we're overloaded. Too many runs to handle. I'll be okay. And besides — Ernie and I will just be on call. In case there's anything else while the on-duty squad handles Jackson Avenue."

She and Malik were at the door now. Malik walked out ahead of her, marching toward the truck as if it were him and not her who would be answering the call, going about the important work of saving lives. That gave Molly a brief private moment with Jake.

"We don't know," she said. She held the front door open so Malik could see that she was coming.

Jake was puzzled. "You don't know what?"

"We don't know what happened to Malik. Eventually you'll get around to asking me — everybody does — and I just wanted to save you the trouble. He was born at home. It wasn't easy, but my mother didn't have the money to go to the hospital. Or any way to get there, for that matter. No paramedics in Briney Hollow. Not back then, anyway." She laughed a short, hard laugh, a laugh born out of her current expertise and the bitter realization of what a difference it might have made at the time. Jake was guessing about the origin of her laugh, but he knew he was right. "Malik didn't get enough oxygen during his birth," Molly went on. "So that's why he's the way he is. Developmental delays and disabilities. My mother and father are both gone. I take care of him now. When I'm not working. Other times, I pay a lady to come in and make his meals and watch over him." She spoke in a straightforward, matter-of-fact way, but Jake could sense the emotion that crowded up behind the words. Like him, Molly had learned the trick of delivering unpleasant facts in a bland manner. It was a mixed blessing, he thought; it enabled you to do your job, but it was a difficult skill to turn off when you wanted to, when you were in another kind of setting. A gentler one.

"Okay."

"And by the way." She was interrupted by the truck's horn, a series of three impatient-sounding bleats. Molly waved to Malik. "Be right there, buddy," she called out. "Hang on." She turned back. "Look, I know that matchbook doesn't prove a damned thing. You can throw it away. But he was just so excited about finding it. I'd told him about our night and all the overdoses. He's been listening to me go on about the drug gangs.

So when he saw those men by the Dumpster — and when he found the matches . . ." She shrugged. "He wants to help. That's it. He just wants to be a part of things. Pitch in. Coming by here this morning — I know it was a lot to ask, having you listen to Malik. But he was thrilled to meet you. I've told him all about you. So I hope you don't mind."

I've told him all about you.

Jake let the phrase wash over him. It gave him a distinct, specific pleasure, limited but intense.

"No problem," he said. Lame — but he couldn't think of anything else to say. He was too nervous. She made him that way. He was mad at himself; after all, he was supposed to be a funny guy, a real smart-ass, the life of the party. Around her, though, he was stupid and boring. Christ. What was he — fourteen years old?

His cell belted out its ringtone. He had left it back on the coffee table. Molly put a hand on his forearm. "Bet they're calling you in, too," she said. "So much for a day off, right? Doesn't look like either one of us is gonna be getting any rest. See you around. And thanks again."

Jake was not able to watch her go, as much as he wanted to; he had to return inside and

172

answer his phone. And yet during his brief conversation with Sheriff Harrison — that's who was on the line — he was less focused on the information being conveyed, as urgent and dire as it was, and more on Molly Drucker, letting his mind stray into territories of rank speculation. She had probably patted Malik's knee when she got back in the Silverado, and told him everything was going to be okay. She probably had to say that fifty times a day.

Jake's forearm still felt the press of her hand from when she had touched him there, quickly, casually, offhandedly. It was a random gesture. It didn't mean anything to her.

It meant everything to him.

"I need you to clear the Jackson Avenue scene," the sheriff was saying. Jake forced himself to concentrate on her words. What the hell was his problem? "Squad already left with the victims. Just poke around, ask some questions. See if you can get any leads on the dealer. Then you can run down the names you sent me."

"Okay."

The sheriff coughed. Jake heard a deep tiredness embedded in that cough, a rattling spasm of profound exhaustion. He recognized it because he'd let loose with the same kind of cough himself more than a few times, after an extended shift with a lot of complications. "I know it's your day off, but it's all hands on deck today," she added, once her cough had run its course. "Jackson Avenue might be the end of it. And then we can move on."

They both knew better than that. But they still did not know — because no one could know — just how bad it was going to get.

SHIRLEY

11:58 A.M.

Knob Creek. Ketel One. Wild Turkey. Absolut. Grey Goose. Stolichnaya. Cuervo Gold. Tanqueray. All the rest.

Each bottle lined up across the double-decker shelves behind the bar bore a label, a name. But Shirley paid no attention to that. She wasn't interested in the names. She saw only the shapes of the glass, because the bottles themselves were so lovely: blues and creams and silvers and blacks and browns and lilacs. Each bottle seemed to catch the light and hold it, and while holding it, transform it. The light did not make the bottles any more beautiful than they already were; rather, it revealed the essential truth about beauty itself, the fact that beauty was not a single static thing but a revolving constellation of possibilities. Beauty could be anything you wanted it to be. You could find beauty anywhere. And everywhere.

This was the Mud Creek Tavern. Its name had long ago been shortened to the Creek. If Shirley had a weekday off from work, she sometimes found her way here. Lately, in the wake of the news given to her by the specialist in Charleston, she had been coming in even more often. The colored glass was a comfort. The rows of bottles soothed her. She did not know why.

She took a seat at the bar, leaned forward, hooked the heels of her boots around the bottom rung of the wooden stool. After leaving the church she had run a few errands. Then she had parked at one of the meters along Main Street in downtown Acker's Gap.

Before she had even gotten out of her car, however, the text from Bell came through:

Sorry — can we make it another day? Swamped.

Shirley had texted back:

No prob. Call me later.

Truth was, Shirley felt relieved. The relief washed over her like a cooling spray. Her plan had been to tell Bell at lunch — tell her the part about her diagnosis, anyway. The rest of it would come later. The minister had suggested that she break the news into two parts, and thus not load up a single encounter with such an immensely heavy burden. It made sense to Shirley.

But she was off the hook now, at least for a little while longer. So she could settle herself down at the makeshift art gallery at the Creek: the rows of colored glass illuminated by the tiny lights screwed into the front edge of the shelves behind the bar.

Midday was the perfect time to come here. Shirley didn't like bars at night. Too many people, too much noise, plus the heavy, layered smell of heat and sweat and cheap cologne, and of raw, pulsing, human need. Fresh out of prison a few years ago she had enjoyed that, even craved it; nowadays, she couldn't abide it. During the day, though, a bar felt very different. It was a neutral place. It featured only a few people, and they generally didn't bother you. They were here for their own reasons. They didn't care about you, and that was fine with Shirley; she had accepted the world's indifference a long time ago. Counted on it. It was a relief.

During the day you could stare at the bottles for as long as you liked, and nobody thought you were coyly avoiding eye contact with some potential hookup. Nobody thought it was a ploy.

She didn't order a drink. She almost never did. She wasn't an alcoholic; that wasn't what stopped her. She disliked the sensation of alcohol moving hotly through her body, turning the hard parts of her into something softer, more pliable. She wanted to stay hard.

The bartender — at midday it was usually Jerry Snell — had a small, harmless crush on her, which she knew about but would never speak of, knowing that he wouldn't, either. Their ritual was this: She paid for her first Diet Coke. After that he topped her off with no charge. If the Creek's owner, Charlie Blunden, had ever caught him doing that Jerry would have been in big trouble. Blunden was a notorious skinflint, and the thought of missing out on a couple of bucks from Shirley Dolan — from anybody — would have sent him over the edge. Jerry risked it, though, because he liked Shirley's company, mostly silent as it was.

"Hey," Jerry said. She had just settled onto her regular stool. Hooked her heels. Settled in.

"Hey."

Shirley waited for him to go away — he was bending over and ducking his head under the counter to fetch a tray of clean glasses — and now she lifted her eyes to the bottles. God. They nearly took her breath away. Who needed stained-glass windows if you had liquor bottles all lined up on a lighted shelf?

"Feels like it's getting to be fall out there already, don't it," Jerry said. It was a statement, not a question. He was visible again, standing up, his stubby hands gripping either side of the plastic tray, thumbs hooked over the ridge. "Coolest summer I can remember."

Shirley shrugged. There must be a law somewhere specifying that bartenders had to spend a certain percentage of their interaction with each customer discussing the weather. Jerry was a decent guy, though, and so her unspoken observation didn't come with any meanness attached to it. He was in his late forties or early fifties and he had, somewhere in the deep undisclosed background of his life, several children and an unspecified tragedy involving one or more of those children. Shirley had heard the rumors, but never pursued the particulars; she liked to keep the world at arm's length these days, and not knowing about somebody's woes made that easier.

Jerry had a red, pitted nose, a droopy eye, and a pair of fat black eyebrows that did not seem to fit with the rest of him. Most of the hair on his head had fled the scene. He combed the remaining gray threads — the

179

total was in the single digits — across the top of his scalp. They looked like seaweed reaching over a rock.

"Yeah," Shirley said.

"You ask me — cooler's better. Can't stand those days when you start sweating before you even leave your bed in the morning, you know?"

"Yeah."

"Hope it don't mean a bad winter, though," Jerry said, tilting his head in a philosophical way. "Sometimes it's like that. You don't get much summer but the winter's a sonofabitch. It's kinda like the seasons're trying to balance themselves out again, remember what's what."

Shirley nodded. He moved on down the bar. He never pressed her to talk more than she wanted to, and she never wanted to. That was his pattern; he would utter a sentence or two and then go on about his business, washing glasses or drying the ones he had already washed, wiping down the bar, sweeping the floor with the broom he kept in the corner, its bristles so bent and twisted that he might as well be doing the job with an armful of dried-out sticks he had gathered on the bank of the Bitter River. Busywork is what it was.

She had been in a lot of bars. During the

years when she and Bobo Bolland were together, she had gone with him on most of his gigs, and most of his gigs were in bars. She had learned to shrewdly assess each one at a glance. She knew by looking at the main area what the ladies' room was going to be like. If the proprietors allowed lipstick-rimmed glasses and wadded-up paper napkins to stack up on the tables, and peanut shells to pile up in crunchy mounds on the floor, then the bathroom would be a disaster. You could just tell. Conversely, if the bar itself was clean, if the stools looked sturdy, if the paneled walls had been washed down more than once a decade, you could count on a fairly decent bathroom. Not that you'd want to touch anything more in there than what you absolutely had to.

She missed Bobo. She told people that she had broken up with him, that she wanted him to get a regular job and he wouldn't, and that was that. But it was a lie. The truth was that his ex-girlfriend, Leila Francone, had resurfaced and — according to Bobo — the only reason he and Leila had broken up in the first place was because Leila thought she was pregnant and Bobo had been a total jerk about it, only as it happened she really wasn't pregnant, but by then she had seen what she called his "true colors." When Leila had showed up again at the start of the summer, Bobo realized he still loved her. Shirley didn't know what to say to that. Living with Bobo was no picnic, but it was what she had decided to do, and so she did it. Now, all at once, she had to find somewhere else to live, and another focus for her life.

The worst of it wasn't so much the loss of Bobo. The worst was his parting shot. She was a hot mess, he told her on a night in early June that would end up being their last real conversation. The metallic scent of coming rain was in the air. They sat on the stoop of their garage apartment. He told Shirley that she was unstable and erratic, and he was frankly tired of putting up with her "emotional bullshit." She lived too much in the past, and in her case, he said, the past was such a crappy place that only somebody "totally batshit crazy" would want to go back there. This was a few weeks before Shirley found out she was dying of lung cancer. It felt as if the world was piling on.

And it feels that way, she told herself, *because it is.*

The only person she had told about the diagnosis — before her visit to the Rising Souls Church that morning — was her friend Connie Boyd. She did tell a few people about the breakup with Bobo. She had to, because she was moving. Her mailing address would be changing. Her landline number would be changing. Bell's reaction was subdued: *Okay, well. Let me know if I can help with anything.* Shirley knew why her sister was being that way; she and Bobo had broken up a few times previously, but they had always reconciled. Bell didn't want to get caught in the middle — caught saying something negative about Bobo, only to have things be awkward later on when Shirley showed up with him for, say, Thanksgiving dinner. Bell didn't like Bobo. Not one little bit. But she tucked that behind a façade of abstract cordiality. Bell was good at tucking things out of sight.

You were right about him all along, little sister.

Bell was always right these days. That had taken some getting used to. When they were kids, Shirley was the one who was right. She was ten years older than Bell, and she was the one who knew more. The one who was savvy and calculating and effective. She had taken care of Belfa, protected her, watched over her, made sure their father never touched her. Except of course that he did, after all. They lived in desperate fear of him, a fear that made the trailer a charged and volatile place.

Dead as he was, his handprints were still visible all over their lives.

"Another Diet?"

Shirley reluctantly shifted her eyes down from the beautiful bottles. Jerry Snell had come back to her end of the bar. There were only two other customers in the Creek right now, both of them male, each of them sitting at one of the little round wooden tables that cluttered up the laminate floor. Jerry had done his duty and freshened their drinks, leaving him free to return to Shirley.

"Yeah," she said. "Thanks."

Jerry's eyes made a quick circuit of the room, as if he suspected surveillance. "You can smoke if you want to. I can dig up an ashtray. Still got one, from back when it was okay. Not supposed to let you — but that don't matter." He lifted his chin to indicate the other two customers. "Those fellas won't give a shit. Trust me."

"No, that's okay."

"You quitting?"

She shook her head. "Just taking a break." The truth was, she had pretty much lost her taste for tobacco. The impulse this morning in the minister's office had been just that — an impulse, arising out of long habit rather than present desire. From the moment of her diagnosis, something had shifted inside her, and no longer was she susceptible to the blissful release provided by systematic drags on a Pall Mall, a release that was like the spreading-open of a flower bud. But she did not want to discuss that with Jerry. Or with anyone.

"You want some popcorn? I can make some."

Again she shook her head. An overwhelming sadness had sneaked up behind her and put a heavy hand on her shoulder, almost as if one of those strangers sitting at a table had abruptly gotten up and crossed the bar and accosted her. She wished it *had* been a real person. Then she could have shoved his hand away and told him to go screw himself. But sadness — sadness was different. You couldn't get rid of it in ordinary ways. Sometimes you couldn't get rid of it at all.

"You hear about what's going on out there?" Jerry said. He nodded toward the door, to make it clear that "out there" meant the world beyond the Creek. "Bunch of overdoses. Them folks're just falling where they stand. You ask me — I say 'Good riddance to bad rubbish.' Let 'em kill themselves. Anybody who puts that crap in their bodies doesn't deserve to —"

"What?" She was only half-listening, catching every other word.

"Addicts," Jerry clarified. "Bunch of 'em dropping like flies. All over the place. Heard about it on my way into work. Two of 'em died. No names yet, but we'll be finding out pretty soon." He picked up the bar rag and flipped it over his shoulder. "Something's got mixed in, they say. With the drugs." Perplexed, he elevated his black eyebrows. "Guess we shouldn't care — I mean, nobody's begging them to take the stuff, right? Nobody's telling them to stick needles in every damned spot they can find. But still."

Shirley didn't say anything out loud, but Jerry's bulletin made her think about Belfa. This news would mean more work for her sister. Her job as prosecutor automatically put her in the center of every bad thing that happened in Acker's Gap.

That was why she hadn't yet told Belfa about her diagnosis. Or the rest of it, either, or her decision that the truth must be told. That was why she had hesitated so far. She did not want to add one more piece of bad news to her sister's load. That was all Shirley had to offer now: bad news.

But soon she would tell her. All of it. She had no choice. As hard as it might be, telling the truth showed respect for the other person. And love, too: It proved your love, especially when it would be so much easier just to let the lie live on in the world. You had to do the hard thing. The minister had helped her see that, as brief as their conversation had been. She had to tell the truth to Bell, every last particle of it. Now she just had to figure out where and when and how.

"Don't know what's happening to this town," Jerry muttered. He pulled the bar rag off his shoulder and started polishing the flat surface, making the same lazy circle over and over again so he wouldn't have to move too far away from her. She knew what he was doing. "I grew up here," he added, "and I don't hardly recognize the place anymore."

He was still talking, but once again she had tuned him out. It was a trick she had perfected in prison: The art of looking as if you were paying attention, when in fact your mind had departed the premises a while back. The one thing the world could not control was your thoughts. People in authority could make you march or stop marching, could make you sit down or stand up, could make you do things that you didn't want to do and that in fact made your stomach turn inside out and sour with disgust — but they had no power over your thoughts. Nobody did.

She had let the lie be. For thirty-five years, she had just let it *be*. When she realized, all those years ago, that the lie had worked — Belfa had no recollection of what had really happened — Shirley was relieved. It meant that Shirley could keep on protecting her. Shirley could stand between her little sister and the darkness. Belfa would have a future, or at least the chance to have a future. She would have her shot.

But now everything had changed.

". . . and so I say, to hell with them." Jerry finished wiping the bar. It looked the same as it did when he started. "If folks wanna kill themselves, wellsir, I say, 'Have at it. Just stay outta *my* way. Don't be messing in *my* business.' "

His attention was caught by something that was happening behind Shirley. The door had opened, letting in a sudden punch of daylight.

She twisted around on her stool. The new customer was an old man in a green Army fatigue jacket and baggy brown pants that dragged the ground behind his feet. His hair stuck out from his head in a spray of gray-white frizz and his beard picked up on the same theme; it, too, was copious and out of control. His gait was a slow, hunched-over shuffle. He paused in the center of the room. His skin — the tiny portion of which was visible — was red-brown and looked as tough as jerky. He was several feet away from her but Shirley could smell him; it was the rancid smell of body odor and turned-up earth and old, dead things.

"It's coming," the old man said. His voice had a fluttery edge to it, a gravely vibrato. "It's coming. It's coming."

"Shut up," one of the other customers snapped at him. He was young and heavyset, and he wore a flat-billed baseball cap with a Cabela's logo on the crown. "Get the hell out of here. You and your crazy shit."

The old man lifted his arms like a maestro in front of an invisible orchestra. "It's coming!" he called out. There was desperation in his voice now, a kind of strangled fury.

Cabela's grabbed the amber-colored bottle of Bud in front of him and banged it back down on the table. Clearly, this was last-straw time. He stood up in a rush, the chair shooting out from under him with a squeal and a scrape. "I told you to shut up, asshole."

"Hey, now," Jerry said. "Come on, fellas. There's no need for —"

"IT'S COMING!" the old man shrieked again, and now his body swayed in an erratic gyration. He stumbled forward in the direction of the bar. One hand dived under the folds of his coat.

"Look out — he's got a gun!" the second customer yelled. He, too, was on his feet now, knocking over the table next to his as he lunged.

The two men tried to grab the old man, but both were overweight and further compromised by the number of Buds they had consumed. They looked, Shirley thought fleetingly, like a couple of bears roused too soon out of hibernation, lumbering and off-balance.

The old man pulled something out from under his coat. The two men ducked. It was only a stick. He waved it around and turned in a circle, as if dozens of marauders surrounded him. And then he seemed to lose track of whatever it was that had summoned him. He dropped his arms. The stick went back up under his coat. He turned and shuffled back out the door, mumbling a softer-voiced but no less agitated version of his warning: *It's coming. It's coming.*

Cabela's sat down. He raked his chair back under the table, shaking his head. What a world: That was the plain meaning of the headshake.

"Jesus," Jerry said.

"Who's that?" Shirley asked.

Jerry shrugged. "Don't know. I've seen him around town. He started coming in here a few days ago. Screams a lot of bullshit and then leaves again. Crazy old bastard."

She let her gaze drift back up to the bottles behind the bar. But the spell was broken. The old man's rant had chased away the magic. And the beautiful scraps of glass that had brought her such solace just a minute ago faded back into reality, revealing what they really were: bottles of booze stacked on the shelves of a crummy bar in a small West Virginia town in the middle of an August day.

JAKE

12:12 P.M.

The victims were long gone by the time he arrived at the apartment on Jackson Avenue, but there was still plenty of evidence of what had happened here. You didn't always need a body to know that someone had died. Death changed the air.

A clump of people blocked the hallway leading to apartment A-12. Jake had to shoo them away. At first he was polite about it — "Excuse me, folks, coming through" — but that did not work. One old woman flattened herself against the wall to allow him passage, but the rest of them just stared at him, truculently immobile. They were old and young, female and male, black and white, placid and agitated, but they shared a common hostility. So Jake grew less polite: "Step aside or I'll search your apartments, too. You want that?"

No, they did not want that. They definitely

did not want that. The crowd broke roughly in half and swung open like a gate. Jake moved through. He had to turn sideways — they left him only a narrow gap — but he didn't want to quibble. The front door of the apartment was not a factor; the paramedics had had to break it down, and shards lay across the threshold in a crisscrossed scatter of cheap shellacked wood.

"Fucking cops."

Jake heard the murmured insult as he passed the last bystanders, a couple of teenagers in T-shirts and cargo shorts. The black kid snorted; the white kid issued a loud cackle. Jake wasn't sure which one had cursed at him but it didn't matter; every single person here wanted to, he knew. Somehow, during the escalating daily race between order and chaos in Raythune County, law enforcement had ended up being construed as the enemy. He was the bad guy. Jake didn't get it — he had done nothing to these people, and in fact the sheriff's department had stopped arresting addicts a while ago, because it was pointless — but their contempt for him was like a bad smell that leaked from the pores of their skin.

Any other day, Jake would have laughed it off. Not today. He stopped and turned around.

"Shut the hell up," he snapped, and he was saying it to all the people hanging around the hallway, but especially to the two punks in cargo shorts.

"You got no call to talk to them boys like that," said an older man in a plaid shirt and sweatpants. A large chunk of flesh was missing from his nose, like sand scooped out of a sandbox. "We been through a lot today. All of us. So help me, Jesus." He was barefoot and he reeked of booze.

Alcohol, Jake thought. *Those were the days.* He was almost nostalgic for it, remembering back when alcohol was the anesthetic of choice. That seemed like child's play now. It wasn't, of course; he had seen the aftermath of too many accident scenes where a drunk driver had smacked into a guardrail or sailed over a median into oncoming traffic. Still, alcohol just seemed . . . tamer, somehow, compared to drugs.

Their neighbors had been carried out on stretchers half-alive — and one of them not alive at all — but Jake didn't have much sympathy for these people. They had known exactly what was going on in this apartment. Most of them were doing the same thing in their apartments. They weren't shocked, and they weren't distraught. They were just curious.

"Any of you know where they got their drugs?" Jake asked.

Heads waggled back and forth, indicating a No. Some shrugged. Two girls giggled nervously in unison.

"Nobody?" Jake said.

Most looked down, checking out the floor of the hallway as if it held the answer to a vexing riddle. A few murmured, "No, sorry" and "Naw" and other variations on a theme, the theme being: *We're not going to tell you a damned thing.*

"Fine," Jake said. Knowing it was useless, he added, "Any of you think of anything, you call the sheriff's department. Right away. We're trying to get some bad drugs off the street, okay? We got ourselves a real problem here."

No one spoke. The old lady who had moved aside for him made a clucking sound in the back of her throat. Several people coughed. A kid sneezed and wiped the snot on his palm.

"You know what I'm saying, right?" Jake added. "The stuff you're buying today — the heroin — it can kill you. The suppliers have added a drug to it that's worse than anything you've ever seen. So if anybody knows anything, tell me now."

Nothing.

"Okay, fine," Jake said. "Fine. But if any of you gets a conscience — give me a call." He couldn't resist a coda. "Of course, it'll probably be too late by then. More folks'll be dead. Have a nice day."

Jake turned away from them again and entered the tiny living room. He took note of the grooves in the thin beige carpet that had been made by the wheels of multiple gurneys. It was dark, even at midday; the windows were covered with sheets that had been thumb-tacked directly into the drywall. The place smelled of heat and old food. Crumpled fast-food bags crowded the top of a card table like tumbleweed. Two flung-open empty pizza boxes, tops and bottoms stained with circular tattoos of grease, were spread out across the sagging brown couch. In the small kitchen that was really just an extension of the living room, he saw a black mass of flies hovering over the dirty sink.

The bathroom was where it had all unfolded. The report from the squad had been e-mailed to Jake and he had skimmed it while sitting in his Blazer in the parking lot. One victim — Curtis Sewell, 24 — was found in the bathtub, fully clothed. His wife, Amber Sewell, 22, had somehow gotten him in the tub when he stopped responding, thinking the water might revive him. Curtis Sewell's brother, Bobby Sewell, 19, had been curled up motionless in the corner, next to a trash bag filled with dirty clothes. Bob's girlfriend, LaRue Synder, 20, was sprawled on the bathmat, and LaRue's cousin, Julie Groves, 32, was on her side next to the sink, shivering so hard that her head banged repeatedly against the wall.

It was Amber Sewell who had called 911. She was the only one not affected, and that was because she had not yet had a chance to sample the heroin Bob had brought over that morning. Her kids — Logan, 3, and Matthew, eighteen months — were crying for their lunch. The moment she finished in the kitchen, she had planned to join her guests for the party.

One by one, those guests had injected themselves with Bob's oh-so-thoughtful gift and then collapsed. The 911 recording included Amber's screams, soon joined by the screams and crying of the two children, frightened and confused by all the commotion.

Jake stood in the bathroom doorway. He couldn't help but recall the Marathon bathroom. Were bathrooms now the default settings for tragedy? For the last acts in human lives? Not battlefields, but bathrooms. Some progress.

Soiled clothes seemed to be breeding in the corners. The metal trash can was over-flowing; along with blood-sodden sanitary napkins and dirty diapers, he spotted multiple syringes and tissues gooey with effluvia of various colors, from yellow to red to brown.

Party time, Jake thought.

He left the bathroom. Next door was one of two tiny bedrooms. This must have been the children's room. Toys and stuffed animals were strewn across the floor. He saw a pink bear and a purple elephant. He saw a couple of Matchbox cars. He didn't see any beds, and so he assumed that the wrinkled towels laid out side by side were the designated sleeping areas for the kids. They were under the care of county social services now. Chances were, however, that because Amber Sewell had not ingested drugs herself — today, at least — she would regain custody quickly. Never mind the fact that she had exposed her children to illegally obtained narcotics and the company of known addicts. Or that she was an addict herself. The county facilities were overwhelmed. It was constant triage.

Jake backed out, returning to the living room. The man with the plaid shirt and half a nose was standing there.

"If you're planning on looting the place," Jake said, "knock yourself out." That was Jake's little joke. There was nothing here worth stealing — which was, he supposed, as good a security system as you could likely have. He made some notes in his small notebook, and then he shoved the notebook into his breast pocket along with the short yellow pencil.

The man belched. "I know where they got the stuff they was takin'."

"Tell me." Jake wouldn't beg. The man would talk or he wouldn't talk, and chances were, whatever he said would be a lie, anyway.

"I live right across the hall there." The man pointed. "I see things, is all I'm saying."

"Things."

"Yeah. Like today — I seen Bobby Sewell come in here with a lot of shit he just bought, and he was bragging about it. Next thing I know, you folks're hauling Bobby and Curtis and LaRue and a lady I never seen before right out of here, and the kids are crying and screaming — and Amber, she's running after the stretcher and she's yelling, 'Curtis! Curtis baby, wake up!' " The man shook his shoulders, and the shudder moved through the rest of his body as if

he were a dog stepping out of a pond, flinging off the liquid. "Hate to think of them
kids seeing that," he said. "You know what I
mean? Seeing their mommy all upset. Seeing their daddy laid out like that."

They've surely seen worse, Jake wanted to
say, but didn't. "You said you had some
information about the source of the narcotics."

"Yeah. Yeah, I do. I listen a lot. Folks don't
even know I'm around. I know where Bobby
got 'em. He was bragging up a storm about
it. New gang just got in town the other day.
Been operating out of the Starliner Motel.
Selling this real powerful stuff."

Jake offered no reaction to the information, but inside he felt a jolt of satisfaction.

Score one for you, Malik.

The man was still talking.

"How's these folks doing at the hospital,
anyway? Curtis ain't such a bad guy. Had a
lot of pain in his life, tell you that. Used to
run a forklift. Had an accident a while ago.
Been on disability ever since. Now, his
brother Bobby — he's no good. Wouldn't
give you a nickel for him. Nor for his
girlfriend, neither. But Curtis is okay."

"He's dead." Jake had been texted the ID
on the fatality back in the parking lot. "The
other three are going to be fine."

"So the bastards live and the good guy dies. Ain't that just the way it always is," the man said.

"Ain't it just," Jake replied.

Jake didn't linger. He wanted to get over to the Starliner Motel. And he wanted to run down his list of local dealers, the human bridges between the suppliers, possibly holed up at the motel, and their eager customers. Corner them, ask some questions. For the first time since he had kneeled down next to the body of Sally Ann Burdette in the Marathon bathroom some twelve hours ago, he felt a faint stirring that he recognized as that rarest and most fragile of entities: hope.

BELL

1 p.m.

The names streamed down the screen of her cell, encased inside the light gray lozenge of text type. The text was from Sheriff Harrison. It confirmed everything Bell had most feared about what they might be facing.

Alone now in her office, she assimilated the rolling ticker of bad news, listed in order of incidence:

IRVING WALTRIP, 57
JEAN SMITH, 21
ALMA SMITH, 23
TYLER GEE, 19
MATT FORSECA, 31
SUSIE WEINER, 16
BOBBY BLEVINS, 27

Each one had overdosed within the last hour. Each one had sparked a call to 911 and required tending by a paramedic. Each one was still alive, as of right now, but three were still in the Raythune County Medical Center, and far worse off. The others had been treated at the scene with naloxone, which instantly brought them back to the misery of their lives — and to the very circumstances, Bell reminded herself wearily, which had caused them to reach for the heroin in the first place. And would do so again, inevitably.

While she contemplated the names and their probable fates, two more texts came in, one right on top of the other. The first was from Clay; the second was from Carla.

Sometimes Bell wished texting had never been invented. As easy and convenient as it was, there was something jarring about the juxtaposition of the profound and the casual, the dark and the light. Right after reading a list of addicts who had overdosed, she read Clay's plaintive, *Time 2 talk?* and Carla's peppy *Yea me — aced botany quiz.*

There ought to be a way of differentiating a grim text from a chipper one. Setting it off. An automatic change of font, maybe. Even another language altogether. As it was, the same alphabet that delivered details about ongoing countywide catastrophe also brought ordinary greetings, simple news.

Personal business.

"Can I bring you some lunch?"

Bell looked up. She was so lost in her ruminations that at first she did not even recognize Lee Ann Frickie, a woman she had worked with daily for the past eight years. All at once, Lee Ann's words punched through Bell's preoccupation.

"No, thanks."

"You have to eat. And you told me that you canceled your lunch plans with your sister."

"I did."

"So let me go get you some takeout from JPs. It's Monday. That means the special is the meatloaf sandwich."

Bell shook her head. She held up her cell. "Sixteen," she said.

Lee Ann waited. She did not know what Bell was talking about, but knew her boss would explain.

"Just got a text from Pam Harrison," Bell said. "The total's rising. Sixteen overdoses since midnight. And two deaths."

"Dear God in heaven."

"Yeah. We've had to call in extra squads of paramedics from Collier and Maywood counties. And the ER's stretched to the breaking point."

Lee Ann's hands were clasped in front of

204

her skirt. She dropped her head for a half a second, exposing the pink lane of the center part in her white hair. Bell wondered if she was praying. She was annoyed sometimes by her secretary's displays of piety, and privately questioned her reliance on religion as a means of getting over rough spots; right now, though, it struck Bell as a fine idea. *I'll take help from anywhere we can get it,* she thought.

Lee Ann lifted her head.

"Why haven't we had more calls about this?" the secretary asked. Her tone was grave. "You'd think the news would be all over town."

"Happening too fast."

"I thought nothing around here moved faster than gossip."

"This is a first, then. But it'll catch up." Bell's gaze moved toward the single window in her office. Sunshine picked out the islands of dust on the window and highlighted them. "I've got to go over and see Dot Burdette. Sammy called. She's having a rough time. Can't blame her."

"She did her best with that girl," Lee Ann declared. "I know. I watched her. Sally Ann was doing fine until she got to high school and then — boom. She fell and fell hard. Fell right into that life. One bad boyfriend was all it took. The Ehrlich boy. Junior Ehrlich's son. Worthless — father and son both. What I don't get," she went on, her tone shifting as she mused aloud with a passion that she normally kept under wraps, "is why people do this to themselves in the first place. The drugs, I mean. Life is hard, God knows — but it's hard for everybody. It was hard for my mother. A widow at twenty-four, with seven kids to raise and no income except for a couple of laying hens and a skinny milking cow. It was hard for my grandmother. My grandfather was a horrible man — violent like you wouldn't believe. He got drunk four or five times a week and when he did, he liked to swing an ax over his head and threaten anybody in the vicinity, including his wife and his children. He once killed a man by stomping him to death. I mean — my God, Belfa, it's not like the world was any easier for our parents and grandparents and all the previous generations on this earth. But they didn't poison themselves. Not like this. Alcohol, yes — but not drugs. And why has it hit so hard here? We've already got enough problems as it is. It's not like we needed another one." She shivered. Her fury and her incomprehension had risen to a crescendo and now began to subside.

Bell had no answer. Lee Ann did not expect her to have one. Her secretary just needed to vent. Bell understood that and waited. After a few seconds, Lee Ann said, "Well." She turned to go, but paused. "What about lunch?"

"What about it?"

Lee Ann sighed theatrically, lifting and dropping her narrow shoulders. "I tried. That's what I'll say. When you keel over from malnutrition, that's my defense — I tried."

A weak smile. "Noted for the record. I'll make sure you're in the clear."

Lee Ann turned to go.

"Although," Bell added, speaking to her back, "if you've got any of those peanut butter crackers in your desk, I'd be willing to take a package or two off your hands."

Lee Ann grunted and kept moving. Bell knew she could expect a snack to be lobbed her way in short order. She could catch it one-handed without even looking.

She picked up her cell. The first text went to Carla: an emoji of an upraised yellow thumb. The second was far more difficult to compose. No, she couldn't talk to Clay right now. A minute with him was too long, and a thousand years wasn't long enough. Their relationship was intense and passionate and complicated, yet they always seemed to return to the same simple impasse: He wanted more from her than she was able to give. *Or* willing *to give,* Clay would say, correcting her, if she spoke the thought aloud in his hearing. She loved him. But she did not want to marry him. She did not want to marry anybody.

Call u later, she texted him back. *Love u,* she added, although she knew as well as Clay did that love was not the issue, that her failure to be what he wanted her to be had nothing to do with love, and everything to do with the past and its long, dark, endless reach into the present.

EDDIE

He had finished mopping the floor. Now it was time to rinse out the bucket in the sink. The church's foundation was over a century old and the basement flooded every few weeks, after a hard rain or an extra-big wash load. Today it was the latter that had caused sour-looking gray water to swish across the concrete floor. Among his duties was washing the linens used in the church — hand towels in the bathrooms, napkins in the social hall — in the ancient front-loading machine that crouched in the corner, and if he waited too long between loads, he had to overstuff, with inevitable consequences. Water would come trickling from the base of the machine like a car leaking oil. Nothing major, but he still had to mop it up. Standing water in a basement led to mold and the attendant smell, a nose-crinkling

209

astringency that could waft up to the sanctuary.

Washing towels and napkins. Mopping floors.

Women's work. That's what his father would have called it. Troy Sutton would have had a good laugh if he had seen his son right now, rinsing out a mop bucket in a two-sided utility sink. *Tough guy, ain't you,* Troy would say, pointing at his boy, and then using the same gnarled index finger to push at the bill of his cap, lifting it off his forehead until it sat so far back on Troy's skull that only habit held it on. *Big tough man, mopping floors. You got some sewing to get to later, boy? Some meals to cook, maybe? And here I thought you had the makings of a soldier. Huh.*

Funny how you hear the voices of the dead more clearly than the voices of the living, Eddie thought.

He finished cleaning the bucket. He set it upside down in the sink to let the bottom dry off. He had already wrung the water out of the mop and propped it on the floor next to the sink. He was grateful, truth be told, to have physical work to do. The encounter with Raylene had left him shaking with anger and frustration. He needed somewhere to put all of that excess emotion. Emotions were a problem for him. If he didn't keep them under control, bad things could happen. At the VA hospital, they had taught him strategies for dealing with his feelings when they breached their natural boundaries; work was one of them.

At least he had gotten to see Marla Kay this morning. She was the one bright spot in his life, the thing that kept him going. Last winter a number of setbacks had laid him low, and there was a moment when he really did not think he could hang on for even one more minute — but the thought of his little girl persuaded him to fight back. He could not imagine never seeing Marla Kay again.

He looked around the basement. Along one wall was the small cot on which he slept, and next to it was an aluminum clothing rack snapped together from a kit he had bought at Walmart. Across from the washing machine was the gravity-feed furnace, so old that they didn't make replacement parts for it anymore, and so inefficient that the gas company threatened to red-tag it one of these days. All that held them back was the fact that this was a church. They were probably afraid of the bad publicity. He had learned the trick of keeping it going, nudging it this way or that when it acted up, or jury-rigging a part when the existing one failed. With special pokes and taps and instinctive adjustments, he kept it humming along, enabling the church to spend its limited funds on something other than an expensive new heating system. From the pulpit, Paul Wolford had once called Eddie the "furnace whisperer." The parishioners laughed, but Eddie did not mind; he could tell warm, friendly laugher from the cold, mean kind, having experienced both.

"Hey, Eddie."

"Reverend." Eddie wiped his wet hands on the front of his work pants before shaking Paul's hand. Paul often strolled down to the basement to chat with Eddie. Eddie had not heard his approach, but that wasn't unusual; when he started thinking about Marla Kay, his mind went to another place and he wasn't attentive anymore. Things got past him.

"So I guess there was a bit of a fuss over at Lymon's today," Paul said.

Small towns, Eddie thought. *Damn.* He had grown up in this area, but still had trouble reconciling himself to the fact that in a town like this, your life was always on display. Privacy did not exist. Sometimes he felt as if he was still back in an Army barracks, where you couldn't take a dump without everybody knowing about it and likely commenting on the shape and color.

Before he could answer, Paul spoke again. "Don't mean to embarrass you, Eddie. Or call you out. It's your business. But one of my parishioners saw you arguing with Raylene outside the store. Just wanted to make sure you were okay."

"She's doing it again." Eddie tried to keep his voice calm. Paul would be looking for signs that he was ready to blow. "Just like that time before. She's out begging for money. Telling people that Marla Kay's sick. It's disgusting."

"It's also against the law," Paul said.

"Yeah, but — you know."

They had discussed this, the two of them, last spring when Raylene first tried her little scheme. Yes, it was fraud. And yes, Eddie could go to the authorities. He could tell them that when Raylene ran short of cash, she picked a spot and put up a sign claiming that Marla Kay was dying of cancer. She collected enough to pay the rent or buy a new pair of shoes and then shut down the operation until the next time her checkbook gave her the bad news. When Eddie had threatened to turn her in, she threatened him right back: If he did that, he would

213

never see Marla Kay again. Eddie had signed away all parental rights on the day the little girl was born. He was still in a fog back then, still fighting the effects of his brain injury, barely able to speak or walk properly, or dress or feed himself. He was better now. But the only way he was able to see Marla Kay was if Raylene decided to let him. He could not take a chance on pissing her off.

He knew what people said behind his back. *Maybe the kid's not even yours. Don't be a fool.* Raylene had a reputation. She was an attractive woman, and it was the kind of attractiveness that never stayed still but was always active, always on the prowl, just like the raw materials for any other scam. She and Eddie had only been intimate once. They had met at the church. For a time, Raylene was employed there, too, as a housekeeper. She handled the dusting and the sweeping in the rectory, while Eddie took care of things like lawn care and the furnace. Once Raylene got pregnant, Jenny Wolford told her to find other employment. Raylene didn't mind. The job was too hard, anyway, and Jenny was "a real bitch," she told Eddie. "Nothing I do is ever good enough for her."

Raylene's pregnancy had been a surprise

— but for Eddie, it was a good surprise. He wanted to take care of Marla Kay. *I got my benefits,* he told Raylene eagerly. *I'll help raise her. Do whatever you want me to do.* She made it clear, however, that the only help she wanted was his money. They were not a couple. They would never be a couple.

"How are you feeling these days, Eddie?" Paul asked.

Eddie shrugged. He never knew how to answer that question. The headaches were still terrible, and he had no stamina; if he didn't get at least ten or eleven hours of sleep each night, he couldn't function the next day. His memory was shot. His limp was getting worse, not better, no matter how diligent he was about doing the exercises recommended to him by the physical therapist. But then again, he had that little girl in his life.

"I'm okay."

"You ever need to talk — you find me, all right? My office door's always open."

"I know." He liked Paul, but sometimes the reverend asked too many questions about his feelings. It wasn't that Eddie had anything to hide. He just didn't know how to answer the questions. Paul reminded him of some of the people at the VA. They meant well, but they did not seem to understand that sometimes their relentlessly positive natures and their constant pushing — *You can do this, you'll be fine, life's going to work out* — were oppressive and hard to deal with. Paul wanted to make everything go right. But his care felt like a burden, an expectation. When Eddie failed, he had the double whammy: He had to deal with the fact of his failure *and* with the fact that he had let Paul down. It was too much.

"The situation's not ideal," Paul said. "I know you'd like to see a lot more of Marla Kay. But the good news is — one day she'll be old enough to do as she pleases. And she can come and see you on her own. Raylene won't have a thing to say about it." He looked around the basement. The low ceiling made the place feel like a cave. Cobwebs swung from the sweating walls. Junk was stacked up every few feet: broken pews, old bookcases, half-filled buckets of paint, a chair with a busted seat. "You sure you don't mind all this? You've been here for a few years now. Maybe it's time for a change. We can find somewhere else if you'd like. An apartment, maybe. We can help with the rent. Or maybe —"

"It's great." Eddie spoke hurriedly. "Really great. I don't want to . . ." He paused, trying to regain his equilibrium. "I don't want to be anywhere else, Paul. This suits me fine. I'm not real good with people. I can do my work and then come down here and be comfortable." His words had slowed down in the middle, but they speeded up again as the anxiety rose in him.

"Hey, hey — settle down. No problem. I just don't want you to ever feel stuck here. Okay, buddy?"

"Okay."

He didn't feel stuck. He was profoundly grateful to Paul and Jenny. On a winter night seven years ago they had found him huddled in the church doorway, babbling and shaking. He had soiled himself. He hadn't eaten in a week. They took him in, cleaned him up, fed him, got him medical help from the VA; in addition to the physical problems from his brain injury, it turned out that he suffered from undiagnosed PTSD from his Army days in Afghanistan and had been self-medicating with alcohol. His unit had come under fire as they cleared a village, house by house, and Eddie took shrapnel in his head. The brain injury caused seizures and a variety of other problems. The medicine he took for the seizures made his thoughts feel slow and heavy, but it was a trade-off Eddie could live with. That was the key word: "live." Paul and Jenny Wolford had enabled him to live again. It wasn't perfect, but he was better than what he had had before. He wasn't homeless. He had a bed and a place to wash up.

And he had Marla Kay.

Paul moved a few steps toward the furnace, so that he could thump its side the way you might gruffly greet a beloved old farm animal, the kind that has no useful purpose anymore but that you keep around out of sentimentality. The furnace was large and round and dirty, and the ducts rising out of the upper portion of its sides looked like striated gray limbs lifted in supplication.

"How's this old thing doing?" Paul said.

"She'll make it through another winter. After that, I'm not sure."

"Well, I'm not sure about *any* of us, Eddie, truth be told." Paul laughed. "But it's good to know you can nurse her a while longer. Cupboard's pretty bare, budget-wise."

Eddie had something else on his mind. He cupped a hand around the back of his neck. "Paul, can I ask you something?"

"Sure."

"You and Jenny — you never had any kids, right?"

"That's right."

"Sometimes I think that would've been better for me, too. Sometimes I wish I didn't know about Marla Kay. Because I miss her so much. I see her with Raylene and I get so mad at what I see. How she's raising her — it ain't right. But all I can do is wish she was here. Wish I was with her more often. It hurts, you know? And so I think, 'If I didn't have a kid, I would be better off.' "

This was possibly the longest speech Eddie had ever made in Paul's presence, and Eddie's growing awareness of that fact was making him feel even more awkward than usual.

"It's always a risk," Paul said, gentleness in his tone. "Loving somebody, I mean. Like you do Marla Kay. Biggest risk you can take. Because things happen to people. Good things, bad things. And when we love — we're vulnerable. There's nowhere to go to get away from the pain." Paul glanced at his wristwatch. He frowned. "Afternoon Bible study starts at two. Gotta run, buddy. You need to talk later — you let me know. I'm around."

"Thanks."

"Anytime." Paul hesitated. Eddie could sense his concern. Something in Eddie's demeanor was worrying him. "You're okay, right?"

"I'm okay."

"Because if you're not, I can —"

"I'm okay. Really."

"Dinner's at six. Jenny's making hamburgers."

"Sounds good."

As soon as Paul was gone, Eddie walked over to a dusty, broken-down cabinet in the corner. He kept some of his stuff in here, in the one drawer that still worked. He pulled it open. He lifted off the red wool blanket that he had carefully arranged so that anyone doing a cursory search might not find what was stowed beneath it.

With great care he drew out the rifle, and then he closed the drawer.

Bell

"Why?"

Bell heard the word but she could not see the speaker. The room was too dark. The blinds had been shut tight, the curtains pulled together and tied. A darkened room in the middle of the afternoon told its own story. It was never a happy one.

The word came again. It sounded like the aural embodiment of pain:

"Why?"

Thirty seconds ago Dot's brother, Sammy Burdette, had opened the front door of his sister's house for Bell. Then he stood to one side. "She's in there," Sammy said, tilting his big bald head toward the closed pocket doors separating the front hall from the living room. He didn't say anything else.

The first "Why?" came when Bell slid open the pocket doors. She closed them behind her, because that was how she had

221

found them, and it wasn't her place to change things. Once the room was dark again, she had to watch her step. She had only been here twice before. She did not remember the layout of the room — the location of couch or chair or ottoman — and she had to move slowly, so as not to bump into solid objects, or trip over them.

A third time:

"Why?"

A dark shape resolved itself into something familiar, and Bell saw the woman who was repeating the word. Dot Burdette slumped forward in an armchair, holding her head in her hands.

"Hey, Dot," Bell said softly. "I got a call from Sammy. He asked me to come by."

That was not true. What Sammy had actually said was: *I've never seen her this way. I think she might do harm to herself. I'm scared for her. For God's sake, Bell — she needs you. She needs somebody.*

And so here Bell was, using up time she didn't have, on a day that was turning out to be worse than anyone could have imagined, with no end in sight. She had no idea what to say to Dot. They weren't close friends. In high school, Dot had been at the exact center of the most popular group, the girls who had the right clothes and the right hair and the perfect boyfriends. Belfa Dolan was at the extreme other end of the social spectrum. She was the outcast, the kid in foster care whose sister was serving a prison term for killing their father. Her clothes were all wrong. Her facial expression never varied beyond a scowl. Bell did not recall a single conversation with Dot Burdette during their high school years. Not one. Dot's laughter had an arch, haughty sound to it, and you could hear it every morning when Dot and her friends hung out in front of their lockers, gossiping, whispering about who had done what with whom the night before, making fun of other people. Bell remembered walking by that group a time or two, and feeling a deep humiliation when the trailing comments reached her ears, studded with words such as *loser* and *freak.*

Then Bell had gone away and changed her life. She had graduated from a prestigious law school, retuned to Acker's Gap, won the election for prosecutor. Dot was named vice president of the bank her father ran. They were professional women in a town where the majority of people spent the workday saying, "Do you want fries with that?" Wordlessly, a truce was struck between Belfa Elkins and Dorothy Burdette; they would pretend that they were old

223

friends. Bell went along with the charade. But she never forgot the words that had been used about her. And she never forgot the sound of Dot's laughter in the halls of Acker's Gap High School, a sound that carried in its wake privilege and exclusion, as well as pettiness and snobbery.

None of that mattered now.

"Mind if I turn on a light?" Bell asked.

No reply.

"Okay, well — I'm going to do that," Bell said. "If it bothers you, let me know." She had spotted an object on a round table next to Dot's chair that looked like a lamp. Groping, Bell found the base, and then the switch.

Dot seemed to shrink back from the sudden light. Her body recoiled, but she still did not lift her head out of the nest of her intertwined fingers. Only the top of her head was visible. Bell had yet to see her face. Dot was wearing an old shirt, trousers, and tennis shoes. The kind of clothes you wear when you aren't paying attention to what you are wearing. Bell had rarely seen her in casual clothes.

The room was a masterpiece of quiet elegance. The Burdettes had money, they had always had money, and there was something about family money that gave a house an extra measure of dignity. The furniture, the carpets, the wainscoting on the walls — everything spoke of an assumption that the people who lived here were worth all of this luxury. Whereas with new money, the accouterments always seemed to be trying too hard, eager to prove that it wasn't just a fluke, a mistake.

None of that mattered now.

Dot was in mourning. Her grief made her indifferent to everything but her own suffering. There were many people, Bell was sure, ready to point out to Dot that she had lost her niece a long time ago, that in effect the young woman had disappeared years before, when she became an addict. But the gulf between a metaphorical death and an actual one was profound. Dot had tumbled into that crevasse. She was still tumbling.

"Why?" Dot repeated. "Why did this happen?"

"I don't know." Bell sat down across from her on a mauve love seat. It was just as uncomfortable as it looked, in the way of expensive furniture that could be admired but never loved.

"She was a good girl," Dot murmured. She raised her face. It was swollen and red. Her eyes were wet. Snot had dried between her nose and her upper lip, and crusted on

225

her chin. She looked terrible.

None of that mattered now.

"I know," Bell said.

Dot laughed. It wasn't the cold, merry laugh of her youth; it was as hard as the bark of a seal, a sharp, ugly sound. "No, she wasn't," Dot corrected herself. "She wasn't a good girl at all. She was selfish and spoiled and she took everything I gave her and she threw it back in my face. She called me a bitch. I called her a whore. You hear that, Bell? I called my own niece a whore. I did. That's the last thing I ever said to her. It was a couple of weeks ago. I found her in here. She'd moved out a long time ago and I didn't know where she was living or what she was doing — and I came home for lunch one day and here she was, right in this very room, wadding stuff in a pillowcase, stuff she was going to steal from me and then go out and sell. I was so mad I was *shaking,* Bell. I was — I was . . ." Dot caught her breath. "I called her a whore. I said, 'Get out of here, you ungrateful whore.' I don't talk like that. But I did. That day, I did. I was so disappointed in her. I thought I was way past disappointment — but I wasn't."

"You lost your temper. It happens."

"Why? Why the drugs, Bell? Why?"

Bell did not answer.

"Your girl," Dot went on, leaning forward in her chair, hands cupping her elbows. "Carla, right? That's your daughter's name?"

"Yes."

"Okay. So how did you do it? How did you keep her away from it? What did you *do*?" Desperation haunted Dot's voice.

"Every child is different. What happened to Sally Ann is not a reflection of what you did or didn't do for her. You can't look at it that way. You'll just drive yourself crazy. All kids make mistakes. Some of them push on through, anyway, in spite of those mistakes. Others don't. But you loved her, Dot. I know you did."

"I did. I did love her." She seemed to become aware, all at once, of who she was talking to, and her voice ratcheted up in intensity. It was the same tone of voice she had used on the phone earlier, a tone of accusation. "You're the prosecutor. So it's your *job*, right? Catching the bastards who sell this shit? So why aren't you doing your job? Why are you just sitting here? *Do your job.* Go do your freaking job."

Lashing out was a good way to deflect grief. Bell understood that. Dot would bounce between sorrow and anger a thousand times today, and every day for the next several weeks or months. Maybe for the rest of her life. And she would aim her anger at the very people who tried to help her, such as Sammy, such as Bell, because they were close by. It wasn't fair, but this wasn't about fairness. It was about survival. Dot would become impossible. Old friends would gradually stop coming around, stop making the effort. They would not want to risk being insulted and screamed at. They would not want to feel Dot's eyes on them as she asked that impossible question: "Why?"

Bell stood up. This wasn't just a condolence visit. It couldn't be. There was too much at stake.

"I have to ask you something, Dot. I know Sheriff Harrison has already gone over this with you, but I want to you to think about it one more time. Because it's getting worse out there."

No reply.

"You can help us do our jobs," Bell continued. "We all want the same thing — to get these drugs off the streets. So I need to ask you to think again. Do you have any idea where Sally Ann got her drugs? Any clue at all? Something she said, maybe. A name. A place. An off-hand remark. Anything."

Dot shook her head. "I didn't talk to her anymore. And she sure as hell didn't talk to me."

She wasn't looking at Bell. She was looking at a spot across the room. There was nothing there. Suddenly Bell was reminded of those times in high school when she would pass Dot Burdette in the hall and Dot would ignore her, would act as if Bell was invisible or — worse — a piece of garbage. Bell was something that had blown in through an open door; you waited for the custodian to pick it up or sweep it away.

How desperately Bell had wanted to belong, and how much it would have mattered to her if, just once, Dot had said hello to her, or made eye contact, or acknowledged in some small way — a way that would have cost Dot *nothing* — that Belfa Dolan was a human being.

None of that mattered now.

PAM

The tally had risen to twenty. It was time to send Bell another text, hard on the heels of the text that Pam herself had just received. Time to forward the names and ages of the latest overdose victims, a list that had been supplied to the sheriff four minutes ago by Agnes Cooper, an ER nurse at the Raythune County Medical Center:

MELANIE STOVALL, 27
REX SMITHIES, 30
ANN MARIE MCCORKLE, 22
SAM WEEKS, 24

No fatalities in this bunch. At least not yet.

Pam hit the tiny arrow on her screen. She sat back in the driver's seat of the Blazer. She had just left her office and relocated herself behind the wheel of the massive

230

black vehicle parked in front of the courthouse. It was the first time she had relaxed all day. The respite would last only a few minutes. Maybe less.

The black leather made the interior uncomfortable on summer days. She could turn on the engine and crank up the AC, sure, but that would be a waste of county resources in a place that had nothing to spare.

She could feel the heat on the headrest. It made the back of her scalp tingle. Pam hated hot days. She had grown up in an unheated log cabin in a remote area of Raythune County, miles from any paved road, and she found cold to be a deep comfort. Heat, on the other hand, made her nervous. Things changed in the heat — they melted, they ran together or fell apart or were otherwise ruined. Whereas in the cold, things became more like what they already were, sealed up inside their frozen essence. Hard. True.

It wasn't just the heat that was irritating her. Bell had asked for constant updates on overdose victims and each time Pam provided one, she was reminded of how profoundly she opposed this strategy. Keeping tabs on addicts, chasing a dealer who probably didn't know that he or she was selling a lethal form of the usual product — it was a waste of time. There were so many other duties she'd had to put off for this. It offended her on a level so deep that she felt as if she was walking around in a state of low-simmering rage.

Pam and Bell often disagreed — but usually it blew over. They would never be friends, but they respected each other. They had very different personalities. They had very different jobs to do. They would agree to disagree. And then they would move on.

Not this time. This time, the disagreement seemed to have opened up a profound rift between them. It felt as if it might be permanent, lasting long after the current crisis was handled.

Did Pam want addicts to die? No. Of course not. But was it the responsibility of the sheriff's department to talk people out of killing themselves, if that was what they wanted to do? Carfentanil might be deadly — but nobody was force-feeding it to them. They had already made the decision to ruin their lives.

Pam didn't like the heat in here, but she relished the quiet. So she stayed right where she was for another minute or so, head still angled back against the headrest. It was an indulgence. She was already late for an emergency meeting with Dr. Vernon Childress, head of the medical center. The squads and their loads of overdose victims would, from this point forward, be diverted to the much larger hospital in Blythesburg, but that presented myriad jurisdictional issues and a whopping load of extra paperwork — which was, of course, exactly what she had signed on for. It was what a sheriff did. Her job was more about solving problems and deploying resources than it was about shooting a gun or chasing down some bottom-feeding scuzzball.

She had learned that from Nick Fogelsong. She had been his chief deputy for five years. When he resigned, she told him she wanted to run for the office. She asked for his blessing. He gave it, although he asked her twice if she was sure that she really wanted the job. She said, "Yeah. I do." He looked at her a long time. Then he nodded and said, "Well, then, I'll support you one hundred percent. You'll be great."

She was. And she would continue to be. She had been proving herself her whole life, because she came from dirt. That was the only accurate way to put it. The Harrisons were a notorious clan of petty thieves and lazy liars and mean drunks and nonstop troublemakers who lived in a daisy chain of dingy trailers out by Charm Lake. The only one who had made something of himself was Pam's father; he had joined the Marines the second he was old enough, served in Operation Desert Storm, received citations for marksmanship and commendations for bravery. When he returned from Kuwait he took his daughter — his wife, Sharon, refused to leave the trailer compound — and moved to a small cabin on Indian Ridge, determined to put both geographical and psychic distance between his family and himself and his little girl. He and Pam did fine. The cabin was off the grid: no electricity, no running water. He taught her to shoot. They ate what they killed or trapped. It was good preparation for being in law enforcement: If you don't hunt, you don't survive. Her father was a good man, but he was a hard man, too. If he had not been hard, he could never have escaped his family, every single member of which — including his wife — he hated. He would not let them anywhere near his daughter. By teaching her about hate, he taught her about love.

A thought came to her, not for the first time, but more powerfully than before, in the light of the day's ongoing trauma: Maybe that's why she had no sympathy for addicts. Because they were weak. They had given up. And the man who had raised her was a fighter. He'd trained her to be one, too.

The *rap-rap* on the window startled her. The woman doing the interrupting — she had a big smile, a chunky build, and a fussed-over hairdo — was well known to her. After Pam pushed the button to roll down the window, Tina Lawton waved and said, "Hey, Sheriff — how're you doing?"

The enthusiasm jarred her. So did the smile. Pam's thoughts were so tightly entwined with the past and the heat and the day's rush of emergencies that it took her a moment to recover. Most people, she reminded herself, didn't yet know about what was going on all around them. Most people didn't work in law enforcement. Most people didn't live with a radio on their right shoulder. For most people — including Tina, a courthouse employee whom Pam had known for years — it was an ordinary late-summer day.

So far.

"Fine," Pam said. Her standard answer. This was not the time to get into it. Tina was being friendly; she did not really want any details. "How 'bout you?"

"Doing well. Thanks. Oh, I did want to tell you that the man's back again. The one hanging out by the bus station. In the Army jacket."

It took Pam a moment to catch up. "Right. From last week."

"Yeah. I was coming back from lunch and saw him on the street. He's all hunched over. Smells bad, too."

"I'll keep an eye out. Not much I can do, though, unless he commits a hostile act."

"He has a stick. Waves it around."

"Not sure that would be considered a hostile act."

Tina scrunched up her nose. "He yells at people going by. Something like, 'It's coming.' And he gets a real funny look in his eye. He ain't right in the head."

"Maybe not. But still, my hands are pretty much tied until he's an active threat." *Being crazy isn't a crime, Tina,* she wanted to say. *Neither is smelling bad. If it were, I'd have to lock up three-fourths of the county.*

"Okay, Sheriff. Just wanted you to know."

"Appreciate it."

"Have a good afternoon." Tina waved and began her slow climb up the courthouse steps.

Pam watched her. In a way, she envied people such as Tina. They did not know. They would know soon enough, because the information was already on the move, as rapid and unstoppable as an injection in the bloodstream, but for now, they were in the brief lull before the storm. They could enjoy their lives for this last little bit.

That was what being sheriff was all about. You never had that lull. You always got the bad news first.

Well, second: It sounded as if the crazy man with the stick had had a little advance notice.

She fired up the SUV. Back to work.

JAKE

"Hey. Hey, you." Jake had pulled the Blazer to the side of the road, next to the skinny kid with the blowsy pants and the flapping red shirt and the bobbing, jittery walk. Dust boiled up from under the Blazer's tires, on account of the swerve and the sudden stop.

"Hey, you," Jake repeated. "Hang on, okay?"

The deputy leaned over the passenger seat, trying to talk through the open window.

The kid fluttered to a halt. He put both bone-white hands on the bottom of the window frame and leaned in toward Jake the same way that Jake was leaning toward him. If somebody was watching from a distance, Jake thought, it might look like he and the kid were long-lost lovers about to kiss. The thought was both revolting and funny.

"Yeah?" the kid said. Jake placed his age

238

at seventeen, eighteen. Certainly less than twenty. His eyes had a smeary cast to them, and his body stayed in motion even as he propped himself up against the Blazer. He tapped a rhythmless solo with his thumbs on the frame. He was high on something. Probably pot, Jake surmised. The kid's step was too springy and his mood was too loose and cool for it to be heroin. In Jake's experience, pot and pills made them mellow, oozy, whereas heroin made them paranoid, wound them tight. This kid wasn't tight. If he'd been a watercolor, the reds and blues and browns would be running all over the road.

"Need your help," Jake said.

"Sure." Big grin. "Whatcha need?"

"Bad batch of heroin making the rounds today. Folks getting real sick. Any idea where it's coming from?"

The kid bunched up his face. It wasn't distaste at the idea of ratting somebody out; it was the arduous effort of thinking. Of answering a simple question, when all he really wanted to do was wallow and boogie in the sunshine.

"Nope." The kid's face relaxed. He had done his duty. He had thought about it.

Jake decided to press a little harder. This was the third time he had stopped during his ride out to the Starliner, the third time

239

he had undertaken a spontaneous interrogation of someone who obviously had first-hand experience with the illegal drug trade in Raythune County. Long shots, every one of them, but he had to try. Twenty people had overdosed since midnight, including four more since he had left the courthouse. Steve Brinksneader had just texted him with the names.

"People are dying," he said to the kid.

"Whoa."

"Yeah. So have you heard anything about a new supply coming in? Starting yesterday?"

"Nope."

Jake waved at the kid and sat upright in his seat again. "Okay. Thanks." He jerked the Blazer into gear and hopped back onto the road. There was no use pushing. He had tried that with the first two people he stopped, and all he got for his trouble was a loogie plastered on the side of the Blazer and a brackish flurry of muttered obscenities. He could wash the vehicle, and the curse words were actually pretty tame when compared with the names he was typically called in the course of a workday, but the point was, it was a waste of time.

And with every minute that passed, somebody else was risking death with the bad heroin.

Wait. As opposed to all the good *heroin that's out there? Jesus.*

Jake shook his head. How did any of this make sense? Why were they even bothering?

He must have asked himself that a hundred times so far today. Two hundred, maybe. *This isn't like a river that some greedy company's filling up with pollution — and folks have to drink the water and so innocent little babies die. This is shit people do to* themselves. *Voluntarily. Why not let them die? Why not let them kill themselves? Saves us the time and trouble of sending out a paramedic and a deputy every damned time one of 'em keels over.*

That was Steve Brinksneader's view. He and Jake had discussed it briefly back at the courthouse, when Jake stopped in after receiving the sheriff's summons. Steve was new enough at the job that he still thought in straight lines. He believed the world was a matter of black and white, good and evil. His mind was calibrated to absolutes. Jake recognized his own younger self in his colleague's implacable hardness. Steve, leaning up against the big humming Pepsi vending machine in the hall outside the jail, had said, "Who gives a crap if there's one less junkie in Raythune County? Or five less? Or ten? I mean — come on, Jake. It's called natural selection. World's better off." Jake understood. There was a part of him that saw it that way, too. But as he pointed out to Steve, "Last I heard, we don't get to decide who's worthy of being saved. We do our jobs." Steve kicked his boot against the vending machine — it had taken his money but withheld his Pepsi, not the first time it had played that nasty trick — and he grunted, and then both of them went back to work.

The Starliner looked even more slovenly than Jake remembered. In the muted sunshine of late afternoon, it seemed to throb in a sallow, glowering way, like a stubbed toe. There were two rusty cars in the parking lot. Jake recorded the plate numbers in his notebook, just in case.

The office door was open, a circumstance that instantly explained the vast number of flies that lifted off the front counter when he approached it. The manager glared at him. He was used to that. Cops always got The Glare. As in: *What'd I do?* Usually they weren't thinking that at all — Jake had, in less stressful situations, asked people why they looked at him that way when they were seeing him for the first time, and a lot of them said, "Habit" and he believed them — but their faces changed, anyway, going from neutral to bothered and resentful. The woman's short white hair was thin on the sides and even thinner on top. Her weight had pooled around her hips and thighs. She wore a shapeless blue garment that his grandmother, Jake remembered, would have called a house dress. He put her age at about sixty-five. The mean part of him put her IQ in the same general vicinity.

"Whatcha want?" she said in raspy voice. Her lower teeth were brown and yellow and broken. Her upper teeth — well, that was the wrong word, Jake observed. The right word was upper tooth. She embodied every cliché about West Virginia that he had ever heard, which annoyed him. He didn't like bigots to be right. But sometimes they were.

"I'll be real clear here, ma'am," Jake said. "I've got no time to beat around the bush."

She looked nervous now. She snagged her bottom lip with the single tooth remaining on the top row, and then released it again.

"Whatcha want?" she repeated.

"Like I said — I'm in a hurry. I need to know who's registered here." Jake reached for the spiral-bound notebook that was open on the linoleum counter. The page featured a list of pencil-scrawled signatures with corresponding room numbers.

The woman snatched it away before he made contact. Jake did not intend to get in a tug-of-war with her. He held up his hands in surrender.

"Can't letcha see that," she said.

He sighed heavily, to indicate his disappointment in her. He didn't have the authority to require her to hand over the register. Usually he didn't need it. Most people around here well understood that no matter the manner of malfeasance in which they were engaged, the sheriff's department was so short-staffed and overburdened that a deputy would overlook virtually anything that fell short of murder and dismemberment. So people complied with routine requests for information, knowing that any minor offenses that turned up would be conveniently forgotten.

This woman wasn't playing along. Yet there was more going on here. Jake sensed that she wasn't just being stubborn for the hell of it.

She was frightened.

He looked around the office. It was about the size of the front stoop of a trailer, with a single window garnished with a set of bent and age-yellowed blinds. A high wooden stool was jammed in the corner. Next to it was a round particleboard table. A dying plant sat in the middle of the table. Its crispy brown leaves drooped over the edge of the plastic pot in a fatal swoon.

He moved his eyes back to the front counter. Set into the wall perpendicular to it was a half-closed door that looked as if it led into a broom closet. The woman's head did not move, but her eyeballs shifted in the direction of the door. Then they shifted back to Jake. She was sending him a message:

Somebody was crouching in that space. Listening. She was warning him. The person, whoever it was, must have been in the office with this woman when the Blazer pulled into the lot.

In the next few seconds, Jake made a series of decisions. He had no warrant and no probable cause to get one. Hunches didn't count. He needed to find the local dealer, the person who could confirm that the Starliner was where a shipment had been picked up. At that point, Jake could get his warrant, giving him full authority to kick down the doors of every room in this misbegotten place, rousting out the gang members. And he'd be sure to bring backup. As urgent as the situation was, as much as he wanted to stop the tainted heroin from hitting the street, he knew better than to

245

challenge a drug gang on his own. They were generally armed, and armed well. And there was enough money at stake to make it worth their while to fight, and fight hard.

"Okay," he said to the woman.

His silent contempt for her — born of his frank disdain for her bad teeth and her obesity and the fact that she was probably protecting the very bastards who were poisoning her neighbors — was quickly fading. This was a job. Jobs were hard to come by around here. She was fortunate to have it. She did what she had to do to keep it.

She was a victim — just like the addicts he was trying to save. God, he hated the word "victim." But it was apt. You could hate a word and still know that it was the right one. He shrugged. Time to go. For now.

He paused before pushing open the door. He took a quick glimpse back at the plant on the table in the corner, the dead one, the one with the brittle leaves and the ugly brown color, and he wondered what that plant might have looked like if it had been given water, light, the right kind of soil, a little care and compassion. A little hope.

PAM

EDGAR LEE SUMMERSTALL, 28
MARJORIE PEARSON, 52
JIMMY DRAKE, 16

Pam snapped off her cell. *Jesus,* she thought. She returned her attention to Dr. Childress, an austere, thin-lipped, hook-nosed man in a well-cut black suit. He sat very close to the edge of his seat. His back was straight, his posture perfect. Both of his knobby, wormy-veined hands lay flat on the conference table in front of him. He looked poised to flee the premises. She could not blame him. The number of overdoses had continued to climb. The hospital in which this conference room was located — its resources and staffing levels already precariously low — was undergoing unprecedented stress. Its imminent collapse would be on

247

his watch.

Pam's most recent text had come from Deputy Brinksneader. He was manning the desk in the sheriff's office, covering for the secretary, Trixie Scoggins. Trixie had skipped her lunch but she could not skip her bathroom break, for reasons she did not need to spell out to the deputy. Steve had received the call with the names of the latest overdoses — it came from Ernie Edmonds, the paramedic — and immediately texted them to the sheriff.

Twenty-three. The total was now twenty-three. Still only the two fatalities. *Thank God,* Pam thought. But — *twenty-three*?

She felt as if she had fallen into a grain elevator and was being buried under tons of heavy grain. She had seen that happen; rather, she had seen the aftermath of it. A farmer named Ray Fane out by Shawkey Ridge had slipped from the rim and tumbled in, creating a situation that was instantly and irrevocably hopeless. Likewise, Pam felt suffocated by the day's onrushing glut of overdoses. She had no idea when it would stop. And no idea what to do about it.

She was seated to the left of Vernon Childress. It was just the two of them. Pam had taken off her hat and placed it on the conference table, a beautifully smooth woodgrain with a deep honey lacquer that made it look almost edible. The high-backed, black leather chairs were uncomfortably luxurious. Pam was not used to meeting in such places, and in fact had only been in this conference room once before. When she recalled the venues in which she usually held briefings — the front seat of the Blazer, a booth at JPs diner, her cramped box of an office next to the jail in the Raythune County Courthouse — this room with its patterned carpet and fabric wallpaper and professional hush seemed, by comparison, like Buckingham Palace. Of course she had never been to Buckingham Palace. It was only an expression.

Childress was an old man. He was scheduled to retire in four months. Pam could not read minds, but she had a fair idea of what the good doctor was thinking: If he had retired in June, his original plan, he would not have to be dealing with this. But the hospital board had persuaded him to stay on until the first of the year. And so here he was.

"We've ordered more naloxone from Charleston. It should be here this afternoon by FedEx Ground," he said. His voice was empty of inflection. It was a straight line seeking out the swiftest route from A to B.

249

"The nursing supervisor has been on the phone all afternoon. She's getting commitments from four other counties to send us additional support. Nurses, physicians, EMTs, patient-care techs. We're even running out of gurneys, if you can believe it. And clean linens in the ICU."

"Sounds like our own version of nine-eleven," Pam said.

Childress's head swiveled quickly in her direction. "What did you say?"

His reaction startled her. It was just an analogy. What was his problem?

"Nine-eleven," she repeated. "Raythune County-style. I only meant —"

"Don't." He cut her off, anger flooding his voice. "*Do not* say that. You don't get to say that. Not in *my* hospital." Now she heard something else in that voice: disgust. A raw, visceral disgust.

It was the first honest emotion Pam had ever seen within the person of Vernon Childress. He had been, in all of her previous encounters with him, serene and unflappable. He had practiced internal medicine in Charlottesville, Virginia, for forty-four years but now he was a strictly an administrator, a man who spent his days amidst charts and numbers, not human beings clutching their bellies and bleating with

250

pain. He rarely found himself in the presence of feelings, and he surely had no need anymore to express them himself. Thus Pam assumed he had probably forgotten how.

He hadn't.

"Pardon me?" she said.

"Don't you *dare . . .*" He took a deep breath, one that caused his bony shoulders to elevate and fall. It did not succeed in dissipating the emotion. "Don't you *dare* make that comparison in my hearing. The victims of nine-eleven were *professionals.* Bankers and attorneys and executives. People who *mattered.* But these — these *addicts* — did this to themselves." He had said the word "addicts" with such barbed malice in his tone that Pam was taken aback. "They *caused* this. They're weak. They're selfish. They don't care about anybody but themselves. They're lucky we don't just leave them out on the street to die. That's what they deserve."

The thought that came to Pam Harrison was simple and stark: *Hope to God I don't sound that like.*

Because the truth was, she shared Childress's opinion. Or at least she had — until she heard him speak it aloud. There was nothing quite like hearing your own view espoused by a snobby, judgmental old bastard who, on account of his money and a couple of initials after his name, was able to glide through the world on a moving sidewalk of automatic privilege to show you the error of your ways.

First thing she would do, when she got back to the courthouse, was talk to her deputies. And Trixie Scoggins, too. Anybody who reported to her. Make sure they weren't cutting corners or taking their time responding to dispatches for possible overdoses. Make sure they understood: *We take care of everybody. You want to stand in judgment of people? Go apply to be God. Or go be a doctor. Hang on — it's the same thing. Just ask any doctor.*

"Okay," Pam said. She picked up her hat. Childress, in his own way, had clarified things for her. She stood up. At the same moment, her cell signaled a new text. She checked it. Then she looked at Childress's grim, sallow face, which he had tilted up toward her, awaiting confirmation of whatever fresh hell this was.

"Another OD. And you got your wish. It's one of your professionals this time. Fenton McHale," she said, naming an attorney whose work for the coal companies had made him a millionaire several times over. He was a well-known man, as opposed to the nameless, faceless, anonymous people they had been dealing with thus far. "His secretary found him unresponsive in his office fifteen minutes ago. Probable overdose."

"Fenton? That *cannot* be correct. It's a mistake. It must have been a heart attack or a stroke."

Childress had to say it to her back because she was already at the door and only turned around to remind him of what he already knew: No one was exempt from the Appalachian virus.

"Come on, Vernon." She had never used his first name before. It had seemed disrespectful. Now, the only respect she was thinking about was respect for the paramedics and the others who were in the field trying to save lives. Not hanging out in fancy conference rooms with black leather chairs and honey-lacquered tables. "You know as well as I do that anybody can lose themselves to addiction. It doesn't matter how much money you have or what your title is."

"Impossible. Fenton McHale was no drug addict."

Pam couldn't stick around to argue. She didn't have time.

Twenty-four, she thought, jogging through the hospital corridor on her way to the main entrance and, beyond that, the Blazer. *My God. Twenty-four.*

SHIRLEY

"So what's going on?" Shirley said.

She took a quick drink of her coffee. She knew when Bell was upset. The tip-off: Her sister wouldn't meet her gaze. It had started the moment they sat down on their respective sides of the booth. Bell looked around the diner — everywhere but in Shirley's direction. Not a good sign.

"Lots," Bell said.

Shirley set down the mug. The coffee wasn't hot enough, which made the problem unsolvable. If it was too hot, you could wait for it to cool; if it was too cool already, you were screwed. You could flag down a waitress and ask for another cup, a hot one this time, but Shirley didn't like to make a fuss. She had made enough fusses in her life already.

"Do tell," Shirley said.

JPs was a good place for a private chat.

You wouldn't think so, based on an initial glance; it was small, and the booths were shoved together haphazardly and too close to one another, and everyone knew everyone else. Oddly, though, those elements made it as private as a confessional. Had the room been bigger and filled with strangers, every gesture would have been an object of intense scrutiny. The old-hat familiarity made people relax in JPs. They let down their guard. Things slipped by. Bell had once joked to Shirley that she wouldn't have been surprised to find Amelia Earhart in a booth in the back, sipping a glass of buttermilk and going over flight plans, having found the perfect spot in which to hide out for lo these many years.

"Just a really hard day," Bell said.

She was being evasive. Shirley didn't know whether to push or to let it be. They were back in each other's lives now on a regular basis, after all that time apart, but they had missed out on so much. Hence their interactions could suddenly nose-dive and become rickety, uncomfortable; they did not enjoy the easy, effortless give-and-take of sisters who had spent a lifetime getting to a good and solid place.

"Hard how?" Shirley said.

"We've had an unprecedented number of

overdoses since last night. Double digits."

"Jesus. I heard some chatter about it, but not the numbers."

"Yeah. The heroin's been laced with something much more potent than usual — that's how it looks, but we won't know for sure until we get the tests back." Bell regarded her coffee cup as if she had never seen such an object before, and did not have the least idea what to do with it. Her mind, Shirley could tell, was very far away from the diner.

"You're worried," Shirley said.

"I am. There's no way to warn people. I mean — how would we do that? Addicts don't come by the courthouse too often to shoot the breeze. And . . ."

"And?"

"And even if we *could* warn them, would it do any good? Probably not." She paused. "It's not nice to talk about, but there's another issue, too. The money this is costing the county — it's tremendous. Enough to fix a dozen torn-up roads or feed every hungry child in Acker's Gap for a month. Between the squad runs and the deputies who have to respond and then the medical costs . . ." Bell stopped. She shook her head. "It won't surprise you to know," she added, sarcasm rippling through her tone, "that not many addicts keep up with their health insurance premiums."

Shirley turned her mug around in a circle. The tabletop was bumpy and scarred. There were cigarette burns, too, from the days when people could smoke in public places. She had not reached for a cigarette since her meeting that morning with Paul Wolford. Funny. All those years as a smoker, and it only took a one-sentence diagnosis to shoo away the desire for good.

"So why don't you want to talk about it?" Shirley said. "You wouldn't be telling me this now if I hadn't pushed."

"True." Bell gave her a rueful smile. "I guess I figure you have your own problems to deal with."

You don't know the half of it, little sister, Shirley thought. Out loud, she said, "For my money, you've got the toughest job in the world."

"I think some Navy SEALs might disagree with you. And a few brain surgeons, too, might have an argument." Bell's smile vanished. "But — yeah. It's hard. You know what? People are always coming up to me and asking why we don't do this or that. Why don't we prosecute the addicts? And track down more dealers? And get rid of the drug gangs hiding out up in the mountains?" Bell made her voice high-pitched and persnickety, imitating the kind of people who constantly accosted her on the street with their moralistic fervor: " 'Don't you know that drugs are *ba-a-a-d*? Hmm? Don't you *want* to get rid of those terrible dealers? Do you *enjoy* watching the young people around here kill themselves with that poison?' " She took a quick, vicious drink of her coffee. The swallow was followed by a wince. Her voice returned to normal as she addressed her invisible audience. Earnest now. "Yeah. Yeah, folks, I know what drugs are doing to our town. I do. And if I had an army, I'd send it up into the hills and roust out every last gang I could find. I'd hunt down the local dealers. And if I were Bill Gates, I'd take all the addicts and I'd get them into a rehab program and when they got out, I'd find them decent jobs and decent places to live, and then I'd . . ."

She stopped talking. Shirley had reached across the table and put her hand on Bell's hand, settling her down.

"God, Shirley. I'm sorry," Bell said. "First I cancel lunch. Then I meet you here and I start yelling. You had something you needed to tell me. This is supposed to be about you, not me. So what's up? I know the breakup with Bobo was hard on you." Bell hesitated.

"Do you need some money? Because I can . . ."

"Hey — no. No, Bell. Come on. I wouldn't ask you for money."

"You didn't ask. I offered."

"Well, the answer is no. I wanted to talk. That's all." Shirley sat back against her seat. "I got some news."

"News."

"Yeah."

Bell waited. Before Shirley could speak again, Bell's cell rang. She held up an index finger and mouthed *Just a sec,* then pushed the phone against her ear.

"Elkins," she said.

Shirley watched Bell's face. There was no movement in it. Nothing to indicate the nature of the news. *You would've been a hell of a poker player, little sister,* Shirley thought.

Bell ended the call. She slipped the cell in her purse.

"Tonight," she said to Shirley.

"Pardon?"

"I have to run. I'm sorry. But why don't you come over tonight? We'll sit on the porch and talk. I'll text you the minute I get home and you can head on over."

"That call just now. Another OD?"

Bell waited. She seemed to be deciding whether to share more bad news with

260

Shirley. Lowering her voice, she said, "Yeah. Which brings the grand total to twenty-four overdoses since midnight. And it's not a kid this time. It's Fenton McHale."

"That sleazebag lawyer? The Richie Rich?"

"That's the guy."

Shirley gestured to Bell with a brief wave of her right hand. "Go," she said. "Do your job."

"Okay. Thanks for understanding." Bell slid out of the booth and stood up. She took a last swig of her coffee and winced again. "So like I said — come by tonight, okay? We can talk. Things will settle down by then."

Hope so, Shirley thought. She felt the old Appalachian fatalism stirring again, curling around her brain like red on a peppermint stick. *Wouldn't bet on it, though.*

JAKE

5:40 P.M.

Coal had been good to Fenton McHale.

It had bought him lots and lots of nice things. It had bought him this large building on the outskirts of Acker's Gap, a former shoe factory that had been extensively and expensively remodeled into a sleek, airy, three-story headquarters for McHale & Associates. It had bought him a variety of shiny, showy vehicles, many of which, Jake noticed, he parked in the sprawling lot adjacent to his office — because why bother having things that other people can't afford unless you can rub their noses in your good fortune and their lack thereof?

Coal was no longer the ruling behemoth it once had been, but that change had had no appreciable impact on Fenton McHale and his lifestyle. He had already made his money. It had come flooding his way from black-hearted coal company executives eager to fight disability claims and civil suits involving workplace safety — and McHale proved to be a shrewd courtroom showman, all flailing arms and insidious accusations against the shy, shuffling, powerless plaintiffs. McHale had used that money to make more money — lots and lots of it. And *that* money, in turn, was used to make more money still.

Coal money had bought him political influence and social prestige. Coal money had bought him a Gulfstream G650 and a thoroughbred with Derby potential and a minority stake in a Major League Baseball team. Coal money had bought him five wives and four divorces.

But it had not bought him happiness.

At least that's what people hope, Jake thought. The idea of Fenton McHale, filthy rich but desperately unhappy, was one of the few pieces of gossip of which Jake could approve. It kept folks going — the notion that, with all of his possessions and all of his power, with his jet and his Jacuzzi, he still wasn't as happy as they were with their honest, simple lives. It was a necessary platitude. One that helped them survive.

Jake parked the Blazer next to the ambulance. Its back doors were flung open, awaiting the return of the gurney. The outside markings said MERCER COUNTY. It wasn't Molly and Ernie, then, but a squad on loan from an adjacent county. He wondered how her day was shaping up; she was probably off on another call. Another crisis.

He shook his head. *Focus, Jake.*

McHale's secretary stood behind the giant reception desk. Creamy waves of long, bright blond hair pooled over both of her shoulders. *Maybe eighteen,* he thought, trying to guess her age on the fly. *Twenty at the outside.* Tears had made a muddy mess of her eye makeup. One arm clutched her slender torso. The hand at the end of the other arm was pressed to her mouth, which was open.

At the sight of Jake's uniform, she uttered a small cry and tightened her grip on her torso.

"He's — they're — I . . ." Each time she tried to go beyond a single word, the anguish caught in her throat and stopped her. Her shoulders bobbed up and down. She was seized by what appeared to be a violent attack of hiccups. She was quite beautiful, but it was a sealed, homogenized beauty that reminded Jake of a sandwich under a heat lamp in a convenience store, the kind that comes wrapped in a plastic sheath you have to peel off before you can get any real sense of the contents.

She gave up trying to talk and pointed to her left. Past the spacious reception area and its array of sumptuous furniture was a pair of double doors that had been heaved open. On a plaque next to the doorway were two lines of gold lettering, festooned with little curlicues: FENTON MCHALE ATTORNEY-AT-LAW. From inside, Jake heard urgent voices.

He crossed the threshold but stayed well back from the action. He didn't want to get in the way. McHale lay on his back in the middle of the plum-colored carpet, his giant belly sticking up, his white shirt parted at the point where it had come untucked from his trousers, allowing an unfortunate peek at the actual skin, at that massive white mound of flesh. He did not seem to be breathing. There was a raised lump on his forehead, a bruise that was just getting under way.

He watched the paramedics work. Both of them were on their knees, on either side of McHale. Because they were normal-sized and the victim was obese, the scene reminded Jake of a movie he'd seen once of *Gulliver's Travels,* when Gulliver is lying on the ground surrounded by the Lilliputians. The former sheriff, Nick Fogelsong, used to tease Jake about having seen the movie versions of books instead of reading the books themselves. Nick read all the time. *Like it makes you any happier,* Jake always wanted to snap back at him, because he was stung by the remark, no matter the lighthearted way in which Nick delivered it. *Like those books of yours have ever helped you, one damned bit.* They hadn't. Nick Fogelsong was the saddest man he knew.

One paramedic fitted the bag-valve mask over McHale's slack gray face and squeezed. The second paramedic looked up at Jake. He was rolling up a blood pressure cuff. Jake noted that both of the paramedics were male. Most of the time he didn't pay any attention to details like that; paramedics were ubiquitous, just professionals doing a job. Male or female, black or white, young or old — it didn't matter. They were a blur of blue.

Except for Molly Drucker.

"No pulse," the second paramedic said. He had a gray goatee. "Hope you'll help us get him on the gurney. Otherwise, we're gonna need a forklift. Guy weighs a ton." It was a crude, cruel remark, and if anyone other than colleagues had been present, he would never have uttered it.

Jake nodded. The first paramedic — he

was much younger than Gray Goatee, and he had curly red hair that reminded Jake of strawberries that had been mashed in a blender — was still squeezing, still squeezing, but there was no return on his investment of labor.

"Where was he when you got here?" Jake asked.

"In the desk chair," Gray Goatee answered. He inclined his head back toward the enormous desk by the window. Its front was decorated with intricate marquetry carving, a sweeping panoply of swirls and curves and horns of plenty disgorging plump fruit. "Head down on the desk. Secretary found him that way." He waggled his eyebrows. They, too, were gray. "Did you see the boobs on her? Jesus Christ. Don't know why he needed drugs for fun, you know what I mean?"

Once again, Jake was not offended. People in their line of work found a variety of ways to offset the grisly realities they encountered daily. Wisecracks and inappropriate raillery worked fine. Jake had been known to make similar remarks himself — although not when he was working a scene with Molly.

"So the secretary called it in?" he asked.

"Yeah, but she took her sweet time," said Gray Goatee. He continued to work while he talked. "They always think we can't tell how long they waited. Bet she had to get rid of the drug paraphernalia. Part of the job description, no doubt. Cover for the boss."

"How do you know that's what she did?"

Gray Goatee uttered a sound that Jake would've described as a guffaw. "Come on. Not my first rodeo, man. Check the top drawer. Left-hand side. Don't know why, but it's always the left-hand side."

The paramedics never stopped moving, trying this, trying that. Jake looked around the office. It was grand but cold. Despite the fancy furniture and the paintings on the walls trapped in their heavy wooden frames, the room seemed empty to him. The whole building struck him that way. There was no activity, none of the usual crackle and bustle you expect in a workplace. It seemed more like a museum than an office. Everyone knew that McHale didn't really practice law these days; he had made too much money from the coal companies. There was no point to it anymore. So he played a lot of golf. He came to this chilly monstrosity of an office every morning, whereupon his first and only order of business was to make his lunch plans.

Which might explain why he was, at this

very moment, flat on his back with his belly stuck in the air, gray-faced and pulseless, having injected himself with something to take his mind off his nonexistent troubles.

All kinds of prisons in this world, Jake mused. *Some of 'em are downright spiffy.*

Getting McHale onto the gurney was, as expected, an ordeal. The three of them finally managed it. They pretended to hurry, but there was no reason for that; the man was dead, and they knew it. *Three fatalities,* Jake thought. *And twenty-four ODs.*

Once the paramedics departed he asked the secretary to sit down. She was still crying, but quietly. They retreated to two chairs in the reception area, the high-backed, heavily padded, floral-print kind. They reminded Jake of chairs in the anteroom of a palace. He drew out his small spiral notebook and his pencil. He asked her name.

"Jill Cousins." She watched him write it down. "Do you think he'll be okay?" she said, in a voice so soft that Jake had to ask her to repeat herself, a bit louder. She did.

"Can't say," he replied, but of course he could, if he had so chosen. It wasn't his place. "The paramedics will do their best. So will the doctors at the ER."

She nodded. She sniffled. She unhooked her hands, which had been clasped in the lap of her tight black skirt, so that she could use the backs of them to wipe at her cheeks. That smeared the streaming mascara even more. She didn't seem to care — *she must have a fair idea of what she looks like,* he thought, *after all the crying* — which, to his surprise, made him respect her.

"What happened?" Jake asked.

"What do you mean?"

He thought the sentence was clear, so he repeated it. "I mean — what happened?"

She nodded. She'd just been buying time.

"So I was out here at the reception desk," she said. "And I heard this thump. In Mr. McHale's office."

He looked at the considerable distance between the reception desk and the office door. "That far away, his office door would've had to be open. For you to hear something in there. His office door was open?"

He could tell from her eyes that she had just been caught in her first lie. His respect for her was diminishing rapidly. *Nothing like being lied to when you're trying to save lives,* he thought, irritation building up in him. *Like everybody in the damned county didn't already know that Fenton McHale would snort, lick, smoke, rub, or inject anything that would give him a good buzz.*

"Yeah," she said. Uncertainly. "He usually keeps it open. All the time."

"Really. I have to tell you, Jill, that I find that surprising. I mean, most attorneys — they're having private phone conversations with clients all day long. They can't take a chance on visitors overhearing. And so it's odd that McHale would keep his office door open." He looked down at his notes. " 'All the time,' as you put it."

"So it wasn't always open. Just some-times."

"And it was open today. Which is how you heard the thump."

"Yeah."

He put the notebook back in the breast pocket of his shirt. He buttoned the flap.

"Jill, I'll be frank with you. I don't have time for this." He kept his voice even. Get-ting mad at her would accomplish nothing — in the present moment. Later, yes. "We're in the middle of a crisis here, Jill. There's some bad heroin out on the streets. It's kill-ing people. I need to find out where it came from — who's selling it. Once I find out who's selling it, I can find out who they're selling it to. And I need to find out really, really fast, so that more people don't die."

Her black-ringed eyes grew wide with hor-ror.

"You — you don't think Fenton is *dead,* do you? I thought the paramedics saved him. I thought they were taking him to the hos—"

"Jill. Listen to me." Jake made sure he had her eyes, that they weren't still flitting nervously around the room anymore. "I think you were in the office with McHale. I think you saw him inject himself with the heroin. Like you'd seen him do lots and lots of times before. Only something went wrong this time. Instead of sitting back in his big chair and falling asleep, he fell forward. His face hit the desk. Right?"

She thought about it, and then she nodded.

"Okay," he said. "Now we're getting somewhere."

"I couldn't stop him," she said, sounding stricken as the words gushed out. "He did what he wanted to do. Yeah, I was in the office. He liked to have me with him when he — well, like you said. But I was always telling him it was wrong. I told him he ought to get some help. Go to rehab. You know. Like the TV show. *Intervention.* That one. Where everybody gets together and they tell you how much they love you and they send you off to a rehab place. I told him and told him."

Lie number two, Jake thought. Fenton McHale paid her a nice salary specifically to *not* nag him about his drug use.

He didn't have the energy to call her on it, though, and he really didn't care what she had or hadn't said to her boss. He needed a name. "Jill, I'm not here to hassle you. You're not in trouble."

Her body relaxed. She smiled at him.

"If," he added.

Her face tightened again. " 'If'? If what?"

"If you tell me right now where he got his drugs."

"I don't —"

"Hey. You listen up." Jake's voice was as stern as he could make it without shouting. "People are *dying.* Okay? Even as we're sitting here. Do you want that on your conscience? I don't think so. I think you're a good girl. I think you want to do the right thing. So tell me — who's his dealer?"

She still wasn't there. He could see it in her eyes. "I don't know," she said, putting a small moan at the end of the sentence. "I'd tell you if I did — I *swear* I would. I swear it on the name of Jesus. Like you said — I'm a good girl. I was raised right. And all I know is, Fenton would call me into his office every afternoon and he'd have me watch him while he —"

273

Jake stood up. "Come on. Let's go."

She looked up at him. "Go? Go where?"

"To jail. I'm arresting you for obstruction of justice. You tampered with a crime scene when you hid his drug paraphernalia. I'm sure we'll find your fingerprints all over it. Stand up. Now."

"Wait. Wait. *Wait.*" She stood up, but as she did so, she reached out a hand and placed it on his forearm. "Okay. Okay. So if I tell you the truth — you won't arrest me, right? Right? Okay, so — yeah. I know where he got his drugs."

Jake shook her off. Gray Goatee might have found her attractive, but he didn't. It was all he could do not to shudder with revulsion when she touched him.

"Tell me," he said.

"This guy comes by once or twice a week. He gives me the package. I give him the cash — the cash I get from Fenton. But when it all started, I swear I didn't know what was going on. I didn't know what was in it. And once I *did* know, I told Fenton that he really shouldn't —"

"Give me a name. You have five seconds."

"But I never knew his na—"

"Four seconds."

"Leo Smith."

Jake nodded. It was one of the three

274

names remaining on his list. A known dealer, just as the other two — Raylene Hughes and Tammy Kincaid — were known dealers. He and Leo had tangled before. Two months ago, Leo was selling pain pills in the student parking lot at Acker's Gap High School. Jake arrested him. Leo claimed that Jake had roughed him up. Leo got off with a warning, in exchange for signing a paper stating that he wouldn't pursue the brutality charge against Deputy Oakes. Somehow, guys like Leo always found their way back out on the streets again.

Leo was a lying, pathetic hustler, a piece of shit walking around in human form. Jake had a reasonable idea of where to find him. And maybe that would be the end of it. Maybe Jake could confiscate the rest of Leo's product. Cut off the supply.

And then if Jake was *really* lucky, Leo would help them in their prosecution of the source — the actual drug gang that had brought the poison into their county in the first place. The thought made Jake itch to get back to the Starliner. He was eager to see if his hunch was correct — that the old lady on duty had been trying to tell him that the motel was Heroin Central.

But even if Leo wouldn't cooperate, at least they could get his tainted product off the market. They could stop the overdoses. Stop the deaths. Give the addicts another chance. Give them another day of life — which just might be *the* day, the day they decided to change.

Jake would never express such a hope out loud. Few of his colleagues would ever take him seriously again.

Well, Bell Elkins might. She was a closet optimist. Jake had suspected as much, early on, and had confirmed it to himself during some late-night conversations with her in JPs, after long, frustrating days spent on hopeless cases. Bell was a lot like him: She knew the worst of this world, but never stopped yearning for better things.

Yearning silently, that is. Yearning secretly. The way you yearn for a lost lover. No one can know. You have to keep your dignity.

Jake was back in the Blazer now. He had loaded Jill Cousins's contact information into his phone. Jake had left her sitting in the expensive armchair with her head buried in her hands, alternately sobbing and murmuring "Jesus, oh my sweet Jesus," and asking for strength in this time of trial. She had casually thrown that very same Jesus under the bus just a few minutes before, swearing on his name that she didn't know the identity of McHale's dealer.

Jesus, more than likely, would let her off the hook. *Last I heard,* Jake thought as he fired up the Blazer, *He's the forgiving sort.*

Next stop: Leo Smith's last known address.

He made a quick call. The second the call ended, his cell rang. The caller ID said it was Deputy Brinksneader. Jake had left a message for his colleague earlier, reporting his whereabouts. Steve was probably checking in to confirm that he'd received the message, and to pass along his own location. They were two deputies in charge of a county whose total square mileage meant that it should have been patrolled by at least triple that number. Keeping in constant touch with each other was a must.

"Hey," Jake said. "I'm leaving McHale's office. Got a good lead on the dealer. Remember Leo Smith? Skinny punk who hangs out at that tattoo place on Route 7? He might be our man."

"Better hurry."

"What?"

"Three more. Some kids on the riverbank. Took some shit and then keeled over. Some old guy found 'em."

"Condition?"

"Unknown. Paramedics on the scene."

Jake slowed down in case he needed to

turn around in the next few seconds, heading elsewhere. "Think I should go over there? Or keep tracking Smith?" There were too many places to be and not enough of him to go around. *Story of my life,* he thought. If he went after Leo, he'd need somebody else to question Raylene Hughes and Tammy Kincaid, just in case they, too, were selling the bad stuff.

Steve was as busy as he was. So who could he tap to help? Jake had an idea.

"I'll check with the sheriff," Steve replied, "but I say keep doing what you're doing. Find Smith. I'll go to the riverbank."

"Copy that." Jake speeded up again. He was less than five miles from his destination. He hoped to wrap it up quickly so he could get back to the Starliner. That was their best chance to shut down the gang itself, the root of this sorrow.

"Oh — and Jake. Got a question for you."

"Yeah."

"Kind of wondering what I'm in for around here. You ever see a day like this? Before I joined the department?"

"Nope. Can't say that I have. You know what that tells me?"

"What's that?"

Jake was feeling a little better, despite the latest news. He had a suspect. The end might be in sight. So he risked a joke: "You're bad luck, Stevie-boy."

BELL

Lee Ann Frickie did not talk about her religion. Bell had always appreciated that about her. Bell knew her secretary was a woman of deep and unshakable faith, but that fact had never featured in their working relationship — except for those rare occasions when Bell needed her to work on a Sunday morning. It was not that Lee Ann refused. To the contrary: She always agreed. But her agreement came after she had silently considered the request, standing straight and tall, frowning, an index finger tapping her chin. Bell always wondered what sort of private negotiation went on between Lee Ann and her Maker during those fraught ponderings, what bargain was struck. Did she put a few extra dollars in the collection plate, maybe, to cover an absence from Sunday school? Whip up a sugar-free pecan pie — Lee Ann's specialty

— for the bake sale to raise funds for new choir robes, in exchange for being a no-show at the 11 A.M. service?

Bell never knew. Lee Ann did not discuss it.

Which was why this moment was so odd. It had never occurred before in the course of their relationship, a union that involved mutual trust and ease but that did not ever quite tilt into friendship.

Lee Ann mentioned God.

It happened as Lee Ann was leaving. Her workday was over. She gathered up her purse and her paperback, along with the empty brown paper sack in which she had ferried her lunch. She reused each paper sack multiple times, until the top edge was so crinkled and frayed that it would barely hold a twist, and the bottom was so weakened by the tiny droplets of moisture that sometimes transferred from the sides of the small Tupperware container of fruit cocktail — her favorite dessert — that it was in serious danger of disintegrating.

"Belfa? A word?"

Bell looked up from her computer screen. The door between her office and Lee Ann's domain was open, and she had been generally aware of her secretary's leave-taking rituals.

281

"Sure," Bell said.

She had just received another message from Sheriff Harrison and could use a distraction. Three more overdoses. Three kids found unconscious on the riverbank.

So the total was now twenty-seven. Three of the twenty-seven had died.

Lee Ann stepped into her office. She stood in front of the desk. "Do you know 'Abide with Me'?"

"What?"

"The hymn. The one that starts, 'Abide with me.' "

Bell shook her head. "No." Her face must have said more than she meant it to, because Lee Ann responded immediately.

"I know, I know," the secretary declared. "It's totally inappropriate to discuss religion in the workplace. Particularly a public building. In fact, it's probably illegal. I might as well be trying to put up a nativity scene on the courthouse lawn. Or post the Ten Commandments in the ladies room. Right?"

"We have to walk a careful line. Church and state and all that. Kind of important."

"Yes. Of course."

Once again, Bell's face did her talking for her. It said: *Then why are you bringing it up?*

"Look," Lee Ann went on, "this is just about the worst single day anybody around

282

here can remember. Acker's Gap is going to be a long time recovering from it. If it ever *does* recover, that is."

"No argument from me."

"So this afternoon I started thinking about a certain hymn. With everything going on — well, it just seemed like something you might want to think about, too."

"A hymn."

"Yes." Lee Ann ignored the skepticism in her boss's tone.

"What's the relevance?" Bell said.

"It was written in 1847 by a minister. He was dying. Henry Francis Lyte — that was his name. He was thinking back on his life as if it had been a single day. Thinking about all the sad things that had happened — death and pain and disappointment. Bitterness and doubt. The day was ending and night was coming on. He was afraid. And so he was asking God to help him get through it. Because everybody has troubles and doubts. Mostly, though, they're spread out across your whole lifetime. It's hard when they're all bunched up in a single day, like what's happening today — but you have to keep going. Keep fighting back. And trust in more than just the darkness that's coming down all around you." Lee Ann paused. She looked a little embarrassed, as if she had overstepped. Giving pep talks was not her style. Giving pep talks about God was *definitely* not her style. "I'm sure somebody trained in theology would have a better way of explaining what Reverend Lyte meant when he wrote it," she demurred. "But that's how I've always thought of the hymn. It's based on Luke 24:29. And it's my favorite. When the choir sings it at Rising Souls on a bright Sunday morning, with the sun coming through the stained glass — it helps, Belfa. That's all I can tell you. It really does help."

"How does it go?"

Lee Ann's eyes widened in alarm. "Heavens. You don't expect me to stand here and *sing,* do you? Right here in the office?"

"Just recite the words, then, if that's easier."

Her secretary paused. Bell could see that Lee Ann did not quite know how to proceed. She had not expected Bell to be interested enough to make the request.

"I'm aware of your feelings about organized religion," Lee Ann finally said. "I'd never intrude on that. Never try to change your mind. It's your business, not mine. But today has just been so — so unbelievably awful, with all the overdoses, and the deaths, that I thought it might be good to have

284

some positive thoughts out there, too. But I don't want to offend you or —"

"I'd like to hear the hymn."

"You would?"

"I would."

Lee Ann nodded. "Well, all right. Just the first verse." She set her purse and her book and her empty lunch sack on the edge of Bell's desk. She clasped her hands and held them waist-high. She took a deep breath. In a small, clear voice, using a cadence that made it clear that it was a poem but that did not sound silly or singsong, she recited:

Abide with me; fast falls the eventide;
the darkness deepens; lord with me abide.
when other helpers fail and comforts flee,
help of the helpless, o abide with me.

She waited a few seconds and then she picked up her purse, her book, and her paper sack. She nodded to Bell and left the office without speaking an additional word. Bell understood. After the austere beauty of the lines Lee Ann had just spoken, anything else she said would be anticlimactic. Even intrusive. The words needed to live in the air all by themselves, untouched by lesser words or more ordinary ideas, for a few precious seconds. And then regular life could resume. The day from hell could continue its relentless march toward night-fall.

To her surprise, Bell did feel a kind of serenity. She had instantly memorized the lines. She was aware of a frail, delicate sense of peace. She wondered if maybe they had come through the worst of it.

And then her cell rang.

EDDIE

He loved to watch her swing. Dusk was coming on but he could still see her.

Both of her tiny fists held the linked chain with the sweet earnestness of a kept promise. The swing rose high in the air and the little girl fully extended her legs, almost as if she were gulping air in her lungs instead of catching air with the glorious upward thrust of her legs, and then, as the swing fell back again, she dropped her legs and bent her knees, bringing her heels to the bottom of the seat, readying her legs for the next swoop up and out. Her face was radiant. He could see it clearly, even though his parking spot was across the street from the park, partially shielded by the leafy, low-hanging branch of a silver maple.

God, he loved his little girl, his Marla Kay. She was named for his grandfather, Marlon, whom he also loved but who had died when

287

he was seven, and for Kay, his great aunt, another loved person who had died a long time ago. Everyone he loved seemed to leave the earth before their time. Maybe he was the problem. He was a curse.

Raylene had let him name her. "Least I can do," Raylene said, " 'cause you ain't gonna see much of her, tell you that right now." He could not fight her on it, because at the time he was in bad shape: the spasms in his legs, the headaches, the mood swings from the brain injury, the blank spots in his memory. He could barely recall the single night he and Raylene had spent together, the night that Marla Kay was conceived.

She was going really, really high on the swing now. Eddie wondered if she was chilly. The sun was on its way down, dropping behind the mountains fast and clean, like something with no intention of ever coming back, and she was wearing a sleeveless T-shirt and shorts. She had to be a little bit cold, small as she was, with her hair cut short like that, to fool people into thinking she was getting chemo. Raylene didn't take care of her like she should.

Just look at that little girl go, Eddie thought. *Just look at her.*

There was no one else around. The park was empty.

He had not thought much past the moment. That was better. So many things had gone wrong in his life that he could not see the point anymore of advance planning. Why plan when things were just going to go wrong anyway?

He got out of his truck. One more look around the playground. Making sure.

Nobody.

Raylene could be anywhere, doing anything. She frequently left Marla Kay unsupervised. The only time she really paid attention to the girl, Eddie thought with rising anger, was when she was showing her off as a cancer victim, trying to get money, playing on people's sympathies. It was disgusting. Raylene's apartment was a block and a half from the playground, which was why she had chosen it; she could send Marla Kay out to play and the little girl wouldn't get bored. It was the world's cheapest babysitter. The swings, the slide, the monkey bars — Marla Kay had her pick.

The swings were her favorite. Eddie knew that because he had watched her here before. Many times. At first he had been nervous, because the church truck was so recognizable, but then he figured it out: Nobody cared. As nosy as the people in this town could be sometimes — when he first returned from the service, total strangers would stop him on the street and ask him why he limped like that — they could also be obtuse, once they had gotten used to you. They were caught up in their own problems. He had watched Marla Kay in the playground dozens of times and nobody ever came up to the truck window and asked him what the hell he thought he was doing, spying on a child that way.

"Hey, sweet pea," he said.

She had not seen him approach. She had slacked off on her swinging and was dawdling now, spinning the seat around, tracing circles in the dirt with the toes of her flip-flops. When he spoke, her head quickly turned his way. Her smile was an astonishing thing; it broke across her small face like a mini-sunrise. Her eyes widened in uncomplicated pleasure. She jumped off the swing and ran toward him. He caught her and he picked her up — not too far off the ground, because he was not able — and he swung her around. It hurt his back and his legs, it hurt like hell, but she loved it and so he did it.

"Daddy!" she cried in delight. "Daddy!"

He gritted his teeth and hoisted her up on his shoulders, arranging her legs on either side of his head. That made her giggle. She grabbed onto his thick hair. He crossed the street. He faltered once, his leg suddenly wobbly and unreliable, but he regained his balance and pretended to be joking around, staggering in a comical way.

When he reached the truck, he opened the passenger door and leaned forward, enabling her to climb off his shoulders and tumble onto the seat. She giggled again.

"Where're we going, Daddy?"

They were almost back to the church by the time she asked. Until that moment, she had talked about neutral things while they drove along: How much she loved to swing, why blue was her favorite color although sometimes it was pink, why she liked shorts better than dresses. And then she asked about their destination. She did not ask anxiously, or suggest that they needed to let her mother know that she had left the playground. She was simply curious. She trusted him.

Eddie replied that they were going to go to his house. Was that okay with her? Marla Kay nodded as if it made perfect sense, even though she had never been there, and then she said, "Why doesn't Mommy like you, Daddy?" Kids picked up on things. He knew that. He didn't mind her asking. He answered her the only way he could: "Don't

know, sweet pea." It was true. He understood that Raylene considered him a nui-
sance, and that she wished he was out of
her life entirely, but he wasn't sure why. His
very existence seemed to annoy her. Yes, he
had argued with her over the cancer scam,
and yes, he had a fair idea of the other thing
she did for money and he did not approve
of it, and when he told her so she said it
was his fault because he never gave her
enough — but her irritation seemed far in
excess of any of that.

He parked the truck in the alley behind
the church, as he always did. He did not
want to vary his routine, in case anyone was
watching. He reached behind his seat. He
had re-wrapped the rifle in the plaid wool
blanket. He had wanted to have it with him,
just in case. Now he needed it for the next
phase. She didn't ask what he was carrying.
That, Eddie had discovered, was the way it
worked with a five-year-old; you never knew
what she might ask about. She would ignore
a big, obvious thing and then her attention
would be snared by something small and
ordinary.

There was an entrance to the basement
just off the alley. Marla Kay was fascinated
by the three steps down and then the door
itself, which was round and red and wooden

and had a funny latch. It looked like a door in a story, she told him. A fairy tale. That had never occurred to Eddie until he saw it through his daughter's eyes.

"Right in here," he said.

They walked side by side through the doorway and into the basement. He pushed the little wooden door shut behind them.

"This is where my daddy lives," she said, as if she were narrating a TV show.

He thought she might be scared in the basement, or at least unsettled. It was a big concrete box, with a low ceiling and an old, moldy smell, and it was filled with junk. The glass block windows only ran along one side, and the light they let in was a murky, underwater light, faint and vaguely sinister.

But she was fine. She ran straight over to the furnace and pounded on the round side, as if she were making friends with a nice giant. It gave off a deep plangent echo.

"What's this?" she said. "It's big."

"It's a furnace, sweet pea. Keeps the church warm."

Next she scampered over to his clothes rack along the wall. "These are your shirts, Daddy," she said, touching the plaid sleeves of his work shirts, one by one. She had recognized them right away.

"Yep," he said.

"And here's your kitchen." She touched the utility sink, the small microwave, the mini-fridge.

"Yeah."

"And here's your bed. Is this where you sleep, Daddy?"

He set the wrapped-up rifle on the card table that he used as a staging area. "That's right."

"And is this where I'm going to sleep?"

She had found the small cot on the adjacent wall. He had bought it that afternoon at the mall, on his way back from Lymon's after his confrontation with Raylene. He had also purchased a set of sheets. They showed a scene from the movie *Frozen:* two girls with long hair and sparkly gowns. He hadn't seen the movie himself, but he knew how much Marla Kay loved it because for a period of time that was all she talked about on the few occasions when he was permitted to see her. She knew the songs by heart. One of them had the refrain, "Let it go," and when Marla Kay saw the sheets, she giggled and said, "Hey, Daddy — you got me some 'Let it Go' sheets!"

Before he could answer she was running back across the room toward him. She hugged him hard. His knees trembled — as small as she was, her headfirst smack into his kneecaps packed a wallop — and he had to reach out a hand to the wall to steady himself. With his other hand, he touched the top of her head. He hated the fact that Raylene had shaved it, to make her look sick, but part of him did like being able to feel her skull, to know for sure how solid it was, how substantial. She was a good, strong girl. His Marla Kay. He loved her so much that it almost made him dizzy.

I will never forget this moment, he promised himself. *No matter what happens tonight, I will remember this moment forever. I will carry it in my heart. No one can take away this feeling. They can take everything else — but not this.*

"Hey, Daddy," she said, breaking away from his knees so that she could gaze up at him. She grinned. "I'm hungry."

JAKE

Leo looked like hell. *No use beating around the bush,* Jake thought.

"You look like hell, Leo," he said. "Guess all that healthy living isn't paying off yet, right?" He laughed. He was in a hurry — he was in a desperate hurry, actually, because the clock was ticking and people were dying — but he needed to keep that fact from Leo. He needed to act like the same old smart-ass Deputy Oakes, easygoing, cool. If Leo figured out that Jake was pressed for time, he would take special delight in tormenting him, drawing out their conversation. The balance of power would shift.

He had found Leo in the back room of a tattoo shop located in a strip mall along a stretch of Route 7 that included a gun and ammo store, a video game store, a tanning place, a pizza place, and two taverns, one at either end.

The tattoo shop had a rusty awing and a bad lettering job on the grimy front window: SKIN U ALIVE. Mack Cruikshank, the owner, had hired his cousin to do the lettering because the price was right, but as Mack's wife, Juniper, had put it, with a saucy toss of her long white-blond hair that indicated she thought she had coined the phrase: "You get what you pay for." The words "SKIN" and "U" were okay, but by the time Randy Rutherford got to the "Alive" he realized he should have measured the space. He had run out of real estate. Thus "Alive" was written with the same giant *A* and *L* with which he had rendered the "SKIN" and the "U," but after that there was a smaller *i*, a tiny *v* and finally a virtually nonexistent *e*. The store's name looked as if it was being sucked sideways into an unseen vacuum cleaner somewhere off to the right.

There was always a Harley Softail Slim parked on the patch of gravel in front of the shop. The bike belonged to Mack. At present the lot also sported two other bikes and a Dodge Charger, which meant this was a busy night at Skin U Alive.

But that, in turn, did not mean that several people had suddenly up and decided that they needed a Tweety Bird or a leering skull or a weeping Jesus or a red rose with a trailing vine of thorns tattooed on a chest or neck or bicep. Skin U Alive was a distribution point for certain varieties of illegal drugs. Jake knew that. All local law enforcement personnel knew that. But knowing that did not mean that there was one damned thing they could do about it.

Mack was an entrepreneur. He didn't sell drugs himself; that was too risky. What he did was provide a venue in which drugs could be sold. There was a difference. He was not especially clever, and he didn't keep a high-priced lawyer on retainer, but he had a knack when it came to dealing with the law. He knew that in a poor county with much more serious crimes to worry about, a man who kept his head down and didn't flaunt his success and never got too greedy would be allowed to run his business. In a lesser-of-two-evils world like this one, Mack Cruickshank made sure he was always the lesser. If it came to a choice between assigning a deputy to either solve a murder or bust Mack for providing an outlet for the sale of pot or oxycodone, the Raythune County Sheriff's Department had to pick the former.

So Jake had a good idea of what the comparatively high number of vehicles in the lot meant. He pushed open the door. It always stuck and had to be cajoled. A little bell tinkled from the top of the door.

"Deputy Oakes. As I live and breathe," said Mack.

A lamp on either side of the cash register provided the only light at the present moment. Dim or not, there was no missing Mack Cruikshank. He sat with regal ease in a big leather armchair. He was a giant man — he had passed the three-hundred-pound mark a decade ago and just kept right on going — and he sported jeans that rode well below his prodigious belly, heavy black boots, and a sleeveless black leather vest, the better to show off the handiwork of his wife, Juniper. She had decorated both of his arms with colorful depictions of rearing dragons and hooded wizards and twisting strands of barbed wire. Mack's gray hair was pulled back into a greasy ponytail that rode his back like something you'd find in a marsupial pouch. His face was a giant cratered mess of flesh and fissures. His deep-set dark eyes never ceased to calculate and weigh and measure the world; even in the dimness, Jake was aware of the work of those eyes, ceaselessly sizing up everything that came within view, gauging its strength, its propensity to put up a fight.

The small room was lined with mirrors. Jake never knew quite where to look in here; the mirrors seemed to double and triple the space, so that you could fool yourself into thinking you were facing an army when it was really just three guys and one young woman, also leaning back in leather armchairs.

Nobody was getting a tattoo.

"Hey, Mack," Jake said. "How's it going?"

"Going good." Mack had yet to sit up straight in the chair. He was tilted back with his belly spread out across his thighs like bread dough set out to rise on a kitchen counter. Sitting up would have indicated that he either feared or respected the deputy. Neither was the case.

"I'm looking for Leo."

"You are, are you?"

"Yeah. I am."

"Well, now."

No one else in the shop had moved or, as far as Jake could tell, even breathed. In the shadowy half-light, their immobility and the sense of menace they exuded gave each one the ambience of a poisonous lizard splayed across a rock, slithery tongue ready to strike.

"Yeah." Jake took another step forward. He didn't have time for this. *And neither do they,* he thought. *They don't know what's out there.*

"Haven't seen him lately," Mack said.

One of the customers spoke up. "Sure you have, Mack. He's in the back. Sick as a dog. Been there all day."

Mack's big head swung around slowly, slowly, slowly, in the man's direction. The man realized he had spoken when he shouldn't have. Jake saw him cringe and shrink back into his chair. Mack did not speak aloud to the man, but the message was clear enough: *Get you later for that, you shit-for-brains.*

Mack eventually would have told Jake that Leo was on the premises. But first there would have been a little give-and-take, a conversational checkers match that amused Mack and annoyed the deputy — which would have amused Mack even more. Now that he had been diagnosed with diabetes and had to watch what he ate, Mack's pleasures were considerably diminished in kind and number; verbally jousting with a deputy sheriff was one of the few left to him, a non-caloric but deeply satisfying treat.

And then Shit-for-Brains had gone and wrecked the whole thing.

"Gimme a minute to think about it," Mack said amiably, as if he appreciated the

301

poke with a memory stick. Showing anger took all the fun out of the negotiation. Anger meant you gave a damn. "Yeah, I guess old Leo *is* in the back room. Slipped my mind."

"Thanks." Jake touched the rim of his hat. Courtesy mattered in here. People who did not understand that were at a disadvantage.

"You fixing to take him in, Deputy? He's sick, like the man said. Been throwing up in a bucket since yesterday." Mack wrinkled up his broad pug nose in disgust. Human effluvia offended him. For a strong, tough man, Mack Cruikshank was, Jake had learned a while back, surprisingly persnickety and delicate. "And I mean *actual* sick," Mack added. "Not from nothing he took. Juniper says it's the flu. That's why he's in the back. Don't want him spreading his damned germs all over the shop."

"Okay. I won't be long." Jake started to walk down the unofficial keel line of the small room. He paused after three steps. "Something I need to say here. You all can tell me to go to hell. I expect you will. I'm gonna say it, anyway."

No one stirred. But they were listening. He could feel it.

"There's some bad heroin being sold around here today," Jake said. He was careful to keep his voice clipped, informational. No drama. No Paul Revere stuff. "They've laced it with something called carfentanil. It's been causing overdoses all over town. And some deaths, too."

"Heard sumptin' about that."

Jake didn't know who had spoken. This was his chance to warn the people most at risk — these people and the people they knew, the ever-expanding circle of drug users in these mountain valleys.

"Yeah," Jake said. "So get the word out, okay? Chances are whoever's selling it doesn't even know what's in it. I want to get them to stop. And in the meantime, I want folks to know. Any heroin you buy today is probably tainted. Just might kill you."

Mack chuckled. His chuckle sounded like something recorded for a Halloween TV special; it had darkness in it, but the top note was a peppery glee.

"I surely hope," Mack said, "you're not suggesting that there's any drugs being consumed on *this* property at the present time. Because if you *are* suggesting such a thing, I can't let you go into the back room without a warrant. On the *other* hand — if you're just here to say hi to old Leo, then that's fine and dandy. Go right on back,

303

Deputy."

"I'm here for Leo." He didn't bother to add that if Leo indeed had sold the heroin, he might very well be facing murder charges.

"Good."

"But everybody needs to be real careful, okay?" Jake said. "That's all I'm asking."

A voice spoke up from another occupied chair: "What the hell do *you* care what happens to a bunch of addicts?"

"I don't," Jake said. He used his jauntiest tone, the disarming one. He knew better than to preach to them about the value and sanctity of every human life. They wouldn't believe he meant it. Sometimes he didn't believe he meant it, either. "One of you dies — it makes a lot more paperwork for me. And I'm a lazy so-and-so. Just ask Mack here."

A round of chuckles.

Moments later Jake was in the back room, looking down at a sweaty, disheveled and clearly ill Leo Smith, who writhed on a mattress on the floor. That was when Jake told him he looked like hell, and made the additional crack about healthy living. "Leo Smith" and "healthy living" were not words that commonly occupied the same sentence.

"Know that," Leo said with a groan. "Got

the flu." He was twenty years old but he looked fifty, with indifferently cut brown hair and spiky brown stubble that staked its claim to the bottom half of his face and most of his neck.

Jake nodded. He looked around. This was the storeroom for Skin U Alive. Its contents included two leather chairs with ripped seats; the ripping appeared to have been accomplished by a knife with a serrated blade, wielded in a fit of rage, forcing the chairs into retirement. Jake chalked it up to some long-standing grudge against Mack. There were also metal shelves stacked with equipment actually related to the application of tattoos — a surprising discovery, because so few stores in this part of the county were in the business advertised on their sign. He also saw packages of printer paper, rolls of duct tape, a socket set, and a long-handled scraper for use on an icy windshield.

"Sorry you're ailing, Leo," Jake said, in a voice that indicated he was not the least bit sorry, "but I've got a problem. And if I've got a problem, then you've got a problem." It was clichéd stuff, all right, and straight out of a TV cop show, but he needed to keep the conversation light. And he needed to keep it on Leo's level.

"Don't know what you mean."

"Fenton McHale."

"What about him?"

"You sold him heroin this morning."

"Did not."

"I got a witness says you did."

Leo lifted the top half of his body from the soiled mattress, propping himself up sideways on one elbow. "I been puking for the past two days," he said in a weak voice. "I ain't sold nothing to nobody. Never even left this here room."

Jake crouched down so that he would be at eye level with Leo. He hated to do that — Leo smelled like fruity vomit and sweat — but it was necessary.

"Leo, there are people dying out there from this particular batch of heroin. I need you to stop selling it. And I need you to tell me where you got it."

"I done *told* you. I ain't left this roo—"

Jake snatched the long-handled scraper from the shelf. In a flash he had angled it like a vise to capture Leo's neck, twisting Leo's body so that he faced away from Jake. While Leo squirmed frantically and clawed at the scraper with desperate fingers, Jake tightened it up under the man's chin.

"Shut up," Jake said, his lips nearly touching Leo's left ear. "You got it? Shut up. No more lies. Where'd you get the heroin you sold to McHale today?"

"I — didn't —" Leo's voice was an air-starved rasp. "Didn't — sell —"

Jake dropped the scraper. He stood up.

"Tell me the truth," he said, "or I'll do that all over again. Harder. Don't think I won't."

A panting, frazzled Leo spit out a chunk of phlegm. It landed on the mattress. He barely noticed. He coughed, pulling his wrist across his mouth.

"I didn't say I never sold to that asshole McHale," Leo said. "I just said I didn't sell him anything in the past couple days. Don't know who did, neither. Been too damned sick."

Jake felt a cold trickle of doubt. The customers in the front room of Skin U Alive had no incentive to lie for Leo. And they had said the same thing: Leo had the flu. He had been flat on his back and helpless during the time when somebody sold Mc-Hale — and a lot of other people, too — the tainted heroin.

Leo flopped back down on the mattress. He clutched his belly and rocked back and forth, letting out a low moan.

"Hey. Jill." Jake had punched in the numbers Jill Cousins had given him earlier that day. "Deputy Oakes again. Nope — no more information on McHale." Let her find out on her own that she would need to seek other employment. "I asked you who'd sold him the heroin. And you said Leo Smith." Hearing her reply, he felt like crushing the phone with his bare hand as if it was an empty soda can. "Okay. You're right — I asked who his regular supplier was. I didn't specify *today*."

He slapped the cell back in his pocket. He was no closer to finding out who was selling the bad batch.

"So it wasn't you." He nudged Leo's backside with the toe of his boot. "McHale got it on his own today. From somebody else. Because you didn't show up. You were telling the truth. Getting the flu makes you one lucky SOB, Leo."

Leo coughed, spat, and moaned some more. "Ain't feeling none too lucky. Pass me that bucket over there, willya? Something's comin' up again."

BELL

In the summer, dusk was her favorite time to drive. It was different in the winter; she didn't like driving in the winter twilight, when the murky, fast-fading light meant that you couldn't tell the state of the pavement. Black ice was always lurking on mountain roads, ready to yank the asphalt out from under you like a tablecloth in a magic act.

But summer dusk was sultry, with the consequent benefit of no ice on the roads. What you couldn't see wouldn't hurt you. She loved the guilelessness of summer dusk, the languor, the glide. Driving at this time of day, at this time of the year, relaxed her.

Usually.

Not tonight. Tonight, she was tense and wary. *Might as well be winter,* Bell thought.

She looked over at Rhonda. The assistant prosecutor was reading a note on her phone.

309

The screen's light illuminated Rhonda's broad face, a face that carried hints of at least eight generations of Lovejoys and Beauchamps who had lived and died in these hills. Bell had met more than a few of Rhonda's relatives — in a county as small as this one, every person you knew came stapled to a trail of other people you would get to know, too — and she was always struck by the way one face merged into another, by the subtle replicating echo that moved from face to face. There was something consoling about that, to Bell's way of thinking. It was as if certain ideas never perished from the earth, even if they could only be expressed in something as fragile as a human face. They constantly found new life in a different venue.

"Here it is," Rhonda said. "Just got an e-mail back from her parole officer. The last address he has for Tammy Kincaid is an apartment complex out by Charm Lake."

"I don't like the sound of that — 'the last address he has.' He's her PO, for God's sake. Shouldn't he know for sure where she lives?"

"Yep. He surely should. Let me put it this way. When God was handing out the gene for work ethic, Ross Parker called in sick that day."

"Okay, fine." Bell flipped on her blinker. Time to make the turn onto Nash Pike. From there, they would head east to Charm Lake.

Jake Oakes had called her an hour ago. He needed Bell to help him run down the last two names on his list of local dealers: Tammy Kincaid and Raylene Hughes. He had received Sheriff Harrison's blessing to make the request. They were shorthanded and the toll of overdoses was climbing; there wasn't time to ponder the propriety of a prosecutor pitching in on an investigation. Bell had done it before. She would do it again.

"Really appreciate you coming along, Rhonda," Bell said. Her next call after signing off with Jake had been to her assistant prosecutor. "If Kincaid looks like a dead end, we'll go see Raylene. From what you've told me, it sounds like she's not averse to picking up a few bucks on the wrong side of the law now and again."

"I didn't know she was a dealer, though," Rhonda said. "I was pretty surprised to see her on Jake's list."

"You mean she might have some moral strictures?"

"Lord, no. I just didn't figure her to be that ambitious."

Bell laughed. "Desperate times call for desperate measures, I guess."

"Just wish I could've tracked her down earlier," Rhonda said, exasperation in her voice. "Saved us the trip."

"I know you do. It's always a trade-off between job and family. How's your cousin doing, anyway?"

Rhonda's cousin, Rafe Ferguson, was recovering in a Charleston hospital from his emergency surgery for an abdominal aortic aneurysm. The call had come into Rhonda's office that morning, just as she was winding up her conversation with Penny Latrobe. Rhonda left minutes later to drive her mother and father to the hospital to see Rafe for what might be the last time.

"Rafe's a fighter," Rhonda said. She waited a beat. "Unfortunately, he's also a smoker and a drinker, and he's never turned down a second helping in his life. Nor a third. The doctors have been clear with Neena — that's his wife. Unless he's ready to make some changes in his lifestyle, he won't be around to see his grandkids grow up."

Bell nodded. She heard that story a dozen times a month in Raythune County. Diseases related to cigarettes and whiskey and obesity — and now drugs — had settled

312

into the area like a turkey vulture on a fence post. Waiting to swoop in and feast.

"So Parker's meeting us there, right?" Bell said. Out of politeness she had asked the questions she needed to ask about Rhonda's family. Now they could get to work.

"Yeah. He says that's best. Tammy can be a mite skittish. You don't want to mess with her unless you know what you're doing."

"What the hell does *that* mean?"

"It means she served a fifteen-year sentence at Lakin for aggravated assault for pumping a couple of slugs into her ex-girlfriend's backside. Once she got out, she took up with the wife of a gun dealer named Blake Pugh."

"Surely to God the conditions of her parole don't allow her to have a —"

"No. Of course not. She can't touch a firearm. But as Ross will be happy to tell you, every time he's made a surprise visit to Tammy's apartment, there's LaVerne Pugh, big as life."

"Any guns on the premises?"

"No. So he couldn't revoke parole. But if LaVerne's there, then guns aren't too far away."

"So Blake Pugh approves of his wife's relationship with Tammy Kincaid?"

Rhonda shrugged. "Not necessarily. But

love's a funny thing. According to Ross, Pugh would rather share LaVerne with Tammy Kincaid than lose her altogether. And no matter how pissed off Pugh might get with his wife, he'd still give her a gun if she needed it."

"And she'd give it to Tammy. Meaning Tammy might be armed and ornery."

"Bingo."

The next several miles passed in silence. Bell spotted the sign for Charm Lake. She made the turn.

"I'm still surprised by today," Bell said. "The OD numbers, I mean." The apartment complex — a sagging gray square — was visible at the end of the road, past the trailer park and the log cabin with the German shepherd chained to a dead tree in the front yard. The dog had given up; sitting impassively on his skinny haunches, he watched them pass with a resigned look in his kohl-ringed eyes.

"Really," Rhonda said.

"You're not surprised?"

Rhonda shrugged. "After it's all started, it's too easy to say, 'I saw this coming.' "

"But you did."

"The way things have been going around here — yeah, I kinda did."

"Then why didn't you say something? So

we could've stopped it?"

"Because there *is* no way to stop it."

Bell nodded. Point taken. She parked her Explorer in the dirt lot in front of the complex. The other two cars in the lot were both marooned on cinder blocks, surrounded by a scattering of rusty engine parts and hand-squashed beer cans.

Before they made it to the metal stairs clamped to one side of the building, Ross Parker drove up in his state-issued white Ford Fiesta. He was a short, frail man with center-parted brown hair and a slight limp. He wore a blue plaid suit jacket, a white shirt, and what looked suspiciously like a clip-on necktie. His black glasses rode too low on his nose. The entire time she was speaking to him, Bell had to fight off the urge to use her index finger to push the glasses up where they belonged.

"You gals ready?" he said.

Bell was not overly fond of the word "gals," but her years in Acker's Gap had taught her to pick her battles.

"Yes," she said. "And just what is it we should be ready *for*?"

Parker's expression was a lofty and superior one. "Well, with Tammy Kincaid, you just never know."

"That's helpful," Bell murmured. She

intended to murmur it too low for him to hear — but if she had miscalculated and he *did* hear, she didn't really care.

Parker led the way, followed by Bell and Rhonda. As they climbed the metal stairway, Rhonda said, "What's your instinct, Ross? You think she's dealing again?"

"Well, with Tammy Kincaid, you just never know."

"Any suspicions of any other parole violations?" Bell asked.

"Well, with Tammy Kincaid, you just never —"

Bell interrupted him. "Got it. You just never know." Her irritation with Parker had reached a fine peak.

The door of apartment A-3 was scuffed and dented. Parker gave it four hard knocks, winced, and then pulled back his fist and cradled it in his other hand.

The woman who opened the door did not match Bell's expectations. She wasn't large or muscular. She was petite, with wide brown eyes and soft features. She didn't look tough; if anything, there was a daintiness about her. Her brown flannel shirt was tucked into olive khakis. She had raised the collar of the shirt to cover, as best she could, the tattoo on her neck. Alas for that effort, Bell could see that it was a Chinese charac-

316

ter, with swirls that reached from the bottom of her ear to her clavicle.

"Parker," Tammy said. She gave him a grim little smile. "Another one of your surprise visits." She seemed more amused than apprehensive. "Come on in. I see you brought some friends with you this time."

Parker didn't respond. Nor did he introduce Bell and Rhonda. Tammy waved them into the small, tidy apartment. It featured thrift-store furniture and a window that framed a distant view of the river.

In one corner sat a particleboard desk. Seated at the desk was a woman with long dark hair that fell around her face like a thick drape. Her bare feet were stacked on a cardboard box. Three books were open on the desk, next to a can of Diet Sprite. She looked up at them with a slightly foggy expression, a pencil between her teeth.

"Hi, LaVerne. How's it going?" Parker said.

Tammy stood between him and LaVerne.

"Leave her alone," Tammy said. "You're here for me, right? Not her."

Parker snickered. He turned to Bell. "Told you. Plenty of sass in this one."

Bell ignored him. "Tammy, I'm Belfa Elkins. Raythune County prosecutor." She waited to see Tammy's eyes change at the word "prosecutor." They didn't. "And this is Rhonda Lovejoy, assistant prosecutor."

"Lovejoy," Tammy said, musing on the name. "I dated a Lovejoy once. Way back in high school. Before I got a clue that boys ain't my thing. Tommy Lovejoy. You related?" Before Rhonda could answer, Tammy laughed. "Of course you are. You look just like him. Whatever happened to him?"

"Married with six kids," Rhonda said. "He's my cousin's son. Lives over in Gallipolis. Doing real good."

"Well." Tammy smiled. "Glad to hear it. Nice guy."

"You're right. He is."

For a moment Tammy seemed lost in the shadowy thickets of the past. Then she recovered. "What do you all want? Me and LaVerne're kinda busy."

Parker, annoyed at being ignored, folded his arms aggressively. "Busy doing what? I got a right to ask you that."

Tammy nodded. "Damn right you do. And I'm happy to tell you. LaVerne's studying for her GED. I'm helping her. I got mine at Lakin. That's what those workbooks are for."

Parker didn't say anything. It was not the answer he had expected.

"How about you?" Tammy said, turning to Bell. "You got some questions for me too, looks like."

Time was short. Bell opted for the direct approach.

"Did you sell heroin today?"

LaVerne answered first, kicking away the box and popping up from her chair. "Blake told you that, right? It's a damned lie. We ain't left this apartment in two and a half days. Been right here studying. Why the hell would you —"

"Hold on, honey," Tammy said. "They can ask me whatever they like. But the answer's no. I don't do that anymore." A ruminative expression crossed her face. "Pretty unusual for two prosecutors to come all this way to ask me something that Parker here could've handled. What's going on?"

"Bad batch of heroin," Bell said. "It was cut with carfentanil. Know what that is?"

"I was in prison for fifteen years. Yeah, I know what that is."

"So you're not dealing anymore. Which means you had nothing to do with the heroin sold in the last twenty-four hours."

"That's right."

"Like she *already told you*," LaVerne put in, her voice huffy with outrage.

"So I guess," Parker said, taking a step

319

forward, "you won't mind a random drug test. Just to make sure you're not involved with that life anymore."

Tammy shrugged. "Knock yourself out."

She had called his bluff. He didn't want to bother today. He would have to make a call, arrange for the test, deal with the paperwork. He gave her a glare. "Any firearms on the premises?" he said.

"Nope."

"You got no problem with me searching the place, in case I don't feel like taking your word for it?"

"No problem at all."

Another bluff. He wanted to go home. Bell could smell the laziness on him. It was like bad aftershave.

"Anything else?" Tammy said. LaVerne had retaken her seat. She flipped through one of the workbooks with brusque impatience. Translation: *I need to get back to my studying.* Tammy stood behind her, hand on her shoulder.

"Any idea who might've sold the heroin?" Bell asked.

Tammy shook her head.

"Or where they're getting it these days?"

Another head shake. "I've got nothing to do with that shit anymore. When I first got out — yeah, maybe. Maybe a little. I was pretty mixed up. But you know what I realized? It wouldn't do a damned thing for me except put me on the road to a nice long prison sentence. No reason in the world to go back to it. And a real good reason not to." She moved her hand on LaVerne's shoulder, rubbing it. LaVerne put a hand on top of Tammy's hand.

Bell looked at Rhonda. Over the years they had handled many court cases together. They had perfected their own brand of wordless communication.

What do you think? Should we believe Tammy when she says she's not dealing?

That's what Bell was asking her assistant. Rhonda's instincts about people were excellent; she could tell when they were lying or even thinking about lying. She could sniff out a masterful bluff. One look was usually all she needed. She could read the truth right off someone's face.

And maybe there was something else going on here, Bell thought. Maybe, just this once, they were actually witnessing a happy ending. Maybe love really had changed Tammy Kincaid. Surely the probabilities of life — even life in Acker's Gap — meant that, once in a blue moon, somebody changed for the better, cleaned themselves up, took hold, moved forward. Like the statisticians say: If you flip a coin and it comes up heads a hundred times in a row, what are the odds it will come up heads on the hundred-and-first flip?

Fifty-fifty.

So there was always hope, no matter what had gone before.

"I think we're ready to go here, Bell," Rhonda said. It was her way of saying: *Yeah. Trust her.*

That was good enough for Bell. "Do me a favor, Tammy," she said. "If you run into any of your old friends, you warn them, okay?"

"Not likely. I don't hang out in those circles anymore. But I hear you."

Bell didn't bother to say good-bye to Parker. She and Rhonda headed to their vehicle, he to his. The sun was riding low on the horizon. Darkness was almost here.

"Okay," Bell said, as she swung the Explorer back onto the main road. "Raylene Hughes. Where does she live?"

Rhonda checked her cell. "She moves around a lot, but according to what Jake found out, her last known address is over by the park."

Back when Bell and her sister were growing up in Acker's Gap, that had been a fairly nice area. Houses set back from the street.

Big yards. Climbable trees. But not any-more, she knew. Vacant lots outnumbered the houses now. The houses left behind were tumbledown shacks with no curtains on the windows, but with big satellite dishes squat-ting in the front yards. A lot of the houses had been chopped up into separate apart-ments.

"Hell of neighborhood to pick to raise a kid in," Bell said.

"Not sure Marla Kay's much of a prior-ity."

RHONDA

She had heard a story once about a judge
in Manchester, England, and a drunk driver
who shows up for sentencing. The judge
asks the drunk why he continues to do this
to himself. He's ruining his life. He's been
to jail many times. He's lost his job, lost his
family, lost his self-respect, lost all of his
money. *So why in heaven's name do you
keep drinking?* the judge asks.

Your honor, the drunk replies, *it's the quickest way out of Manchester.*

The story stuck with her. When she was
asked why so many people around here used
drugs and alcohol, Rhonda always wanted
to say, *Well, it's the quickest way out of Acker's Gap.*

She thought about the story again while
they walked to the front door of the dramat-
ically shabby house in which Raylene
Hughes and her daughter lived. The win-

324

dows were covered in dirty plastic. The aluminum siding was sliding off in horizontal hunks. Leaking bags of trash leaned lazily against one another on the porch. There were four black mailboxes nailed crookedly to a strip by the door. The second one from the left had a Post-it Note with HUGHES scribbled on it, and below that, NO. 2.

The door was unlocked. They stepped into a grimy foyer with a checkerboard tile floor. It smelled like last night's supper. Four doors, two on the left, two on the right, led to apartments carved out of what had once been a single-family home.

Bell knocked at No. 2.

Nothing.

She knocked again, harder.

Still nothing.

This time Bell used her I-mean-business knock, which always drew Rhonda's admiration. If you heard it from inside, you'd probably deduce that the house was on fire and a mass rescue was under way.

When the door finally opened, Rhonda was stunned. And perturbed.

Raylene Hughes looked just as she had in high school. Didn't somebody say that you paid for your sins with your face? Raylene had certainly sinned — but her face was beautiful. Creamy skin, plump lips, visible cheekbones, and all of it surrounded by bouncy, shiny hair that was straight out of a shampoo commercial. She wore a white silk robe. The matching silk sash was coming loose at her waist, as if it had been tied in a fumbling hurry. There was a dizzy, drowsy quality to her movements; she'd been roused from sleep, or from something else.

Dammit, Rhonda thought. She didn't curse often, not even internally; she tried to save it for a special occasion.

This was that occasion.

Would a wrinkle or two have been too much to ask for?

In addition to her flawless face, Raylene also hadn't put on a single pound since senior prom. Truth was, Rhonda had not attended that prom; the only guy who asked her was somebody she didn't much like and even back then, she'd had her pride. So she said no. But she knew how Raylene had looked that night because there was a picture of her in the yearbook. She was stunning.

Was there no justice in the world?

Funny thing for an assistant prosecutor to ask, Rhonda thought. The answer was clearly no. No, there was no justice in the world.

Before Raylene could speak to them, she

was bumped out of the way by a brown-bearded lummox of a man who had been standing behind her. He frowned aggressively. He took up all the space in the doorway.

"The fuck you two want?" he said. He'd clearly put on his flannel shirt in a hurry; it hung open, exposing a hard round belly that was shiny-wet with perspiration. The drawstring of his gray sweats was untied. He was barefoot.

"We'd like to talk to Raylene," Bell said.

"She ain't got no time," he said. He started to close the door in their faces.

"Wait." Raylene leaned forward. "Hang on, Corby. I know this lady." She peered at Rhonda. "Acker's Gap High School, right?"

"Right."

"Okay, yeah. I remember you," Raylene said. "You hung out with Sandy Blanton, right?"

Rhonda shook her head. "No. That was Ellie Trainor." Another overweight girl in their class. To Raylene, they were interchangeable.

Corby was getting restless. "We got things to do," he muttered. "You two git on outta here."

Bell flashed her ID. "I'm Belfa Elkins, Raythune County prosecutor. This is

Rhonda Lovejoy, my assistant. We have an emergency, Miss Hughes, and we're hoping you can help us save some lives."

Raylene had grinned at the "Miss Hughes," but the grin faded by the end of Bell's sentence. "Save lives? What the hell?"

"Look, I don't have time to be coy here," Bell said. "Somebody's selling bad heroin. We've had a record number of overdoses and even some deaths. We know you've dealt drugs in the past. If it's you this time — if you sold heroin in Acker's Gap in the past twenty-four hours — we need to have whatever's left. And we need to know where you got it. Right away."

"Drugs? *Drugs?*" Raylene said. "I don't know *what in the world* you're talking about. I'm a *mom.* I wouldn't —"

"Shut up, Raylene," Corby said, at a volume that was just short of a yell. "You shut your mouth and you keep it shut. You don't got to say nothing to these bitches."

The commotion had an effect. The door to the apartment next door opened. An elderly woman stood warily in the threshold, one hand on the inside knob, the other on her walker. She looked exhausted and alarmed. She was wearing two sweaters and a pair of brown corduroy pants — odd for August, Rhonda thought, but maybe not if you were over eighty, which she obviously was.

"Hey, there," Raylene said, waving at her neighbor. She addressed Bell again: "That's Dreama Gaddis. She can tell you."

"Tell us what?"

"Tell you that I've been right here at home for the past twenty-hour hours. Me and Marla Kay. And Corby, of course." She giggled and flinched. Apparently Corby had pinched her rear end, because Raylene reached around behind her back and smacked at his hand. "Corby, be*have* your-self! You're a real bad boy!" Back to Bell: "I couldn't have been selling no drugs. We were right here. All of us."

Bell turned to the old woman. "Mrs. Gaddis?"

"Yes." Gaddis looked as if she would rather do anything else in the world than supply an alibi for Raylene Hughes, but she was compelled to speak the truth. "Yes," she repeated glumly. "Walls are thin as paper." She narrowed her eyes at Raylene and Corby. "You don't want to know how much I can hear. The two of you — it's a disgrace."

"And nobody stopped by?" Rhonda said. She wanted to keep the old woman focused. Maybe Raylene's customers came to her, instead of the other way around.

"No," Gaddis answered. "And I keep a good watch. Always." She brightened. "Wait." She pointed triumphantly at Raylene. "You and the girl left this morning. You were gone for at least two hours."

Raylene nodded. "I was getting ready to say that. I did leave. I went over to Lymon's. Lots of folks saw me there. They can tell you I didn't sell no drugs."

Rhonda felt a renewed sense of frustration at the fundamental injustice of the universe. Raylene's little scam was getting her off the hook.

They had no choice but to leave. They had no warrant to search Raylene's apartment, and no probable cause to get one.

If it wasn't Leo Smith and it wasn't Tammy Kincaid and it wasn't Raylene Hughes, who was selling the tainted heroin? Somebody new, perhaps. A local dealer they didn't even know about yet.

They were quiet for most of the drive back to the courthouse. When they turned onto Main, Rhonda decided to speak.

"So doesn't it bother you?"

"What?"

"That awful place. Raylene. Her raising a kid there. All of it."

Bell thought about it. "Things aren't as

330

bad for Marla Kay as they could be. I mean — sure, no child ought to be used for fundraising by her slutty mom. But you know what? Better that than being around drug deals. Maybe Raylene's given up dealing for good. And the girl's got a roof over her head. Clothes on her back. Food to eat. That's more than what half the kids in this county have."

"So that's the choice? A mother who's a con artist or a mother who's a drug dealer?"

"We can't save every kid."

"We can try."

Bell shook her head. "No, Rhonda. We can't. We don't have the staff or the resources. Or the legal right. You and I might not like the way Raylene is bringing up her child — but it's not up to us. I'll ask a social worker to stop over there, but you know what they're going to say. They've got their hands full with children who are being actively abused, physically and emotionally."

"And this is supposed to be cheering me up?"

"If we catch Raylene in a parking lot, claiming her kid's getting chemo and taking money on that basis — great, we'll haul her in. A judge will fine her and warn her. She won't pay the fine or listen to the lecture. The fact is, if she's not dealing, we have to let her be."

"Doesn't seem right." Rhonda flung herself back against the seat.

"Didn't say it was. I just said we had to learn to live with it."

MOLLY

The child would not stop screaming. She decided to make it Ernie's problem.

"Get that kid to hush, will you?" Molly said. Typically she was good with children, and liked them, but under the circumstances — no.

It was hard enough to work inside a crowded car while holding a flashlight without having the additional problem of a terrified toddler yelling and crying. They didn't want to move the unconscious bodies — two in front, two in back — until they knew what they were dealing with. The kid was strapped in a car seat between the two people in the backseat. The kid was fine; they had checked that, first thing. But it would be another few minutes before they could liberate him from the car seat.

"What do you want me to do?" Ernie said.

"Sing to him. Read him a story. I don't

333

care. Just get him to shut up."

Molly and Ernie had arrived at the intersection a few minutes ago. Four people in the stopped vehicle. Heads thrown back or twisted to the side, limbs flaccid, mouths open.

They took vital signs, ascertained that all four adults were still breathing. Breathing meant they were alive. Alive was good. Alive was better, certainly, than dead. The paramedics also had needed to ascertain that the car had not been in an accident, and that the four had not suffered traumatic injuries — subdural hematomas, say, or spine or neck fractures — which would mean they shouldn't be moved until another squad could be summoned with backboards and other accouterments.

They finished the checklist quickly. No injuries consistent with a collision.

So now they knew what they were dealing with. Same thing they'd been dealing with all day: overdoses.

"You got kids, right?" Molly said, snapping on her gloves.

"Four. Plus two of my wife's."

"Six kids. Okay, so do a little dad magic back there, Ernie. Get the kid to quit screaming."

The car had coasted to a stop at a red light

on Sayman Street, and when the light turned green, the car stayed right where it was. That lack of motion had caused the driver of the car behind it to honk, curse, shake a fist, curse more, honk more, and then get out of his vehicle and charge forward to give the other driver a piece of his mind — at which point he discovered that the other driver had passed out, as had the three additional adult occupants. There was a child strapped in a car seat in the back. The child, understandably confused and distraught but unhurt, had begun to scream.

The driver called 911. Arriving at the scene, Molly and Ernie opened all four doors. Then they began reenacting the ritual in which they had engaged throughout the day: checking vitals. Administering naloxone.

Leaning in one side of the car and then the other, front seat and back seat, Molly squirted the aerosol dose up the nostrils of each of the four adults while they were still slumped over and motionless.

Ernie, meanwhile, reached into the backseat, keeping clear of the passed-out person leaning against the car seat. Ernie touched the screaming kid's hand. Once he had his attention, Ernie made funny faces: sticking out his tongue, pulling on his ears. The kid was either amused or appalled. Either way, he stopped crying.

"A kid in the car," Ernie muttered to Molly while he entertained the kid. "Can't believe you'd have a kid in the car when you're shooting up. Christ."

Molly had finished administering the naloxone. The driver was waking up. He was in his early twenties, she guessed. Same age for the woman beside him. She, too, was quivering back to consciousness. The first word she said was, "Shit," followed shortly thereafter by, "Why the hell'd you Narcan me? Feels like hell. Fourth time this summer." Both of them rolled out from their respective sides of the car, chanting obscenities like an incantation. They were black-haired, skinny, pale as ghosts.

The couple in the backseat needed Molly's help to exit the car. They were heavier, groggier, older. They were in their forties, Molly speculated, which was probably why the overdose had hit them harder. Once the man had cleared the door frame he jerked his arm out of her grasp. From the vehemence of his gesture, and from the curl in his lip, Molly guessed that it was the first time he'd ever been touched by an African-American. In Raythune County, that was

336

entirely possible.

None of the four had asked about the kid. Or looked around to locate him. All of them seemed to be in a daze of longing, as they groped for the fading scraps of their lost high, trembling and cursing.

"What do you want me to do with him?" Ernie asked.

He had unhitched the child from the car seat and gently removed him from the car. He held him in his arms. The kid was playing with Ernie's mustache.

"Wait for a deputy, I guess," Molly said. "They'll get a social worker out here." Ernie, she noted, was a natural; he knew just how to hold the kid, whom she judged to be mixed-race. He was beautiful, with a soft round face that looked like an oatmeal cookie, and a stubby mat of curly black hair.

A stench rushed out of the kid's rumpled red shorts. Clearly, a long time had passed since his last diaper change.

"Hey — how are you guys holding up?"

It was Deputy Oakes. Molly had seen the black Blazer arrive at the intersection, but she didn't immediately think of Jake. The county owned three Blazers. The day had been a blur of brown uniforms and flat-brimmed hats and terse exchanges of data. Could have been the sheriff or Steve Brinksneader. But it was him.

"Just heading back from Route 7," he said. "Heard the squad call. What's going on?"

Molly filled him in. The four people had refused transport to the hospital. They were still staggering around the car, alternately retching and threatening the paramedics for canceling their highs with Narcan. A small crowd had gathered on the sidewalk.

"Nothing like a little gratitude to make you love your work," Jake muttered. He waved at the line of cars, indicating that the drivers should be cautious as they wove around the stopped vehicle with the four flung-open doors.

A few minutes later he and Molly took a break, sitting on the back fender of the ambulance. Ernie still had the kid; he walked around, bouncing the boy up and down, swooshing him around and making rumbly airplane noises. A social worker was on the way. Molly had called Trixie Scoggins in the sheriff's office, and Trixie had made the arrangements.

"Yeah," Molly said.

"Hell of a day, right?"

"Hell of a day." She rubbed the back of her neck.

"I keep remembering that girl in the bathroom last night," Jake said. "The first one. Only we didn't have a clue that it was the first anything. If we'd known —"

"I don't know about you," she said, interrupting him, "but I would've run for the hills. Never looked back."

He laughed. She laughed, too. It felt odd to laugh, given the context. They both seemed to feel that at the same time, and their braided laughter trailed off.

Traffic was moving again. Cars and trucks looped around the vehicle. Molly knew she ought to get back to work — if there wasn't a call right at the moment, there would be one shortly — but she gave herself the gift of a few minutes. With Jake.

She liked him. She had always liked him. He had a good sense of humor but he wasn't a smart-ass; that was a fine line, but an important one. He liked her, too. She could sense it. She wondered about his life: Why had he become a deputy sheriff? Some people didn't have a choice; jobs were scarce around here. You took what you could get. Did what you had to do. But Jake, she thought, *did* have a choice. And he had chosen this.

He didn't know, most likely, that she thought about him as much as she did. They were always busy. And when they weren't — when, for instance, she had stopped by his house this morning — she was careful to be neutral and impersonal.

Molly was keenly aware of how close he was sitting. Their thighs bumped a few times, as they shifted their positions on the bumper. Each time they touched, she felt a small jolt of electricity. Was he feeling it, too? She would bet that he was.

She had had only one serious relationship. It happened back in community college, when she was getting her medic training. Pete LeMay. That was his name. A good-looking black man who worked in the college admissions office. He was very good with Malik. Malik, in fact, still asked about him. "Where's Pete?" Malik would say, out of the blue. Ten years had passed since Pete was in their lives but Malik would still blurt out the question, prompted by — what? Molly had no idea. She never knew what made Malik suddenly remember Pete, and maybe remember, too, the way he and Pete had tossed a football around the backyard, even though the yard was very small and Malik was so uncoordinated that he never caught a pass. Not once. Ever. He'd scoop it up off the ground after missing the ball and fling it back toward Pete. And Pete — long-legged, graceful, a natural athlete, would catch it and throw it back, and Malik would fumble the catch again, scoop it up, fling it back. When Molly got ready for work she would keep her bedroom window open, even on chilly nights, just so she could hear the two of them in the backyard, laughing, talking.

And then it was over. Pete broke up with her. He'd met somebody else, he said. She thought it was more than that. Malik took up a lot of time, required a lot of effort. Playing ball in the yard was one thing; organizing life for someone with Malik's many needs was something else altogether.

Or maybe she was kidding herself. Maybe it wasn't about Malik at all. Maybe he just didn't love her anymore. It happened.

Molly saw them once, Pete and his new love. At the mall. They were strolling along, wrapped up in each other, literally as well as metaphorically; his arm was tight around her bouncy little butt, her arm was tucked into the back pocket of his jeans. He was much taller than she was. Every few steps he would lean down and kiss the top of her head. The woman — Molly never knew her name, didn't want to know — responded to that by tilting up her face and then they *really* kissed, a deep, long, luxurious kiss that seemed to go on for about a day and a half. It was excruciating for Molly to witness.

Did they see her watching them? She didn't know. It didn't matter.

I am going to die. She remembered having that thought as she observed them that day at the mall. Kissing. The pain was that bad. Those were the precise words in her head: *I am going to die.*

She didn't die. She finished her course that semester at the community college and then she finished the other courses. She became a paramedic. Her pain over Pete changed. It didn't go away, but it became bearable.

Anyway, the worst part for her wasn't her own pain. It was trying to find a response to Malik's question, "Where's Pete?" Sometimes, even now, a decade after the fact, he would get in a rut with it, following her around the house, increasingly anxious: *Where's Pete? Where's Pete? Where's Pete?*

She was acutely aware of Jake's presence there beside her on the back bumper of the ambulance. The sun, its light softened by its gradual decline, made the moment feel intimate. She knew he was feeling it, too. She admired Jake. She liked the way he did his job, the way he carried himself. And there was more to it, too; of course there was. She felt more than just admiration. But she couldn't go through all of that again. She couldn't stand hearing Malik say, *Where's Jake? Where's Jake? Where's Jake?*

She was black and he was white. It would have been challenging. In West Virginia — oh, God, yes. But that wasn't why she pretended that she didn't know how he felt about her. She couldn't take the chance. *Where's Jake?*

And that wasn't all. That wasn't the only thing that made it impossible. There was something else, too.

"Thirty-one," he said. "These four bring it up to thirty-one."

"Yeah." She had done the math, too. "Unbelievable." There wasn't much more to say about it.

A car pulled up. It was the social worker. Their moment was over. They needed to clear the scene, finish their separate reports.

Molly and Jake stood up. Work to do.

EDDIE

"You know what, Daddy? I love Tater Tots. They're my favorite."

Marla Kay was sitting down but she still kicked out her feet every few seconds. It was almost as if she was back on that swing. Her legs hit his knees under the card table, causing him pain, but he didn't mind.

"I like them, too," he said.

"Are they your favorite?"

He thought about the question. He had promised himself he would never lie to her, not even about trivial things. He had listened to Raylene lie to her too many times. Well, Raylene could do whatever she liked, but for him — no. He would always tell his little girl the truth.

"I like them a lot," Eddie said, "but they're not my favorite."

Marla Kay grinned. "Then what *is* your favorite, Daddy?"

344

"Probably hot dogs."

She wiggled all over and kicked out her feet. He had never noticed before how much she wiggled, as if there was so much life and joy in her that sometimes it just had to bubble out of the top, like a carbonated beverage. There were so many things he did not know about her, because he had spent so little time with her, all told. Raylene always made it difficult for him to see her. But now he was making up for that lack. He was noticing everything, all the little nuances.

He had cleared off the top of the card table so they could have their supper there. He had fetched two folded metal chairs from the corner of the basement and he'd unfolded them, setting one on either side of the table. Then he dumped a package of Tater Tots on a paper plate and put it in the microwave. The *ding!* signaling they were done made her giggle. While he divided up the Tater Tots, Marla Kay had placed a napkin and a plastic fork at each of their places.

It was the third course of the meal. She had a ferocious appetite, which surprised him; as small and delicate as she was, he had assumed she would be a picky eater, the kind of child who frowns at her food while propping up a tilted head with a fist in a small cheek. But no: She roared through two slices of the frozen cheese pizza he had heated up, and then ate an apple. When he asked her if she liked Tater Tots, her eyes answered him even before her words did.

What a night it had been.

Best night of my life, he thought. He tried to keep that kind of thinking at bay, however, because he didn't want to jinx it. But it was. Definitely, it was.

"Do you like living down here, Daddy?"

"Yeah."

"I like it, too." She was swinging her legs in rhythm with her words. "I like the big thing over there." She looked over at the furnace. "I was scared of it at first but I'm not now. You're not scared of it, right, Daddy?"

"Nope."

"I'm not, either." She picked up a Tater Tot, holding it between her thumb and her index finger the way a jeweler would lift a precious stone to the light. She turned it around, licked it, popped it in her mouth. "I love Tater Tots."

"Go ahead and finish your dinner, then."

"What're we going to do after that?"

"Do you like to play cards?"

"Sure, Daddy." Brightly, eagerly. A moment passed. "What's cards?"

"You know. Like, Go Fish."

"Oh, yeah. I like it."

"Okay, then that's what we will do."

He looked at his watch. It was almost eight thirty. It was getting dark outside now, which meant he could start to get ready. He was nervous, but it was the good kind of nervous, the kind that keeps you sharp, alert.

He had changed his mind about what was going to happen tonight. This was a better plan. He had moved the rifle over to his bed. It was still wrapped in the plaid blanket. Paul knew he kept a firearm down here. They had discussed it. Paul said he wasn't comfortable with anyone having a firearm on church property. *I'm a veteran,* Eddie countered. *I've got medals for marksmanship. Guns are part of my life. Plus — it'll help me protect the place.* Paul said a firearm should never be discharged in a church, even if someone was breaking in. And Eddie said, *You don't understand, Paul. The point of a gun is that once folks know you have it, you don't have to use it.*

They sat at the card table and played three rounds of Go Fish. He taught her to play Crazy Eights and Kings in the Corner. She was good at card games, which pleased him;

she was a smart girl. Her only problem was that her hands were too small to hold more than two cards at a time. She couldn't spread them out the way he did, making a fan, and it frustrated her. After twice dropping a bunch of cards, she pushed all of her cards to the floor and sat back and crossed her arms, fuming.

"Try not to get upset like that," he said. "Don't be the kind of person who gets upset. Won't serve you."

He started to tell her what his temper had done to him — how it got him in all kinds of trouble when he couldn't control his anger. He held back. She would ask him more questions about it. He didn't want to lie to her. But he did not want her to know that he had hit a man in the head with a bowling ball because the man had pissed him off, annoyed him, and the man was now blind in one eye, and had a dentedin place on the side of his skull. Eddie did not serve much time for that. He was just back from Afghanistan and his thinking was totally messed up. The judge, thank God, was a veteran, too.

She was instantly contrite. "I won't, Daddy. I promise I won't get upset."

"Good. If you do, though — just count to ten. That helps."

"I can count *way* past ten," she said, scoffing at the idea that ten was her limit. "I can go to twenty-five."

"I know, sweet pea. But that's not what I mean. I mean that if somebody makes you mad, you can count to settle yourself down. One, two, three, four, five — you get a rhythm and it takes your mind off it. So you're not focusing anymore on being hurt or upset."

"Does it work for you, Daddy?"

"Yeah." He reached over and nudged her paper plate, rattling the rest of her Tater Tots. "Can you finish these?"

"Yeah," she said. He had the impression that she had said "Yeah" just now because he had said "Yeah" before, and she wanted to be like him.

That was an astonishing thought. Never before had anyone wanted to be like him. He was always the negative example, the person you did *not* want to be like. But Marla Kay wanted to be like him.

It occurred to him that this night could be his whole life. He could live it all right here, right now. Live it right down to the stub, like a candle that burns all the way out. Morning, noon, and night: He could live it all in the next few hours. With his little girl. After that, he didn't care what happened to him. He had read about certain insects that did that: They lived a lifetime in a single day.

He looked at his watch. It was all going by so fast. It was almost 9 P.M.

Part of him wanted to tell her what was going to happen, so that she would appreciate it, too. So that she would understand. They had to pack everything in together, the two of them. They had to pack a lifetime of nights into a single night.

This night.

"Am I going to spend the night here, Daddy?"

He was tempted to say, *Yeah, sweet pea.* He really wanted to say that. The idea would please her; she was comfortable here, at ease, and she would look forward to sleeping on the *Frozen* sheets. That had been his original plan. Then he had changed his mind; this was one of the first places they'd look for her.

But he had promised himself he would not lie to her. Ever.

So he said, "No, not tonight. In fact it's just about time to go."

"Go where, Daddy?" Excitement in her voice. Anticipation.

"It's a surprise."

She nodded. She trusted him. He was her

daddy and he would take care of her. She kicked out her legs, her body bouncy and free. She turned her head. She noticed the long thin object on the bed, the one wrapped in the plaid blanket.

"What's that, Daddy?"

PAUL

9:07 P.M.

The meeting with the church elders had run long. It always ran long but usually not *this* long. They had gotten a late start; Paul had an errand to run before joining the seven old men in the church rec hall. He had met Dot Burdette at the morgue. She had wanted to see her niece's body.

By the time Paul said good night to the last old man and walked into the rectory's small kitchen, Jenny had just about finished preparing their dinner. Mondays were his night to cook.

"Hey," he said. "Smells terrific. But it was my turn."

"If I'd waited for you to extricate yourself from your adoring flock," Jenny said archly, "we wouldn't eat until midnight. Those old guys really love the sound of their own voices, don't they?"

"Yep." He kissed her cheek, which was

flushed from the heat of the stove. She shooed him away. She was busy. "But as somebody who's notorious for giving long sermons," he added, "I've got no room to criticize."

She laughed. "Too true." She dished up two bowls of beef stew and they sat. The table was a long wooden one with bench seats. Jenny had discovered it in an antiques shop in Virginia and thought it looked vaguely churchy.

"Too hot for stew," she conceded, "but I felt like making it."

"I thought you were leaning toward hamburgers. That's what I told Eddie."

"Changed my mind. And he never came up, anyway. Guess he's not hungry."

"Well, the stew's good." He had yet to take a bite.

"You haven't even tasted it." Annoyance creased her voice. "That's so *you,* Paul. You praise something just to be praising it. It's got nothing to do with what you actually believe."

He took a long sip. "Okay, but it really *is* good."

She had complained about that before, about his need to make everybody feel better. He took responsibility for all the emotions in the room. He always had. Even as a

353

kid, he had felt a serious need to ensure the happiness of everyone he came across. He was the kind of boy who would deliberately miss a jump shot if his team had a big lead, in order to give the other side a chance to catch up. When his older sister admired his bike, he tried to make her take it. She wouldn't. Instead she had looked at him and said, "What? No. You're crazy. I don't want your stupid bike. I want one of my own that's just as good as yours. Or better." In college he never told his dorm roommate how much he hated Pearl Jam. Cliff loved their music, and so Paul said he loved it, too, and it was fine if Cliff wanted to play it loud.

And that was why he became a pastor. He could do professionally what he'd always done — which was to soothe the world, to keep it smoothed-out and safe. Round the edges. He was handsome in a square, middle-of the-road way — medium build, straight brown hair, straight teeth, regular features — and that helped, too, with the minister thing. People liked to confide in a good-looking young man. His mentor, a preacher at his home church named Elbert Trammel, explained that to him. It sounded simplistic, but it ended up being true. Paul saw it all the time: Women and men who came to him because they were troubled would visibly relax in his presence. Paul was, as the Reverend Trammel put it, "easy on the eyes." Trammel was not; he had rubbery lips, frizzy gray hair, bad skin, a melting-candle physique. People were made anxious by ugliness, he told Paul, especially in a man of God. *If you're such a good and faithful servant of the Lord, then why do you look like ten miles of bad road?* That, the old man insisted, was exactly what they were thinking when they sat in their pews on those Sunday mornings and listened to Elbert Trammel preach at them. *At the very least, wouldn't a just and loving God have taken care of that face of yours? I mean, really.*

Paul met Jenny at his first church assignment: assistant pastor at Stone Ridge Baptist in Poplar Springs, Tennessee. She was twenty-nine and still lived with her parents. She worked at the Gap, and on one of their first dates, she explained to him — at his request — the proper way to fold a T-shirt. *I do this all day long,* she told him. *You wouldn't believe how often people come into the store and mess up the stacks of T-shirts, just for the heck of it.* Jenny was short and heavy and wore glasses. She was not what anyone would call attractive, but there was an energy about her, an earnestness, that many people, including the new assistant minister, found appealing. She was volunteer coordinator at Stone Ridge and her greatest desire, she told Paul on that same first date — after she had demonstrated the proper folding of a T-shirt — was to change the world. Make it a better place.

"So what were the guys grousing about tonight?" Jenny asked. Before he could answer, she added, "Do you want some crackers with that?"

"No, I'm good." He wasn't really hungry but he knew better than to tell her so. It would be rude, being as how she had worked so hard to make dinner. He had already decided: He'd finish his bowl and ask for seconds. "They're upset about all the overdoses today. Had a bunch of them. All over town."

"I heard." She nodded solemnly. "What does it say about this place that dozens of people overdose on heroin and you and I don't even discuss it until" — she checked the clock on the kitchen wall — "after nine o'clock at night? It's like a regular thing around here now. God help us all."

"Yeah. Pretty shocking."

"What did the elders say?"

"The usual. Everybody's wondering what

the church ought to do." He braced himself. He knew what was coming next.

"So what *should* we do?"

There was challenge in her tone. The "we" was on purpose. He knew his wife's view: A church should be an active force for good in a community. Life was a battle, it was always good versus evil, and they couldn't — they shouldn't — let down for an instant. Work. Strive. Sacrifice. Work some more. It was the same drive she'd brought to the folding of T-shirts at the Gap: Don't stop. Don't even slow down. He admired her. He really did. Except that sometimes he got a little tired of it.

Sometimes he wanted to just eat his dinner. Or not eat it. Whatever. He just wanted to relax without having somebody preach at him about his duty. He knew his duty. He knew it better than anybody else.

He owed her. The bargain they'd struck six years ago was unspoken, but unspoken bargains often were the most binding of all. He had learned that. The bargain was: If he agreed to take the job as head pastor of the Rising Souls Church in Acker's Gap, West Virginia, she would give him another chance. Because that was why he needed to leave Stone Ridge. He had had an affair with a parishioner. Wendy Pang was a forty-four-year-old divorcée who came to him for spiritual counseling. Paul, to his great surprise, fell in love with her. Their lovemaking — passionate, intense, uninhibited — was like nothing he'd ever experienced with Jenny, back when they were still having intimate relations. He was selfish with Wendy. He didn't worry about her pleasure, as he did when he and Jenny made love. It was enormously liberating. Wendy liked his selfishness. She said it turned her on.

They talked of a life together, he and Wendy Pang. He would have to leave the church, of course, in addition to divorcing Jenny. Before any plans could go forward, Wendy announced that she had changed her mind. It was a fling, she said, a short burst of madness, but she had come to her senses. And he needed to do that, too. *I thought it would last forever,* she wrote in her final text to him. *But it didn't.* He confessed to Jenny. The job in Acker's Gap — a place neither of them had ever heard of — seemed like fitting penance.

But his affair had turned Jenny into what she had never been before: A Jealous Person. She was always watching him now, alert for signs and hints. He knew why she had come to his office that morning, ostensibly to deliver the message from Dot Burdette. It wasn't to deliver a message from Dot Burdette, even though, as it happened, Dot Burdette really *had* needed comfort from him, in the wake of her niece's sudden, grubby death.

She had come to get another look at the woman he was meeting with in his office. To gauge the vibe. Was there anything going on? Was there anything that meant something conceivably *might* go on at some point in the future?

No. And: no. That's what Jenny had decided. He could tell. She had sensed no sexual threat from Shirley Dolan.

"I don't know," he said. "But we've got to do something. This town is really shaken up — parts of it are, anyway. The rest doesn't even know what's happening." He leaned back, then forward. He missed a regular chair with a back to it. "I've never seen Dot Burdette the way she was tonight, over at the morgue. I'm not sure why she wanted to go."

"Somebody had to positively ID the body, I guess."

"Sammy had already done that. I don't suppose it much matters if it's an aunt or an uncle." He fetched a deep, discouraged-sounding breath. "What a night. First the morgue and then the elders' meeting. Walter Bee and his buddies, telling me the world's going to hell — and just what do I propose to do about it?"

"Well, that's kind of in your job description, isn't it? Helping people make sense of their sorrows?" She was pushing him, like always. Needling him. "When things go wrong — people turn to their pastors. That's good. Not bad. Right?"

He shrugged. She would never forgive him. Or worse: She would always forgive him. She would make forgiving him her personal hobby.

He had realized that the second they landed in Acker's Gap. It didn't matter what he did or didn't do, it didn't matter if he was the world's best husband or a philandering cad — she would never, ever, *ever* not forgive him.

So to hell with her.

He didn't mean that. He was tired, and he was sad about the overdoses and all the pain he had seen in the eyes of the church elders tonight, several of whom, he knew, had children and grandchildren with drug problems, and who were probably thinking, *There but for the grace of God . . .*

He was glum and he was frustrated. And he didn't want any more damned stew.

"Some of the elders want to start a halfway

house," he said. "Someplace for addicts to come."

"That's a really good idea," Jenny said. "There's not enough room here at the church, but I bet we could find a good empty building downtown that we could —"

"Whoa," he said. "Nothing's been decided yet. We'd have to do a lot of fund-raising first. And get permits and such. It's just an idea right now." *And it's* their *idea,* he wanted to say to her. *You don't have to be in charge of every damned thing. You don't have to swoop in like some angel and start organizing all the good deeds in the world.*

But he did not say that, because it would be cruel. And Paul Wolford was not cruel. He was a good guy. He was the guy everybody liked. When he screwed up, he asked for a second chance, and he usually got it. *Our God is a God of second chances,* he liked to say in his sermons. People liked hearing it.

"What was that?" Jenny said.

He started to give the classic retort to that question — "What was *what?*" — when the sound came again and this time, he heard it, too: A knock, as if someone had dropped something on the floor of an adjacent room.

"Might be somebody at the back door," he said. "I'll check."

"I'm coming, too."

He understood. She didn't want him to go alone. By now it was dark outside. The church's neighborhood at the east end of town had once been considered safe but there was no such thing anymore as a safe neighborhood. Not in Acker's Gap.

They reached the back door. Another knock. Paul flipped on the outside light. When he opened the door, he said, "Raylene" in a startled voice. He wasn't sure if he was saying it to her or to Jenny or to himself.

Raylene was bent almost double, one arm stuck straight out to claw at the door, the other clutching her stomach, heaving with sobs.

"My baby!" she cried. "He got her. You have to help me — please! *Please!* No telling what that pervert might —"

"Is this about Marla Kay?" Jenny said, using her elbow to help her move in front of Paul. "What's going on? What happened?"

"I *told* you," Raylene screamed back at her. She seemed to be offended by Jenny's relatively calm demeanor. "Eddie took my baby girl. His truck's out back so I figure he's got her down there. He grabbed her from the playground. I went to get her and this lady who lives across the street said she saw a man take her — a man in an orange truck with a church sign on it. You gotta help me — *please*." Her voice dropped to a snarl. "By God, if he so much as *touches* my little girl, I swear I'll *kill* that goddamned bastard with my bare hands, just as sure as I'm standing here."

"Settle down," Paul said, in his best can't-we-all-just-get-along purr. "Eddie's a good man. And he loves her. He's not going to —"

"He's got a *gun* down there," Raylene broke in. "He told me once. Did you know that? The man you're protecting has got a deadly weapon. How're you gonna feel if he hurts my girl?"

Before Paul had a chance to answer, the air was riven by the sound of a gunshot from the church basement.

BELL

She had been sitting with Dot Burdette for
over an hour. Their business was concluded
but they were still here, sitting side by side
in the bucket seats in the waiting room of
the Raythune County Coroner's Office.
Everyone else had gone home: Dot's
brother, Sammy; her pastor, Paul Wolford;
the coroner, Buster Crutchfield.

Only Dot remained. And as long as Dot
was here, Bell would be here, too, because
that was what she had promised Dot: *You
stay, I stay.*

The chairs were the cheap plastic kind,
the whole row bolted to a long metal strip.
They were purposefully uncomfortable —
that was Bell's theory, anyway — to discour-
age long visits. Grief sometimes left people
frozen. She could well imagine someone
showing up here to ID a body and then
just never mustering the will or the energy

364

to leave.

Dot might be that someone.

In the hours since she had learned about Sally Ann's death Dot had shifted from one region of sorrow to another, making the change like the swift, clean stroke of an engine. She had gone from active shock and clawing agony to a kind of blank, wide-eyed calm. Dot had not washed her face or changed her clothes. This woman who was always so prideful about her appearance, who rarely left her house without full makeup and heels that matched her purse, wore old pants, tennis shoes, and an over-sized shirt with a raggedy collar. These were exactly the clothes she had pulled on, Bell surmised, when she received that middle-of-the-night visit from Sheriff Harrison. She had spent the subsequent hours sitting in her living room, the room in which Bell had found her earlier that day. Dark room, dark thoughts. Her hair had not been combed. It was flat in some places; in others, it stuck up in strange-looking tufts.

And she doesn't give a damn about any of that, Bell thought.

"Just a little bit longer," Dot said. Her voice was calm and steady. "I'll be ready to go soon. Just not right away, okay?"

"We can stay as long as you need to."

"I know you're busy."

"I am. I'm busy being here with you." The line surprised Bell, even though she was the one who had spoken it. It wasn't like her.

Damn. Must be mellowing in my old age, Bell thought ruefully. *Too much* Oprah, *maybe.*

Dot was correct: She had a million other places, give or take, where she ought to be. At Jake's request she had called Judge Tolliver, securing a warrant for a search of the Starliner Motel; she needed to follow up with the deputy and see if he'd had any luck shutting down the drug gang. She needed to decide whether or not to prosecute the addicts who had fallen and then been revived during the day's devastation. Normally she wouldn't bother hauling them in — an activity she filed under the heading "freaking waste of time" — but already two county commissioners had called and demanded that she do so. Naloxone, they pointed out, cost money. Lock 'em up until they paid the bill for their own rescue. Or rescues.

She had calls to return and evidence to review. She had a sister to meet up with, a sister who had been waiting for this day from hell to end so that she could talk to Bell about something important.

And so what was Bell doing?

She was sitting in a plastic chair in the waiting room at the county morgue alongside a woman who wasn't really her friend. A woman who had, in fact, caused Bell's senior year in high school to be filled with a great deal more angst and self-doubt than it strictly needed to be.

So why *am I here?*

An hour ago, Buster Crutchfield had done his duty. He pulled back the drape on the eye-level slit of a window that enabled Dot to see Sally Ann's body. Family members did not enter the room in which the bodies of their loved ones were stored, supine on long tables, a sheet pulled up to their necks. They were restricted to the small room with the tiny window.

Bell admired Buster. He was gentle with the lost and grieving people who constituted the living half of his clientele. The old man had done this job for decades but never seemed to forget that for most people, this was the first time they had seen a dead body. The shock was visceral.

Dot's presence was not required. Sammy had already identified Sally Ann's body. "But I *need* to be there," she said to Bell, when she called and asked her to meet her there. A few minutes later Dot's minister,

Paul Wolford, showed up as well. Bell had seen him before, but could not recall where; that was what it meant to be in local politics, she reflected silently. You knew just about everyone, although you really didn't know anyone at all. They shook hands.

Dot peered through the window. No one spoke.

Bell had feared Dot might break down; she had been crying all afternoon, and was primed and ready, surely, for more tears. But no. Dot spent several minutes looking through the window at the body of her niece. Then she bowed her head, murmured something in a voice too low to be intelligible to the others, and backed away.

Sammy hugged her. He had to be getting home, he said, and if Dot didn't mind . . .

"It's fine," she said. "Have a good night, Sammy."

Paul put his arm around her and asked if he should stay. "No," Dot said. "Thanks for coming." He said he would pray for her. She thanked him for that, too. Paul departed, and after a few more minutes, Buster did as well. Had the prosecuting attorney not been present, he would have required them to leave when he did. Because it was Bell, though, they could stay. "Just pull the door shut behind you," Buster said.

"Locks automatically."

So now it was just the two of them.

Time passed before Dot spoke. "I remember when I found pot in her room," she said. "The first time, I mean. I wasn't snooping. My hand to God — I wasn't. It was totally accidental. She had just started high school. I was putting some clean socks away in her drawer. And there was just this little stash. In a plastic bag. So I ignored it. I just — I just assumed she'd figure it all out for herself. She was going through a rough patch. She never felt that she really belonged anywhere."

Bell didn't respond. Dot, she sensed, didn't want her to. She wasn't talking to convey information. She was talking to arrange her own thinking. She was talking to make a story out of the raw materials of her memories and her emotions, like paving stones gathered and deployed to make a pathway.

"I tried my best with that girl," Dot went on. "I did. I wasn't always as patient with her as I should have been — but she knew she was loved. She did. I'm sure of it. She did know that." Now a bit of emotion glimmered in Dot's voice. She swallowed hard. "At least I hope so. I wasn't always able to tell her how much I loved her. That's not . . ." Another difficult swallow. "That's not easy for me. I don't come from that kind of family. You've seen me and Sammy. We don't hug — God, no. Grew up in the same house. I know him better than I know anybody else in the world, but we don't relate that way. You saw. You saw how he was tonight. He's just as upset as I am — I *know* he is, I know my brother — but he'd never show it. Never. Not to me, not to anybody."

She shook her head. She was rambling, and she knew it. She didn't want to ramble. She had things she needed to say, here in this bright, cold waiting room with the bad chairs and the terrible lighting. A few feet away, separated from them only by a thin wall in which a small window had been cut, was the body of her niece, a body that Dot had fed and clothed and watched over for many years, but that soon would be out of her reach forever.

"She loved science. Did you know that, Bell? No, you didn't. Nobody knew that. Because she didn't like to talk about herself. She was too shy. But I saw her eyes when she talked about her science classes. She was smart. She loved it when she learned something new. You could see it in her eyes.

"And then," Dot said, her voice hardening, "she just stopped coming home. First time she did it, I called Nick Fogelsong — he was still sheriff back then — and he went and found her for me. She was at that tattoo place out on Route 7." Dot shuddered. "In some kind of back room. Can you beat that? Bunch of mattresses on the floor. Kids lying there — high or stoned or whatever the hell they call it. Kids from good families. Kids with futures. Nick brought her home but I could tell it was over. I'd lost her. After that, I couldn't keep her home. She wanted to go back. She felt better in a horrible tattoo place than she did in that nice room I'd fixed up for her, in the best house in Acker's Gap." A long, deep sigh of incomprehension, followed by a sudden fury: "The drugs — God, Bell, what're we going to do? What are we going to do?"

She seemed, this time, to want an answer. Bell didn't have one.

"I don't know," she said.

They sat together for another few minutes. And then, with no warning, Dot stood up. That was it. She had passed through to another realm.

"Good night, Bell. Thanks for coming. If Sammy and I decide to have a memorial service, I'll let you know where and when. We're not sure yet."

Bell drove home along streets that were largely empty of cars. She pulled into her driveway. She had forgotten to leave the porch light on. She corrected herself: She hadn't forgotten anything. There had been no reason for her to turn it on. When she left the house early that morning, she'd had no way of knowing that she would not return again for more than twelve hours.

Climbing the front steps, she saw a figure sitting on the porch swing. It was too dark to make out any particulars, but Bell did not need them. She could sense her sister's presence, even in the dark.

"Hi, Belfa."

"Hey. You could've gone on in. You still have your key, right?"

"Yeah. I do. But it's okay. Kind of enjoying it out here."

"I didn't see your car."

"I got a ride. Car's in the shop. Heard a funny sound in the engine this afternoon"

"You need some help with that? I know car repairs can be pretty expen—"

"Belfa."

"Okay, okay." Bell sat down on the swing beside her. "Finally. We get to talk. But fair warning — I've got some calls out. I might get a return call while we're talking. I'll have to take it."

"Got it."

"And that's okay, right? You won't get mad."

"Promise."

"Mind if I go get a sweater? Kind of chilly when the sun goes down. You want one?"

"No," Shirley said. "I'm good."

When Bell returned to the swing they sat for a few minutes in silence — that is, *they* were silent, but the world wasn't. The sounds of a late-summer night, the crickets and the spring peepers and the bullfrogs, rose up all around them, a robust natural symphony. The mountains in the near distance seemed to be leaning in just a little bit closer, Bell thought, as if they, too, wanted to hear what Shirley had waited all day to say to her.

"So this thing you need to tell me," Bell said. "I'm sorry we had to keep pushing back our talk."

"It's okay. Not your average day."

"Good God — no." Bell laughed, but it was disillusioned, mirthless laughter. "If it was, I'd resign. Effective immediately."

"No. You wouldn't."

"I wouldn't?" Mild amusement in her tone, with a palpable subtext: *So you know me better than I know me, big sister?*

"No," Shirley said. "You love what you

do. You were born to be a prosecutor."

Bell still had a tease in her tone. "You mean I'm bossy and judgmental?"

"No. I mean you do a lot of good for a lot of people."

"Oh, come on," Bell said. She wasn't fishing for compliments. Shirley should know that. "Lighten up."

"I can't."

"You can't lighten up?"

"No."

Now she heard it: The note in Shirley's voice that told her this would not be like any conversation they had ever had before.

"What's going on?" Bell said. She said it quietly.

"I've had that bad cough for a while. You know that."

Bell felt dread flooding her heart. "Yes. And you had it checked."

Silence.

"You did have it checked, right?" Bell pressed her. "You promised me."

"Not right away. I got busy. What with me and Bobo breaking up and me having to move and all. Anyway, I finally did go. I went last week. I was having some lower back pain, too, and it was really bothering me. Couldn't do my job. Those high shelves at work — with all the auto parts. I'm supposed to keep them stocked and I couldn't. Not with the pain."

"So you got it checked."

"Yeah. They did some scans."

Bell waited. The world stopped turning on its axis.

"And?" she said.

"And I've got lung cancer. Something they call oat cell carcinoma."

Bell could not speak. But she had to. "Did they say —"

"Three months. Maybe six."

MOLLY

"So I had to come by and thank you personally, Malik," Jake said. "Best lead we had all day. And it came from you, my man."

Malik's face remained placid, but something was happening to his eyes. They widened. He was clearly pleased. He didn't quite know what to do with that pleasure, how to express it in an appropriate way.

"Yeah," Malik said. He jerked his body to the left. "When I saw the matchbook, I knew. I knew."

"Well, you were right, buddy." Jake held up a sheet of paper. It was typewritten, with a flourishing signature at the bottom. "This is what's called a warrant. It gives me the legal authority to search the Starliner."

"Because of my matchbook?" Malik said.

"Well, sort of." Jake folded the paper. "It was that and some other things, too. It's signed by a judge. And I'm on my way over there right now."

The house where Molly and Malik lived was on the way to the Starliner. Sort of. It was the "sort of" part that caused Molly to give Jake a sideways, questioning look. She knew how important it was for him to find the gang that was supplying the tainted heroin to the local dealer. And it sounded as if he had a good lead.

So why had he stopped by? Why was he wasting time?

When she'd heard the doorbell, she had looked at Malik, and Malik looked at her. It was late. Who would be visiting them at this time of night? Molly had only been home for half an hour. When she got there, apologizing for being so late to the woman who watched Malik, the woman had scowled. *I've got my own family, you know. This can't happen again, you hear?* Molly wanted to say: *You're right. But not in the way you mean it. This can't happen again. The town can't take it.*

She didn't say that. Or anything close to that. *I'm sorry.* That was all she said. *I'm really sorry, Mrs. Hunnicutt.*

After dealing with the four overdoses — and the kid — in the idling car, she and Ernie had had one more run before they clocked out. Two more overdoses. Two

377

women: Mary Higgs, 19, and Louella Simpson, 24. They were found at the back of an abandoned building downtown, slumped against a brick wall. A little naloxone magic up the nose and in two minutes they were up again, flailing and cursing.

Thirty-three overdoses since midnight. Three deaths.

Molly had barely had a chance to wash her hands at the kitchen sink when she heard the doorbell.

It was Jake Oakes, standing in the yellow circle of the porch light, showing off his search warrant. Thanking Malik. Making Malik happy.

She invited him in. Of course she did. Because she had to. It was only polite. But still: He had to get to the Starliner, didn't he?

When she saw Jake on the job, when he was the deputy present at an accident scene to which she and Ernie had been summoned, or if he arrived at a scene after she and Ernie had already begun their work, she was pleased. She was aware of the spark between them. But that was all it was. That was all it could ever be.

"Can I go to the Starliner?" Malik said.

They stood in the front hallway of the old house with the peeling wallpaper, the three of them. Malik was already in his Superman PJs. Molly was still in her uniform. She had untucked the light blue polo shirt, kicked off her shoes. It felt odd to be sock-footed in front of Jake. And the fact that it felt odd *also* felt odd. Why should it matter whether or not she had her shoes on? Okay, maybe it was this: She had never been less than fully dressed around him.

"No, sorry, buddy," Jake said. "It's too dangerous. But I'll let you know how it goes, okay?"

"Deal." Malik held up his hand to get a high-five.

Jake complied. He remembered what Molly had told him that morning: Malik didn't like handshakes but he liked high-fives. Jake had filed away the information.

"You helped me crack this case," Jake said. "So I owe you."

"It's not finished," Molly said. "Is it?"

Jake looked slightly chagrinned. "Well, no. You're right. I'm meeting Steve Brinks-neader out there. We need to take a look around before we execute the warrant. So I'd better go."

Molly took Malik's chin in her hand, so that he would have to look at her. He didn't want to look anywhere but at Jake. "I'm go-ing to walk Jake out to his truck," she said.

"It's late. Brush your teeth, okay? I'll be right back."

They didn't get as far as the Blazer before she turned on him. They were halfway down the dark sidewalk.

"Don't do this, Jake." She stopped walking. He did, too.

"What?" He seemed very surprised.

"Don't try to bond with Malik as a way of getting to me." There. She had said it out loud. She was glad it was dark, so he would not be able to see her face. She was afraid of what it might reveal.

"I don't know what you mean," he said.

"Yes, you do."

"Look," he said. "Maybe I was out of line. Coming to your house."

"We came to yours."

"I'd given you my address. You never gave me yours."

"Hey — you're right." She tried to sound playful. She wanted to lighten the mood. "How'd you find us, anyway?"

He was somber, answering her as if she had really meant it to be a question. "I'm a deputy sheriff. Finding people is what I do. But it was clearly a mistake, okay? Won't happen again." He walked away from her, toward the Blazer.

She followed him. When he reached the

driver's-side door he turned around.

"I wanted to ask you out," he said. "I thought that maybe one of these days we could —"

"No." She crossed her arms. "No. It's not like that, Jake. It can't be like that."

"Okay. So you're seeing somebody. I get it."

"It's not that."

"The race thing? Is that it? Because I don't see why —"

"No. This is the twenty-first century."

"Yeah," he said. "Twenty-first-century West Virginia. Not the most progressive place on the planet."

"I don't care what anybody thinks. That's not it."

He took the heel of his hand and smacked himself on the forehead. "God, what an idiot I am! You don't feel that way about me. Okay. Okay. Message received. Thanks for clarifying."

He turned toward the door again, reaching for the handle. Before he could grasp it she had spun him around to face her. She was very strong.

She kissed him. She had wondered for some time what it would be like to kiss him. She felt the long delicious thrill that comes with a first kiss. When they broke apart, he fell back against the door. She knew he was slightly discombobulated. She knew that because she was, too.

"That's not it, either," she said.

He was breathing hard.

His cell rang. "Dammit," he said. "I've got to take —"

"Of course."

She waited, listening to his side of the conversation, the terse replies. He hung up and said, "Steve can't make it to the Starliner. He's at an accident scene on the interstate. Bad one. Multiple vehicles."

"How about Sheriff Harrison?"

"She's with him. All four lanes shut down in both directions. They're up to their ears. So I've got to think of something else. I can't go without backup."

She smiled. "Maybe Malik *can* come, after all. He's wearing his Superman PJs." Then she grew serious again. "What are you going to do?"

"I don't know." He had an idea, though. Would it work? He'd worry about that later. Once he was back on the road.

Abruptly he drew her toward him to kiss her again. She pushed him away. Not hard, but her intention was unmistakable.

"Jake — I thought I was clear. This can't happen."

He was taken aback. "But just a minute ago —"

He was right. She was sending him mixed messages. She wasn't being fair.

"That was a mistake. I got carried away," she said. "It's not possible, okay?"

"I don't understand."

"You need to go. You're on duty."

"Fine. I'll go. But just tell me why the hell we can't at least try this. That's all I'm asking. If it doesn't work out — okay. No harm, no foul. But why can't we try?"

She looked at him. She liked looking at his face.

"Why?" he repeated. "Give me a reason."

"Be careful tonight."

"Molly, I —"

"Go."

JAKE

10:38 P.M.

At night the Starliner looked a lot like the Emerald Oasis. It was a low, lumpy shape resembling a giant meat loaf, slumped dismally against the sky. He had parked on a tree-studded ridge above the motel, waiting for his new backup to arrive, and from here he could see the front doors to all the rooms.

The Emerald Oasis was a motel he remembered from his childhood in Beckley. It was surely closed down now, he thought; businesses came and went, and that was a long time ago. Everything changed. The reason it had lodged so permanently in his mind was because, one night when he was five years old, his father had swept him up and placed him in the backseat of the car. They drove. The car stopped, and as his father opened the door he said to him, "Wait here." Jake moved to the center of the backseat so that he could look out the front windshield. A green neon sign with EMERALD OASIS rose up over the roof of the motel. There was a palm tree under the word EMERALD, with lights twinkling along the leaves.

Something happened that night. At five, he did not know what it was. His father came back to the car and they drove home. Jake's questions went unanswered. He found out some details later, of course, and it was as ordinary and sordid as you might expect. His mother was at the motel with another man, one of his father's friends. Jake never knew what was said inside that room when his father showed up. The incident, in retrospect, did not make Jake think less of his mother. He pitied her, imagining the desperation that must have been clawing at her from the inside out, to make her seek the shabby glamour of a place like the Emerald Oasis. Or the temporary solace of sex.

"Jake."

The big face at the open window of the Blazer just about scared the crap out of him.

"Charlie. Jesus, you startled me, man."

"Focus. You need to focus and concentrate, young'un." Charlie Mathers grinned.

He looked like he was having the time of his life.

When Jake called his old colleague from the road, he had fully expected to have to do a sales job. He was prepared to appeal to Charlie's sense of duty, and his pride, and even his manliness. But none of that was necessary. He had explained the urgency and his need for backup, and Charlie immediately said, "I'm there, partner."

Jake was still reeling — in a good way — from Molly's kiss. He had no idea why she had turned him down. He got along fine with Malik. Malik liked him. So what was the problem?

But right now he needed to compartmentalize, and he would. He climbed out of the Blazer. Charlie had parked his Denali down the road, and hiked up the steep ridge. He was panting heavily.

They lay on their bellies, watching the Starliner. Jake aimed his binoculars: The office was dark, with a lopsided SORRY CLOSED sign hanging on the door. The parking lot was lit by only a single streetlight. It buzzed and flickered and seemed about to give up. There were no lights in front of the doors. Four cars inhabited the lot. Three of them were parked close together. The fourth was off by itself at the end of the lot, parked at a sharp angle instead of facing straight in.

The plan was to swoop in with the search warrant, moving very quickly.

"Sounds like a damned raid, not a search warrant," Charlie had mumbled, when Jake went over it.

But Charlie understood. Drug gangs were adept at destroying evidence on the fly; in minutes an entire case could crumble. They had to be quick. In order to be quick, though, they had to be knowledgeable. Jake didn't want to waste time by starting the search in the wrong room, a move that would tip off the others in adjacent rooms, giving them an opportunity to dump the merchandise. From his swift upside-down view of the spiral notebook in the office, he had seen that all of the rooms were rented to a single person: John Parsons. There was no "John Parsons," of course. Whatever the gang leader's real name was, he had paid in cash.

"What's the final tally of overdoses?" Charlie whispered.

"Thirty-three. Three of them died."

"Jesus. I heard about McHale."

"Did you have any idea he was using?"

Charlie shifted the position of his stomach on the ground. "You hear things."

Abruptly they stopped talking. A door opened; a man came out of one of the rooms. He was dark and slender. Jake guessed that he was Mexican. Was it politically incorrect to assume that, based on what the man looked like through a pair of binoculars? Jake consoled himself: The FBI had briefed the sheriff's department a few months ago, and they did not hesitate to call it a "Mexican drug gang." Because that was where they came from.

Jake still had not found the local dealer, the link between the gang in the Starliner and the addicts collapsing in the streets. But he would. He was going at it from the other end now. Instead of using the dealer to ID the gang, he would use the gang to ID the dealer.

And they would get the carfentanil-laced heroin off the streets.

"What's he doing?" Charlie whispered.

The man was walking around the lot, chopping at the gravel with the heels of his boots. He spit.

"Don't know. Maybe just blowing off steam."

They watched as he entered the room next to the one from which he had emerged. When the door swung open, the room's brashly lit interior was suddenly visible, with a clarity like that of a movie screen. The man closed it quickly behind him, but not before Jake had seen what he needed to see: Two long tables were covered with heaps of plastic packages. The packages were filled with white powder. Seated at the table were two more lean, swarthy men, wearing pale green gloves.

This was where the heroin was being cut with the carfentanil.

"Guess they figure they don't need to be too careful way out here in the woods," Charlie whispered. "Pretty damn brassy, doing their business out in the open like that. They don't even have a lookout."

Before Jake could answer he felt his cell vibrating in his pocket. The text was from Bell Elkins:

Coming to join u. Need some diversion. Got to get my mind off something.

Jake texted back a thumbs-up and their position. Her message was a little more personal than usual — Bell rarely gave a reason for her actions, because it was none of his business — but he didn't mind her being there. In fact, he welcomed it. They couldn't let these guys slip away on a technicality. A prosecutor on the premises could ensure everything was done by the book. Minimize the chance of errors that might put these murdering bastards back out on the street.

"Bell's on her way," he said. "Never known her to miss the action."

Charlie grunted. "Ain't it the truth."

Now they waited. Once she arrived, they would move carefully down the hill and then, on Jake's signal, rush the room, brandishing the search warrant and confiscating the drugs. Jake was looking forward to the interrogation. He'd make them give up the identity of the local dealer. And — yeah. Maybe Molly would hear about it. Maybe so.

"Feels real good, being out here," Charlie whispered. "Glad you called."

"You were my third choice, old man."

Charlie chuckled softly. "I bet. So what did the sheriff say when you told her I was your backup?"

Jake didn't answer.

"Come on," Charlie said in a harsh whisper. "You *did* tell her, right? You got permission?"

"Well."

"What the hell are you *thinking*? Technically I'm a civilian. Pam Harrison's going to chop your balls off when she finds out. And then she'll go for mine."

"You're a retired deputy. You've got more

experience than me and Steve — and the sheriff, too, for that matter — put together."

Charlie's whisper still sounded worried. "You've put me in a bad spot here. I told Doreen the sheriff signed off on it. Only reason she let me come."

" *'Let'* you come? Charlie, Charlie." Jake's whisper was lighthearted, but he knew the subtext would hit his friend hard.

"Give me a break," Charlie retorted. "Doreen worries about me. And you know what? Kinda nice to have somebody at home worrying about you."

They didn't talk for a time. The crickets took up the slack, adding their jingly chorus to the rest of the night sounds: the spring peepers, the soul-haunting screech of an owl. Despite the danger, Jake felt the old juices stirring, the excitement. His heart rate was elevating by the second — and he loved it. *Anyone who says they don't get off on this,* he thought with satisfaction, *is a freaking liar.* Even the most sincere and dedicated law enforcement professional was also an adrenaline junkie. Not a thing in the world wrong with that, Jake told himself. Not a thing.

And there was *also* nothing wrong with wanting to share it with Charlie. Wanting to remind his friend what a kick it was: a stakeout on a warm August night. High risk, high reward.

Jake heard a slight stir off to his left. He checked it. Bell was approaching their spot on the ridge on foot. She had parked down the road by Charlie's Denali. She would be there in seconds. If Charlie was going to bail, he would have to do it soon.

The older man's voice sounded troubled. "I don't know. Jake. I'd like to help, but I don't want to piss off Pam Harrison. Maybe I oughta just go back home."

"Hold on," Jake said. "Ask yourself this. What would Benson and Stabler do?"

Charlie laughed softly. There was a brief pause. "Okay, partner. I'm in."

The moment Bell appeared, the two men got to their feet. There were no greetings, just a round of nods. It seemed to Jake that Bell was a little preoccupied. She wasn't her usual highly alert, hard-charging self. She was quieter, more taciturn. He chalked it up to the drama of the moment. Draining this particular swamp would mean a lot to Acker's Gap.

He was glad, frankly, that she had a lot on her mind tonight. Otherwise she would have posed her own questions about Charlie's participation. She'd want to know if Sheriff Harrison approved. Jake would have told her the truth — you don't lie to Bell Elkins — and she might have shut them down. But if she didn't ask, he was in the clear.

And she didn't ask.

They found the steep path from the top of the hill that Jake had scoped out. Down they went, traveling single file through the tangled brush. They moved stealthily across the semi-dark parking lot.

Jake took the lead. He approached the door. Charlie was right behind him. Bell stayed off to the right. She activated her cell's video camera to record the execution of the warrant. No slip ups.

Jake banged on the door with his fist, a rapid flurry of blows. "Raythune County Sheriff's Department," he called out. "I got a search warrant to enter. Coming in."

Nothing.

"Coming in," Jake repeated. He rattled the knob; the door was locked. "Five seconds," he yelled.

He drew his sidearm. He signaled to Charlie. They heaved themselves sideways at the door, using their shoulders as battering rams. The cheap door collapsed without a struggle.

The room appeared to be deserted. The merchandise was still stacked on the tables. From the bathroom, Jake heard the snick of a hinge.

"They're going out the bathroom window," he said. "Charlie, start rounding up this stuff. I'll go get 'em."

"Copy that," Charlie said. He pulled out the gloves and the trash bag from his back pocket. He knew how careful he had to be with carfentanil.

Jake was a fast runner. He had always been a fast runner. And even if he hadn't been fast, he knew that getting three men out a bathroom window, one by one, would take some time. He rounded the side of the motel and there they were, tumbling out the window. He waited for the final man to hit the ground before he flipped on his Maglite and raised his sidearm.

"Okay, fellas," he said. "Let's go."

It had been almost too easy. They weren't armed, and at Jake's command the three men, blinking in the bright light, linked their hands behind their heads. He marched them around to the front of the motel.

Charlie emerged from the room with a garbage bag, now engorged with merchandise. He held it up for Bell to record with her cell.

"Gonna need another bag," Charlie said. "Still got more to pack up. These guys were planning to be in business around here for a *long* time, lemme tell ya."

Jake kept his Glock trained on the three men. He hoped Charlie would hurry. He was unsettled by how easily the gang members had surrendered; there were hundreds of thousands of dollars at stake, and they had capitulated without a fight. Weird.

And he also didn't like the atmospherics. He felt exposed, remembering how easily he and Charlie had looked down on the lot from their elevated perch. As dim as the single streetlight was, it still turned this area into a stage. Anyone could be watching them from the outer ring of darkness. He and Charlie and Bell were sitting ducks.

Jake recited the Miranda warnings to the men. When he asked if they had understood him, one man said, *"Sí."* Jake replied, "In English." That prompted a "Yeah" from each man.

His uneasiness was escalating.

"Let's wrap this up," Jake barked at Charlie. "Finish our business and get these guys back to the Blazer."

Charlie grinned. "Come on, partner, chill out. Don't get your panties in a bun —"

The flat smack of a gunshot echoed across the lot, canceling the other night noises with a single vivid slash of sound. An eternity passed in the next tenth of a second. Jake's head whipped around.

Bell? Did it hit —

Charlie crashed to his knees. The bright wound blossomed on his forehead. He swayed and then toppled, but before he went down, he looked directly at Jake, confusion in his eyes.

"Charlie," Bell cried out. "Oh my God —"

Jake wanted to go to him, but he had to find the source of the shot. He and Bell were still vulnerable. He dropped to a crouch, arms extended, ready to fire. His eyes swept the lot.

And then he saw her.

At the door of the motel office was the manager, the toothless old lady he'd pitied that afternoon. She was holding the 12-gauge shotgun with practiced ease, squinting, taking aim. Her finger was on the trigger. She was ready for the second shot.

"Jake!" Bell called out.

He dropped the old woman where she stood. The gunshot hit her square in the chest and she flew backward, slamming against the screen door. She screamed as she fell.

He and Bell kneeled down beside Charlie. Three-quarters of his forehead was missing, replaced by a bloody cavity. Charlie's eyes were glassy. Fluids bubbled out of his mouth and his nose. He opened and closed his mouth spasmodically, as his body frantically responded to the terrible injury. He jerked and twisted for another second or so, and then he stopped.

"He's still breathing," Bell said. She had her fingers on Charlie's neck, desperate to find a pulse. "Still got a heartbeat." She ripped open his shirt and started performing CPR, frantically pumping with the heels of her hands.

Jake was already on the line with the 911 dispatcher, giving their location, giving all the rest of the information. He never let of go of the Glock. Finished with the call, he lifted his weapon toward the three men, aiming it at their faces, one after the other. If they got away, then Charlie would die for nothing.

"Anybody moves, anybody tries to run — I blow your freaking head off," he said. "Are we clear?"

This time they didn't bother with the *"Sí"* and went straight to the "Yeahs" and the "Sures."

Jake retuned his attention to Charlie. Bell was still doing chest compressions but she was also talking. Her voice was low and affectionate. Charlie was long past being able to understand what she was saying, but Jake was glad she was saying it, anyway. Wherever Charlie was now, he might be aware of a syllable here and there, of the timbre and cadence of her voice, the voice of a friend:

"Charlie — Charlie. Hey, Charlie. This is Bell. I'm right here with you, Jake's here, too. Right beside you. We won't leave you, Charlie. Promise."

Clearly the squad was not going to get here in time. In seconds Charlie Mathers, the good-guy deputy, the man who loved self-help books and *Law and Order: SVU* and chocolate ice cream and doughnuts and Doreen — Charlie was open about his passions, he enjoyed talking about the things he loved — would be no more.

He was dying. Jake knew it, and he knew that Bell knew it, too. But neither one of them would acknowledge it.

Bell had stopped talking. She had stopped the CPR as well, because he wasn't responding, and the violence of it had begun to seem pointless and intrusive. Charlie needed peace now, didn't he? Peace and rest. He deserved that. Jake almost believed he could read her thoughts.

Watching her, Jake felt the spasm in his own throat, the tightening, the seizing up. And this was a time when she most needed to speak, to comfort Charlie. She had access to words that Jake didn't have.

"Talk to him, Bell," Jake murmured. "He needs to know we're here." He wanted her words to wash over Charlie as he left on his last journey. His journey home.

She tried to speak. Nothing. She tried again.

This time, her voice came back. It was thin and unsteady, and she had to push, but she was able to keep going. Jake had no idea of the source of the words. He did not know that she had heard them for the first time herself earlier on this very day, while sitting in her office at the courthouse. He did not know that, when she began speaking them here in the dimly lit parking lot of a seedy motel, as she knelt over her dying friend, they were as much of a surprise to her as they were to Jake:

" 'Abide with me, fast falls the eventide. The darkness deepens. Lord with me abide. When other . . .' " She choked up. Jake put a hand on her shoulder. She swallowed hard and continued: " 'When other helpers fail and comforts flee, help of the helpless, O abide with me.' "

Jake was not a religious person. He did not know if Charlie was a religious person. Or Bell. That did not matter. The words were not about a doctrine. They were about comfort. They were about hope in a place where there was no hope. They were about picturing a life — however long that life lasted — as a single day, from midnight to midnight, and within that span, loving and knowing you were loved in return, and believing, and trusting, and trying.

When the squad arrived Jake and Bell backed off, letting the paramedics do their work. Charlie was gone, and they knew it. But the paramedics would still try. It was their job.

Everyone had a job to do.

"I've got to get these suspects over to the courthouse," Jake said. "And the evidence that Charlie collected." He had done many things wrong tonight. He had been reckless, because he wanted to shut down the drug ring. And maybe because he wanted some glory. Maybe because he was showing off. He had persuaded his friend to join him because he didn't want to postpone the search of the Starliner. It was a bitter thought.

"I'll get the paperwork going for the arraignment," Bell said.

He started to go, but something pulled him back to her.

"There's more," he said.

"What?"

"It's not just Charlie. I know we're both shaken to our cores by what's happened, but from the moment you got here tonight — you've not been yourself."

"Thirty-three overdoses in a day will do that to a person," she said.

"Well, yeah. But . . ." He stopped. Why should she confide in him? He worked with her. That was the extent of it. He wasn't really a friend. Whatever was troubling her, it was her business.

By this time another squad had showed up. The paramedics hopped out, ready to deal with the old lady who was sprawled on the strip of concrete leading to the office. She was obviously dead but they still went through their checklist.

"She was the lookout," Jake said. He said it with disgust. "Wonder how much they paid her."

Bell shrugged. "In the end, she's the one who paid."

They watched as the first ambulance, the one carrying Charlie, pulled away. Soon the red taillights were absorbed into the Appalachian night.

"He's in good hands," Jake said softly. He didn't know why he said that, or what he meant by it. He must have meant the paramedics and the staff at the Raythune County Medical Center.

Yes. That must have been it.

"So," Bell said. "See you back at the courthouse."

He heard a cell ring. Was it his or hers?

"That's me," she said.

Jake watched her face as she listened to the call. It told him that the night, as long and arduous and sorrowful as it had been, was still not over.

PAUL

11:11 P.M.

He had been talking for over two hours now. His throat was hoarse. He was weary to the bone.

He sat on the top step of the three concrete steps leading down to the door of the church basement, elbows on his knees. The dark alley behind him had a pinched and lonely feel, as if it was the last alley in the history of the world, a tunnel lined by the boarded-up back doors of abandoned buildings, leading nowhere. He had propped the flashlight next to his right hip and its light cast a big yellow circle on the locked door. Paul had talked to that door for so long now that he swore he could see hidden pictures in the wood grain: a galloping horse, a Nixon profile, the outline of the state of Texas.

There was something else in that door, too, that kept snagging his eye: a bullet hole.

Jenny and Raylene were behind him, pacing and fuming. He could hear their quick, angry steps on the gravel, Raylene's heels and Jenny's New Balance sneakers. But he could not focus on them. He had to focus on the door, and on Eddie.

And on Marla Kay, who was Eddie's prisoner.

At first they had agreed to take turns dealing with Eddie, trying to persuade him to come out, or at least to let the little girl leave, but that did not work. Raylene could not keep her emotions in check. Twice she had ended up screaming and cursing at him. Jenny, too, grew frustrated after a short while. Only Paul seemed able to remain calm, to keep Eddie talking.

"It's so late," Paul said to the door. He had said it before, but there was no telling what might get through to Eddie. "You've got to be exhausted. And Marla Kay — come on, Eddie. She's five years old."

"She's fine." Eddie's voice was easy to hear through the door.

"Let me talk to her, then," Paul said. "Let her tell me she's fine."

"She doesn't want to talk to you," Eddie said.

Was that a giggle? Paul leaned forward. Had Eddie somehow persuaded Marla Kay that this was a game?

After hearing the gunshot, the three of them — Paul, Jenny, and Raylene — had run out the back door into the alley. Jenny had barely managed to keep Gilead, agitated and madly barking, inside the house.

Eddie Sutton was at the basement door, foot on the bottom concrete step. With one hand he held his rifle; with the other, Marla Kay's small hand.

When he saw them, he pulled the girl back inside. The twist and *thunk* of the dead bolt sliding into place was unmistakable.

"Eddie — we heard a gunshot," Paul had said. He was breathing heavily, palm on the basement door. "What's going on? Open up."

"Back off, Paul. Just go away."

"Is everybody okay? Just tell me that."

"We're fine. Go away."

Before Paul could respond, he heard Jenny's voice behind him. "I'm calling the sheriff. That little girl could be bleeding. For God's sake, Paul, we have to —"

"Jenny, please," Paul said. He gave her a long, meaningful look. "He wouldn't hurt Marla Kay. So let's try to settle this on our own, okay? Before we call the authorities? I think that's best. And I think you know why." He glared at Raylene, who stood next to his wife, a surly, petulant look on her face. "And you know why, too."

Jenny stared back at him. At last she nodded. "Your decision. It's all your doing, anyway."

Raylene had thrust her hands into her tangled red hair. When she got nervous or upset, she would tousle her hair, flipping it up and then letting it fall in bountiful tangles. Her hair was like a separate character in the story of her life. "Believe you me — Eddie's enjoying the hell out of all this drama," she had said with a sneer. "Making us all dance to his tune. He's a bastard. A first-class, grade-A, bast—"

"That's not helpful, Raylene," Paul said quietly.

"Oh, excuse *me,* Mister High-and-Mighty Minister," she snapped. "So sorry that I offended Your Highness." She tried to execute a mock-bow and do a quick little tap dance, but stumbled. The rock-strewn alley was not hospitable to stiletto heels.

When they first moved here, Paul didn't like the fact that Rising Souls was located in a business area, especially since the businesses had all closed down, stranding the church on its own dingy little island. But at the moment he was grateful for that. There were no houses around with nosy occupants who might wonder why three people were standing in an alley arguing with each other — especially when one of the three was a minister.

Or why a gunshot had not prompted an immediate call to the sheriff.

"Eddie," Paul said. "Why did you fire your rifle?"

"I didn't."

"What?"

"I said I didn't. I didn't fire it. That was Marla Kay."

"You let a child near a firearm?"

"It won't happen again. It was a mistake," Eddie said. "She picked it up before I could stop her. It was my fault for having it out like that. I was packing and I lost track of her for just a second. Bullet hit the door. She's safe."

"Oh, my God," Jenny murmured. "Oh, my God. That little girl. And a rifle. Oh my —"

"Yeah, we get it." Raylene interrupted her in a flat, bored voice. "We get that you're real upset. You and your husband are just *so* sensitive. *So* good. *So* —"

"Shut up," Jenny said. "You can't talk to me that way."

"The hell I can't. Who's gonna stop me? That husband of yours?" Her laugh was cold. "I don't *think* so, Fat Ass."

"Watch your mouth."

"Well, *you* watch your husband." Raylene crossed her arms. She struck the same pose she had favored that morning, when she stood in the Lymon's Market parking lot and dared anyone to challenge her right to exploit her child for cash.

Paul ignored them. He kept a hand on the basement door, trying to get Eddie to come out. Then Raylene had taken a turn, and then Jenny, and then Paul again.

Two hours later, Paul was spent. He sat on the top step, still talking to Eddie, but with less conviction that it would do any good. He signaled to Jenny. It was time to call the sheriff. She nodded and pulled out her cell.

"So what happens now, Eddie?" Paul said. "Where do we go from here?"

Silence.

Paul tried again. "Just tell me what you want. I can't promise, but I'll try to help. I will. What do you want?"

The voice on the other side of the door was gentle and wistful, not hostile and demanding.

"I want my little girl."

"You get to visit her, Eddie."

"Not enough. It's never enough."

"Raylene's right here. What if I talk to her?

408

What if I get her to agree that you get to see Marla Kay more often? How would that be?"

Silence.

"Eddie?"

"Keep your voice down," Eddie said. "Marla Kay just fell asleep. Poor thing's tired out. Don't want you to wake her up."

"Okay, Eddie. I'll do that. But listen — you've got to end this, okay? You've got to come out of there."

Silence.

Raylene spoke again. "You're acting like a damned fool, Eddie. Like a crazy person Wait — I forgot. You *are* a crazy person." She laughed. "Crazy, crazy, crazy."

"You hush," Eddie said.

Paul tried to wave Raylene away but she wouldn't stay back. She charged at the basement door, shouting at it. "You're looney-tunes, mister, and everybody knows it!"

"Let me have her, Raylene." Eddie's voice sounded wistful and pleading. "You don't want Marla Kay. Let me take her. Raise her. Let me have my little girl."

"She ain't."

"What?" Eddie said.

"You heard me. She *ain't* your little girl. She's mine but she ain't yours. And if you weren't such a goddamned fool, you would've figured that out a *long* time ago, mister."

The silence that fell upon the alley was unlike any Paul had ever heard before. He knew silences; he considered himself something of a connoisseur of silences. He put plenty of silent moments into his Sunday services. He sought out quiet places so that he could think about his life and how he had fallen so far short of his ideals.

But he had never heard a silence like this one.

All he could think of was, *Thank God Marla Kay's asleep.* She would be spared this. One day she would have to know, but not from hearing it blurted by her mother specifically to wound the one man who had been kind to her, the one man who loved her the way a father should.

A decent father, that is. Not a coward. Not a liar who hid behind pretty words and platitudes to cover up the massive fraud of his life, the compulsions that ruled him. He had tried to make everyone happy and he had ended up making no one happy, including himself.

"What?" Eddie said. "What?"

"Yeah," was Raylene's saucy reply. "You heard me. She's not even yours. You never even asked for a paternity test! What kind of

410

dumbshit don't ask for proof that a kid's *his,* anyway? Who in their right mind takes the woman's word for it? Jesus Christ, Eddie — wise up! You got no rights to her, no rights at all. I only let you think it so I could get some money from you now and again. But you never made enough for it to matter. So fuck you. You bring her out so I can go home."

Silence.

"Who's her father?" Eddie said.

Raylene laughed. "I think you know. I think if you take that pea brain of yours and apply it to the problem at hand, you'll figure out it out. Remember when we were first working here, Eddie? You in the basement there and me scrubbing toilets? Remember how I told you that the good reverend couldn't keep his eyes off my ass? You think on that, Eddie. You think *real hard.*"

The sound of a siren grew ever closer.

Eddie's plaintive voice threaded through the door. "Paul? Is it true?"

Jenny spoke before her husband could.

"Of *course* it's true," she said bitterly. She didn't seem to be talking only to Eddie. "Of *course* it is. That kind of scandal — we'd never survive it. Never. Not another one, like back in Stone Ridge. And what would be next? Where would they send us after this latest little escapade? Where do they send ministers who get their housekeepers pregnant?"

"Jenny," Paul said.

That was all he had a chance to say before the wincingly bright headlights of a Chevy Blazer invaded the alley. The vehicle stopped a few feet away from them. From the driver's side, Deputy Brinksneader jumped out. From the other, a large woman in a hot-pink pantsuit and white sandals.

Paul had met the deputy once before, about two months ago, when somebody broke a window at the church and Jenny had insisted they call the sheriff's office. Paul didn't want to. No matter who had done it, that person would be forgiven — so why make a fuss? Why bother some poor deputy who had more important things to take care of? Paul's attitude had irritated Jenny so much that he backed down and called. They sent Deputy Brinksneader. All he did was look around at the damage, frown, make some notes. *See?* Paul wanted to say to Jenny, but didn't, because that would only set her off all over again. *Told you. Nothing anybody can do. Some things, you just have to put up with.*

Brinksneader was panting. Sweat glittered on his forehead and his neck.

"Stay back, Rhonda," he said to the woman who had accompanied him. "Reverend, this is Rhonda Lovejoy. Assistant prosecutor. You got a hostage situation — that right?" he said, his eyes going from face to face, seeking confirmation. "That's what the dispatcher indicated. Any firearms involved?"

"The SOB's got a rifle," Raylene said, shrieking the words. "Plus my baby." She banged on the basement door.

From inside came the sound of a child's crying.

"You woke her up," Eddie said. "Whoever did that woke her up."

"It was me," Raylene yelled at the door.

"Figures," Eddie said.

Steve cleared the area in front of the door. He looked at Paul. "What's his name?"

"Eddie."

"Okay." Steve turned back to the door. "I'm Deputy Steve Brinksneader," he called out. "I'm asking you to come out of there peacefully and to bring the girl, Eddie. Or I'm coming in. I don't want any trouble. I don't think you want any trouble, either. We've had enough trouble in this town today as it is. Let's end this, Eddie. Right now. I've got a prosecutor here with me and after you come out, we can talk about

413

what's gonna happen next."

There was a murmur of conversation on the other side of the door, a man's voice and then a child's voice.

"I'm coming out," Eddie said. "Not because *you* want me to. I'm coming out because *she* wants me to — my little girl."

Steve stepped back. He kept a hand hovering near his holster as the door slowly opened.

Eddie still had the rifle in one hand, and Marla Kay's hand in his other hand.

"Drop the weapon!" Steve yelled. "Drop it now!"

Something passed in front of Eddie's eyes. A mist, a dream, a memory — something. Watching him, Paul almost felt as if he could hear Eddie thinking: *We can make a run for it. If we can just get to the truck, we'll be free. We'll go somewhere and I can raise her, and we'll —*

"Drop your weapon!" Steve repeated, even louder.

Now a wave of anger seemed to grip Eddie. Once again, Paul felt himself channeling the other man's thoughts: *They can't do this. I won't give her up. I don't care who they say her father is — I'm her father. It's me. I won't let her go. I can't.*

Eddie re-formed his grip on the rifle. To

Paul, he looked as if he had made a decision: He would fight back if they tried to stop him from taking his little girl.

Marla Kay called out in a bright, hopeful voice. "Don't be upset, Daddy! And if you are — count to ten! Remember? Like you taught me? Count to ten, Daddy! Here, I'll help — one. Two. Three. Four."

By the time she reached five, Eddie had lowered the rifle again. He was looking at Marla Kay, not at the deputy who rushed at him, grabbing the weapon out of his hands, and then securing his wrists behind his back with a zip tie. Eddie did not resist. He did not speak. As the deputy led him away, Eddie twisted his neck so that he could keep his eyes on the little girl for as long as he was able.

EDDIE

11:52 P.M.

The woman climbed into the backseat of the Blazer right beside him. She introduced herself as Rhonda Lovejoy. During the ride to the courthouse she told him she was an assistant prosecutor. She explained his legal rights to him, and advised him that anything he said might be used against him in court.

He nodded, but her words meant nothing to him. In his mind he was thinking only of Marla Kay, and of how he had likely seen her for the last time. The ties on his wrist were tight, but he barely felt them. He was in too much emotional pain to pay attention to the physical kind.

Marla Kay wasn't his child.

The deputy did the driving. The big SUV wove through the dark streets of Acker's Gap. Eddie looked out the window, but there was nothing to see.

416

"I want to help you, Mr. Sutton," Rhonda said.

He turned to look at her. He had to use his whole upper torso to do so, shifting his shoulders, on account of his being tied the way he was, hands behind his back.

"Help me how?"

"You'll have to pay for what you did — there's no way around it — but there are extenuating circumstances. I've put in a call to the prosecutor. We have some latitude in deciding what to charge someone with, and what punishment to ask for. We'd like to try to get you some help. You see, Mr. Sutton, I think I know why you did what you did. It wasn't right and nothing excuses it — but I do understand it. You love your child."

" 'Cept now I know she's not really mine."

"That's not true."

"Paul is her father."

"I'm not talking about biology. I'm talking about love. You love Marla Kay. You'd do anything for her. She's more yours than she could ever be Paul Wolford's."

Eddie felt a deep anger stirring in his gut. "Why didn't he tell me? The bastard."

"He was ashamed. And afraid. And maybe it wasn't just that."

"What else could it be?"

"Maybe he saw how much you love Marla

417

Kay. And he saw how much that love helped you. Kept you going. Maybe he didn't want to take that away from you."

"You don't know if any of that's true," he said. He wanted to believe her, but he was also afraid to believe her. Hope could hurt. It could turn on you at any time.

"No. I don't. But it makes sense, doesn't it? Paul's not an evil man. You know that."

Reluctantly, Eddie nodded.

"Okay, then," Rhonda said. "If he's not evil, and he didn't lie to you out of maliciousness, it had to have been something else. I think he was confused. And desperate. And I think he cares for you. Wants the best for you. And he honestly thought that making you believe Marla Kay is your child was the right thing to do."

"How do you know all this?"

"I don't. I'm guessing, based on what Paul said to me while Deputy Brinksneader was getting you in the Blazer. And based on what I know about people."

"You think they cooked up the lie together, the two of them? Paul and Raylene?"

"Yes," Rhonda said. "And his wife helped. They had to clean up a bad mess. Cover it up. When Raylene got pregnant, they had to do something. Saying she was your child — convincing you of it — was just a handy way out for all three of them. But that doesn't matter. What matters is Marla Kay. And you. And doing our best to make sure that you get to see her, once you've served your time. You took her without the permission of her custodial parent, Mr. Sutton, and you threatened people with a firearm. Those are serious charges. But if you're willing to admit what you did and accept your punishment, you may be able to have Marla Kay in your life again someday. I think that's what you want, isn't it?"

"Yeah."

"That's a good thing. Because she's going to need you."

He squinted at her. "Why are you talking to me like this? I don't even know you."

Rhonda pondered his question. "When Deputy Brinksneader called me tonight and told me what was going on, I said I wanted to come along. Isn't that right, Deputy?"

Steve nodded, his big flat-brimmed hat moving up and down, and then he grunted. "She sure did."

Back to Eddie, Rhonda said, "I went to high school with Raylene. I've lived around here a long time. Too long, I sometimes think. I don't see the things I should. They're too familiar. I look right past them."

"What do you mean?"

"The prosecutor and I were over at Raylene's apartment. It was for another case. But it didn't occur to me until much, much later that I didn't see Marla Kay. I didn't ask about her, either. I was too busy stewing in my own juices. We all get confused sometimes, Mr. Sutton, and forget what's really important."

Deputy Brinksneader pulled the Blazer up to the side of the courthouse. The sign on the door, illuminated by a light just above it, said JAIL. An old man in a dirty Army jacket was hunched face-first next to the building, scratching at the stone with a fingernail. His hair was a wild mess and his pants drooped from his hips like drapery.

"Who's that?" Rhonda said.

Steve shrugged. "Some guy. Been hanging around for the last few days. Goes into stores now and again, ranting and raving. Waving a stick around. Seems harmless, but he can get himself pretty worked up. Scares folks. We've tried to chase him off, but he always comes drifting back."

"Might be a vet," Rhonda said. "Mr. Sutton? What do you think?"

Eddie peered out the window. "Might be."

Rhonda nodded. "I'll see what I can do for him. In the meantime, Mr. Sutton, Deputy Brinksneader here will take you

420

inside. And remember — if you can't afford a lawyer, the court will assign you one."

He had something more to say to her. "I never would've hurt my little girl."

"I know that, Mr. Sutton."

JAKE

11:56 P.M.

Thirty-three overdoses. Four deaths, if you threw in the old-lady manager who doubled as a lookout.

No: *five* deaths.

He had forgotten to count Charlie Mathers.

He had forgotten because Charlie did not belong with the others. Charlie wasn't a number. Charlie was his friend, the first friend he'd ever had in Acker's Gap. Maybe the *only* friend he'd ever have in Acker's Gap. Well, he would find out, wouldn't he? Once the shit hit the fan. You always find out who your friends are when things go wrong.

Jake had pulled into the Marathon station. There were no other vehicles in the lot. He parked in front of the glass-walled store. He needed to think. This seemed as good a place as any; it was familiar and easy.

The Blazer seemed to find its own way here, like a dog following a scent.

He knew he faced serious disciplinary action for having used Charlie as his backup at the Starliner. He might lose his job. The sheriff was letting him finish his shift tonight not because he was off the hook, but because she needed him; she had made that clear. The accident on the freeway was just the start of a very bad, very busy night, coming at the end of a very bad, very busy day. Steve was already tied up on yet another call. A hostage situation, Jake had heard. He didn't get the particulars. He didn't care about the particulars. He'd had enough of particulars in the past twenty-four hours. He was drowning in particulars.

The sheriff had told him very little about her visit to Doreen Mathers. Only that she had made it. She offered him no details about Doreen's reaction; it was as if she considered such details to be a privilege, and he had squandered the right to any such privileges. They had yet to release publicly the news of Charlie's death.

Jake knew what he had to do. He pushed the number on his cell.

Doreen didn't sound like herself. Her "Hello?" was like a tattered rag, a thin, insubstantial thing. He had always thought of her as a strong woman, a woman who spoke her mind, did what she wanted to do. Hearing the small, trembling voice was excruciating.

"Doreen, it's me. Jake Oakes."

Silence.

How much had the sheriff told her about what happened at the Starliner? Did Doreen know he had caused Charlie's death?

"Jake," she said. "I thought you might be Charlie's brother. Calling me back. I had to leave a message. Oh my God. Oh my God."

"I know."

"Jake. He was such a good man." Her voice was gaining strength again. It was as if, by talking about the man she loved, she was being restored to herself. "So funny. And gentle. Isn't that a strange thing to say about a deputy sheriff? He did his job. He could be mean when he had to be. Tough as nails. But he was gentle inside. You know that as well as I do."

"Yeah."

"He loved you, Jake. I'm sure he never told you. He thought of you as a son."

Don't tell me that. Jake wanted to yell it at her. But he didn't, of course. He just listened.

"He really did," Doreen went on. "You should have heard him. He was so proud of you. The job you do, the fact that a man like you stayed here. 'Young man like that,' Charlie would say, 'could go anywhere, do anything. But this is his home now.' Oh, Jake."

He couldn't stand it. Not a second more. He couldn't endure the fact that she thought well of him.

"Doreen — I've got to tell you something. You need to know — it was me."

"What?"

"I'm the reason he's dead. I called him. I asked him to help me out tonight. I didn't have permission. I should've checked with the sheriff but I didn't. I wanted him to come. I needed him. And he said yes. It all went wrong. And now he's —"

"Jake."

He waited. He was ready for her to tell him to go to hell. He didn't deserve her kindness, the nice words she had said.

"Jake," she repeated. "I know."

"You —"

"I'd already figured that out. Didn't make sense that the sheriff would sign off on a retired deputy joining an official operation. I'm not sure Charlie got it — but I did. And you know what, Jake? You should've seen him. He was so excited after you called him tonight. He was himself again. Ready to go to work. Taking care of the town. Getting rid of those damned drug gangs and the poison they bring here." She took a few deep breaths. "Don't get me wrong. I'm going to miss him forever. I loved that old man. We had such plans. Wonderful plans. But you know what? I'd see him sitting there in front of that TV set, night after night, and I'd think, 'This is no life for Charlie Mathers. He's going to get real tired of this.' He got to do what he loved to do, Jake. One last time. All in all, I guess I'd rather have it end the way it ended — instead of watching him get bored. Feeling useless. So don't beat yourself up, Jake. Don't do that. Just know he loved you. And Lord knows, he loved this town."

They talked a bit longer. They talked the way grieving people do when they want to keep a loved one in their midst for just a few precious moments more: They told stories about Charlie, funny ones and poignant ones, stories that made them sad and stories that cheered them up again. They knew they had to let him go, and they would, but for now, the stories kept Charlie tethered to them; as long as there was another story to share, he would not disappear altogether.

Finally it was time for Jake to hang up. He

knew she had other calls to make, things to plan. She asked him if he would be a pallbearer at Charlie's service. He said yes, of course. It would be an honor.

Jake put a hand across the back of his neck. The night wasn't especially humid but he was sweating, anyway.

He looked through the Blazer's side window, into the store. He saw Danny Lukens standing at the counter, like always. Jake would have to go inside and say hello before he drove away again tonight. If he didn't, Danny's feelings would be hurt. The kid was sensitive. He acted like a tough guy, but down deep, Danny was a wimp. Jake didn't have the heart to tell him that he wasn't all that crazy about Snickers bars.

His radio crackled. He heard Steve Brinksneader tell the dispatcher that he had cleared the hostage scene. *Good for you,* Jake thought. Steve was a good deputy.

Maybe Steve should have handled the search for the local dealer. Because Jake hadn't gotten the job done. He had arrested the gang at the Starliner, including the man with slicked-back black hair and a surly sneer who appeared to be the ringleader, but he still didn't know who the local dealer was. The homegrown bridge between the out-of-town delivery crew and the customer base. He had never managed to find him or her. That person might still be distributing the carfentanil-laced heroin.

The nightmare might continue.

He had another call to make. Now that he had talked to Doreen, he wanted to talk to Molly. He wanted to tell her about his day, about its frustrations and its disappointments and its fleeting, unlikely beauties. He wanted her in his life. And as more than a friend or a colleague. He wanted to fall asleep in her arms. He sensed — no, he *knew* — that she wanted that from him, too.

So what did he have to lose? He would try one last time.

From inside the store, Danny Lukens waved at him. Jake waved back with his free hand.

"Hey," he said when she answered. "Hope I didn't wake you up."

"No. You didn't." Her matter-of-factness didn't throw him. He was used to it by now. She added, "How did it go with the search warrant at the motel?"

So she hadn't yet heard about Charlie Mathers. Maybe that was best, for the time being. He could tell her the terrible news later.

"There were some complications," he said. "But we got the bad guys."

"Great."

"Think you'll sleep okay tonight?"

"No," she said.

He waited. When she didn't go on, he said, "Does that have anything to do with me? With us?"

"Oh, Jake," she said, and her tone cut right through him. "I won't change my mind, okay? I can't. You have to accept that. Listen — I like you. A lot. I really do. But it can't be what you want it to be. Ever."

He decided to go into Full Salesman Mode. Give it his best shot. "Listen. Malik's no problem, okay? He's a great kid. I know he's your priority. I totally accept that. I —"

"You don't understand." She was crying. It took him a minute to pick up on that, to discern the thickness in her voice. He was startled. He had never expected to hear her cry. He had only ever seen her strong.

"Molly, Molly — please. Is something wrong? Let me help."

She took a deep breath. With no preamble, she began her story:

"We lived back in the hollow. Medical care? A joke. Damned joke. Mostly that didn't matter, though. We got along. When I was six years old, my mother got pregnant with Malik. She had a lot of complications.

429

Things I didn't understand.

"When she went into labor, my father realized we needed help. We didn't have a phone. So he sent me down to the store to use the phone there and call the doctor. Get him to come. Well, I didn't think it was that important. I thought my mom would be fine. Women had babies all the time. All my friends' mothers had ten or eleven kids apiece. I wasn't worried.

"My friend Sheila had a new bike. I was going past her house — and there she was with that bike. Prettiest bike I ever saw. Red and shiny. With a basket and a bell. And she said I could ride it. So I took my time. I rode Sheila's new bike. And then I went on down to the store and called that doctor. Told him we needed him. But by the time he got there — it was too late. Malik was born the way he was born. And my mother died. Because I wanted to ride that bike."

"You were six."

"Old enough to be sent to call the doctor," she said. "Old enough to be trusted."

He didn't know what to say, so he said what was in his heart.

"I can make you happy, Molly."

"I know you can. But that's the problem. I caused my mother's death. I caused my brother to be the way he is. So I don't deserve to be happy."

"You can't —"

"I need to go now, Jake."

"Don't. Please."

"I have to." But she didn't hang up. Not right away. It seemed that she had more to say to him. A summing-up. "I know we have to work together, and that will be fine. We'll do our jobs. We'll do them well. Like we always do. But I'm going to ask you not to call me again. Or talk about this. Or ever think of us as a couple. It can't happen." Her voice softened. "I could love you. I really think I could. But that's the point — do you see? That's why we won't ever be together. It's *because* of the way I feel about you. It's *because* we would be happy to-gether. After the thing I did to my family — I don't deserve happiness. I can't let myself feel that. I can't — I can't deal with the guilt of it."

Jake waited. He hoped she would say something else. She didn't.

A few seconds later he realized she had ended the call. She had ended something else, too, something so unfathomably im-mense that the dimensions of it expanded beyond his emotional line of sight. He could feel the size of it — the size of the life she had rejected, its astonishing possibilities to bring both of them a quiet daily joy for the rest of forever — even though he could not see to the edge of it. It was too vast. Too wide and too deep. He felt it the way you feel thunder, as a distant vibration that you know is filling up the sky, the world, but that you cannot grasp or measure. You can only sense the infinitude of it.

He was numb and empty and sad. He needed something else to think about, and right away. So he looked again through the big lighted window, toward the counter where Danny was tidying things up. Jake had seen the items on that counter so many times that he could name them from memory: the little round dish of pennies; the plastic rack of sunglasses; the cardboard box of air fresheners shaped like pine trees, each with a loop of twine threaded through a small hole at the top so it could dangle from a rearview mirror.

As bright as it was in there, it was still a lonely scene. One guy, working by himself all night long. You'd think Danny would be a little more nervous and jittery, given what had happened here last night. Especially with the video surveillance system on the fritz.

You'd think that, wouldn't you?

Jake cursed himself. *Of course.*

A gas station was a crossroads. People traipsed in and out all the time. It was a perfect distribution point. There was a good reason why Danny hadn't insisted that the owner fix the busted video camera. This way, nobody knew who came and went, or what business they transacted with Danny Lukens while they were in there.

Danny had his days free. So when he wasn't at the station, he could still be doing business, selling to anybody who didn't make it by the Marathon at night. Everybody knew Danny Lukens; he could move around Acker's Gap in an easy way, slick and frictionless, palming a packet of heroin into a customer's hand.

Right?

Yes. Right.

If Jake hadn't been so preoccupied with his feelings for Molly, if he hadn't been acting like a damned stupid lovesick puppy, if he hadn't been showing off for her by going after the Starliner gang with only his old buddy as backup, he would have made the link much sooner. If he'd done his job, this might have been over hours ago.

Jake made a quick call to the sheriff. Her tone was cold, professional — and why wouldn't it be, after what he'd done? — but this was business, and she listened to him.

He told her what he'd figured out about Danny. He was going in. He needed backup, just in case. She would leave the courthouse right now, she told him. She would be there in minutes. No reason for him to wait for her; he could handle it. When she got there, she would help him secure the scene.

He reached for his hat on the seat beside him.

BELL

"You've been here all this time?"

"Sure," Shirley said. "Enjoyed it. Real peaceful. Got to admit I dozed off there for a while. What time is it?"

"Midnight. Or thereabouts."

"Lord. Bet you're glad this day is almost over, little sister."

Bell nodded. She had paused at the foot of the steps. The porch light was off, and no light burned in any house on the street. People in Acker's Gap started their days early and ended them that way, too. Still, Bell could see everything plainly: steps and pillar and porch and swing. And Shirley.

Her sister sat at the far right end of the swing, left hand in her lap, the thumb of her right hand rubbing the metal chain that held up her side of it, massaging the linked rings.

Shirley patted the place next to her. "So

435

where'd you go? I tell you my news and you go flying out of here. I was hoping we could talk about it."

"We can." Bell crossed the porch, sat down. "But at first I couldn't . . ." She tried again. "You're the only family I have. Something happens to you — I'm alone." She shook her head. "Listen to me, will you? Pretty damned selfish. *You're* the one who's sick. Good God."

"No. Not selfish. Just human." A beat. "So where *did* you go?"

"Long story."

Shirley smiled. "It always is."

So Bell filled her in. She told her about Charlie's death in the course of the raid on the Starliner. She told her about the thirty-three overdoses and the three fatalities. She told her about locking up the drug gang, and about still not finding the local dealer.

"Really sorry about your friend," Shirley said. "I remember meeting him once. In your office. Seemed like a real nice fella."

Bell nodded but didn't say anything, and so Shirley added, "This place."

"Yeah."

"And this night."

They sat in silence for a moment or two.

"I'm glad you have Clay around," Shirley said. "Especially now. Because the day is going to come when I won't be —"

Bell interrupted her with a ferocity that clearly startled Shirley: "No. No. *No.* Don't you say it. We're going to get you the best treatment available. Wherever they're doing the cutting-edge research — that's where you'll go. Columbus, New York, Houston — the best. No argument."

Shirley laughed softy. "I figured out a *long* time ago not to argue with the likes of you. No percentage in it."

"Good. So that's settled."

Bell had a fleeting impulse to bring her up to date on her relationship with Clay. It was well and truly over. It had to be.

She said nothing. Shirley had enough to deal with right now.

Shirley was talking again. "I'll try to beat this. Promise. But I think we need to be honest with each other, Belfa. Not a lot of people survive lung cancer. This time next year I might not —"

"No." Bell was feeling panicky again. "We're going to fight. Fight *hard.* And if it turns out that the best doctors are in D.C., well — that's great. Because I just might be moving back there."

"Really?"

"A classmate of mine is starting a new firm. She asked me to join her. And after a day like today — it sounds mighty attractive."

"Bet so." Shirley paused. "I have something else to talk to you about, too. But it can keep if you're too tired."

"I'm okay. I got a second wind. But how about you? You've got to be pretty whipped yourself. Hope you plan on spending the night."

Shirley was rubbing at the chain again with her thumb. Up and down, up and down. She looked at the chain, not at Bell. "Something I've got to say here. Hardest thing I've ever had to do."

"I have no idea what you're —"

"That night." Shirley stopped rubbing the chain. She still wouldn't look at her sister.

"What night?"

"You know which night."

And Bell did know. Of course she did. There was only one night in both of their lives. It had happened a long time ago and it had never really ended.

Bell stood up. She wanted to be able to face Shirley. She looked down at her sister, who sat very still in the swing.

"We don't talk about that," Bell said. "We agreed."

"I can't."

"Can't what?"

"I can't keep the agreement. Not any-more."

Bell's perplexity turned to annoyance. "I don't know what you're talking about. And this is a hell of a time to go there."

"It's the perfect time. There's never going to be a better time." Shirley patted the seat beside her once again. "Come on. Sit back down. We need to talk about it. About what happened. About Daddy's death."

Bell hesitated, but finally complied.

"When I got my diagnosis," Shirley said, "it was like a light had found me. It had picked me out, that light, and it was shining directly on me. It made me realize some things, Belfa. Things I never would've re-alized otherwise. I have to say the truth. I *have* to. I can't leave this world with that kind of lie trailing behind me."

And she told her sister the story of that night. The real story — not the one they had made up together. Not the one that Shirley forced Bell to memorize, repeating it over and over until it had soaked into her soul. Not the one that sent Shirley to prison for a crime she did not commit.

Bell listened. And as she listened, the words made a picture in her mind. The ter-rifying plausibility of it all, a deeply visceral remembrance of three and a half decades ago, descended on her.

"Belfa — what did you do . . ."

Belfa stood in the middle of a kitchen lit only by moonlight. Next to her, their father's motionless body was sprawled in a dinette chair, his arms limp at this sides, his legs sticking out in front of him, his head thrown back, his fat neck torn open and wet with blood.

Shirley's eyes came back to Belfa.

"What did you do?" Shirley repeated, keeping her voice soft, not wanting to startle her. "What did you do?"

"He was coming after me. I stopped him. I had to."

That didn't make sense. A ten-year-old girl, overpowering a grown man? That could not be true. So what *was* true?

Shirley had just arrived home. She had gone out with friends. She had never had friends before — but for the first time, she did. And they asked her to go to a movie. A movie. With friends. Unthinkable. Not something she had ever done. She was sixteen years old and she had never been to a movie.

Until tonight.

"Belfa," Shirley said. "What do you mean? How did you —"

440

"Right after you left. He came after me. He tried to do things. You know." Belfa's stare was intense and solemn. "You know, Shirley. You know what I mean."

Belfa's hands. How had Shirley not noticed her little sister's hands until just now? The small palms were matted with something dark and sticky-looking. The fingertips, too. The back of the wrist.

A knife lay on the floor at her feet. The wet blade glittered in the moonlight.

"I waited for him to fall asleep," Belfa said. "In the chair. You know how he does."

Yes. Shirley knew how he did. Donnie Dolan spent more nights sleeping upright in a kitchen chair than he did on the smelly, tattered mattress in his room. Sometimes it was because he had been drinking and he had passed out at the table; sometimes it was just out of laziness. He ate and he fell asleep, crumbs on his chest, greasy smear of food on his chin. The trailer only had one bedroom and it was his. The girls slept on the couch in the living room.

"He was asleep," Shirley said. "So why did you have to do this?"

Shirley opened her hands to identify the "this": The horror that spread out in the room all around them, a picture silvered by moonlight but still black and unfathomable.

"Because," Belfa said, "I knew he would be coming back."

And then they went to work. They found the gasoline that their father kept under the porch in the red metal cans. They splashed it around the trailer: first the inside, then the outside. The next-to-last thing Shirley did was call 911 and report a fire.

The last thing she did — they were standing outside now — was to light a book of matches and toss it toward the trailer.

They stood and watched the flames devour everything they had ever had in their lives, everything they had ever known, all vestiges of familiarity. All the while, Shirley talked very fast to Belfa, in a low, urgent voice. She put a hand on her sister's shoulder. She would not let Belfa turn away from the fire. She wanted to use the fire to cauterize the lie, to seal it inside both of them. The heat would fuse the seam. It would turn the lie into the truth.

"I killed him," Shirley said. "I did it. I cut his throat with the knife. Do you hear? It was me. Not you — me."

She chanted it a dozen times — two

dozen, maybe, or three, it didn't matter —
and Belfa did not say a word. The little
girl's eyes were wide. She did not blink.
The trailer was far away from the main
road and so Shirley knew she had time.
She had time to let Belfa get accustomed
to the lie, to memorize it. To learn how to
believe it.

Finally, with the up-and-down scream of
the siren growing closer, Belfa looked at
Shirley. Her lips parted. She tried to speak.
She couldn't.

The ambulance was there. A sheriff's car
was right behind it. People were jumping
out of vehicles, slamming doors, shouting,
demanding that the girls back away, BACK
AWAY. A deputy sheriff was coming toward
them, and despite the urgency and the
thunder and the chaos of the moment, he
had a kind face, Shirley saw, and that
made her happy, because she would be
putting Belfa in his hands, hoping for the
best. Maybe they had gotten lucky, just
this once. Maybe he was the one who
would do it, who would help Belfa.

Just before the deputy reached them,
Belfa said, "You cut his throat with a knife.
It was you." And Shirley felt a relief so
tremendous and overpowering that she
wanted to cry, she wanted to fall to the

ground, but she did neither of those things, because she had to be strong, she had to be tough, she had to persuade the world that she was mean enough and hard enough and cold enough to have slaughtered her own father.

"I don't remember," Bell murmured. "I swear to God I don't remember."

Shirley reached out her hand. "I'm sorry. I'm sorry I had to say the truth, after all these years."

Bell began to weep. She could count on the fingers of one hand the number of times she had cried in her life; crying was useless, and she had figured that out while still a child. Crying made you feel weak, and look weak.

Tonight that did not matter.

She had to let the tears subside before she could speak.

"Don't ever be sorry for saying the truth," Bell said.

Shirley still held her sister's hand. She gently squeezed it. "I've been thinking. Maybe it's enough that we've said it out loud. Just to ourselves. So maybe no one else has to know. Maybe we can just —"

"No." Bell drew her hand out of Shirley's grasp. "It can't be that way. Everything is —

everything is *different* now. It has to be. There's no statute of limitations on murder. They'll have to reopen the case. I'll confess. I have to."

Shirley's voice had a panicked edge. "Belfa, no. No. I never meant —"

"Funny thing about the truth. You can't go halfway."

The night air had changed. It was charged now with a kind of desperate electricity that surrounded them, holding them fast within this endless moment of their past. The facts were slowly making their way into Bell's mind; half-remembered shapes and vague sounds and almost-recollected impulses stirred in the wake of Shirley's narrative, resuming their rightful place, pushing aside the false memories.

It was true. It was all true.

She had suppressed the truth all these years, letting Shirley's made-up version be the one they told the world, the one they lived by. She had let her sister go to prison on her behalf. Bell hadn't done it consciously, perhaps — but that was the effect. She had allowed Shirley to give up her life for her.

Bell knew what she had to do. She stood up. She walked to the front door.

"Belfa? Where are you going?"

445

She turned around. "To write my letter of resignation. I can't be a prosecutor anymore. Not after confessing to felony murder. You'll be exonerated, Shirley. You have to be." Rising in Bell's mind were the faces of the people she loved as much as she loved Shirley: her daughter, Carla, and Nick Fogelsong. He was old now, but once upon a time, he had been the young deputy. The one who had taken care of her that night, and who believed in her thereafter, and who insisted she go to college and work hard and create something good and golden of her life, a life that had begun in such pain and violence. Because of him, Shirley's sacrifice had been worthwhile.

Tonight it was all coming undone, unraveling before her eyes. Bell's life was spinning backward, hurtling her into a past she had tried so desperately hard to escape.

Now she knew: The past always has the last word.

DANNY

A little less than twenty-four hours before
this moment, a young woman had walked
out of the night and into the artificial
brightness of the Marathon station. She
wore cutoff denim shorts and a black T-shirt
with the word PINK spelled out across the
front in pink letters.

Danny knew what she needed.

She had asked to use the bathroom, and
he pointed the way. She said, "Okay,
thanks." Their eyes locked. Still looking at
her, he reached under the counter. His hand
brushed against the key to the bathroom
door, hanging from the bent nail, and then
it brushed against the cold edge of the
revolver. Just past the gun, he found it: one
of six small, cloudy-white packets that he
had picked up at the Starliner Motel earlier
in the day.

He had passed the packet to her. She'd

447

handed him a wadded-up bill. A twenty. The bill was wet with the sweat from her hands. While shoving the bill in the front pocket of his jeans, he'd watched her make her way to the bathroom.

That was then. Right now, however, he wasn't thinking about the girl, the one who had died in the bathroom last night. He was thinking about Jake Oakes, who was sitting in his Blazer. He'd be coming in soon, no doubt.

Danny liked him, but there were things about Jake that bothered him, too. Jake didn't really know him at all. Jake underestimated him. Jake thought Danny was just a clerk at a gas station, standing behind the counter and watching the night go by, watching his life go by. The word "loser" seemed to live in the general vicinity of Jake's attitude toward him. Well, fine. Fine and dandy. Because you know what? *Jake Oakes* was the loser. *He* was the moron who didn't know what was really going on. Someday he would figure it out. But by then, Danny would be long gone. Where? Didn't matter. Somewhere. Somewhere else.

He looked out the window again. Jake's Blazer was in the same spot in which he had parked it the night before, after Danny

called him. After that skank — the one with
the PINK shirt — had locked herself in the
bathroom. Tonight the deputy had arrived
on his own, without Danny's summons.
Things were back to normal. They'd laugh,
joke around. Shoot the shit.

Danny waved. Jake waved back. It looked
as if Jake was on the phone. He'd be coming inside soon enough, jonesing for his free
Snickers. And wanting to use the can. Same
as always.

Danny finished restocking the wire rack of
Skoal tins. It wasn't like he was happy about
what had happened to that girl. Or to the
others. But nobody forced them to buy from
him. Business was business.

One more glance out the window. By now
Jake had finished his call and was heading
his way. The moment the deputy passed
under the light that hung from the awning,
Danny got a better look at him; even though
Jake had his hat on Danny could see the
expression on his face, and it was taut,
closed. Not friendly. Not like it usually was.
That was mildly surprising, but then again,
Jake probably had a lot on his mind tonight.
Everybody was talking about the overdoses.
About how the whole place was going to
hell in a hurry.

And all at once it seemed to Danny as if

Jake, who by now had pushed open one side of the glass double doors and was moving relentlessly toward the counter, had somehow materialized out of the night itself, like a piece snapped off from a solid object. It was too dark to see the mountains in the distance but Danny knew they were back there, darkness rising behind darkness. Those mountains had been lording it over him his whole life, reminding him how puny he was, how insignificant. It was little wonder that nobody Danny knew gave a damn about anything. Those mountains cast a spell. They kept you in your place, here in what his grandma used to call this beautiful heartbreak of a world. He wasn't exactly sure what she meant by that. She was just a crazy old lady. Not smart like him.

He had a funny feeling. Jake's face was the tipoff. If Danny was wrong, then so be it; the deputy would never know how close a call this was. But if Danny was right, if Jake had figured it out and was coming after him, he wasn't going to jail. No way.

"Hey, Jake," Danny said. Big smile. His hand slinked under the counter, feeling for the chilly steel. "What's going on?"

ABOUT THE AUTHOR

Julia Keller spent twelve years as a reporter and editor for the *Chicago Tribune,* where she won a Pulitzer Prize. A recipient of a Nieman Fellowship at Harvard University, she was born in West Virginia and lives in Chicago and Ohio. Julia is the author of the Bell Elkins novels, beginning with *The Devil's Stepdaughter.*

The employees of Thorndike Press hope you have enjoyed this Large Print book. All our Thorndike, Wheeler, and Kennebec Large Print titles are designed for easy reading, and all our books are made to last. Other Thorndike Press Large Print books are available at your library, through selected bookstores, or directly from us.

For information about titles, please call:
(800) 223-1244

or visit our website at:
gale.com/thorndike

To share your comments, please write:
Publisher
Thorndike Press
10 Water St., Suite 310
Waterville, ME 04901